FAE

CAPTIVE

THE MAGE SHIFTER WAR BOOK ONE

ELLE MIDDAUGH
ANN DENTON

Elle ♥
Middaugh
xoxo

To hot gangster shifters everywhere.

We've left the back door unlocked for you. ;)

AUBRY

I WAS JUSTICE IN THE NIGHT—DARK, WINGED, VENGEFUL justice and I was gonna end these assholes like a damn apocalypse. I was gonna punch a hole through them and steal all their tomorrows. One of us wasn't gonna walk outta this warehouse alive and I knew who I was betting on.

I wasn't even gonna shed a tear over their furry asses. *Shifter scum.*

At least, that's what I told myself...

I perched on a warehouse beam, my silvery white hair tucked up into a black beanie, my ebony uniform helping me fade into the darkness. I felt like a fae version of Batman, wings spread in the shadows behind me, watching the criminals below scurry back and forth with their stolen cargo.

The moon lit the room through the windows underneath me, until a cloud passed over it and obscured the beams of light. The gloom forced me to squint as I stared down at the shifter gang. That's when I noticed a large figure open the door at the back. He peered inside, watching the boxes move back and forth. I assumed it was a man because of his size, but I couldn't make him out clearly without the moon's aid. He was just a solid shadow, slightly darker than the surrounding blackness, one who took up the bulk of the door frame.

Lackey? Guard? Criminal? Who knew?

Something about him made a shiver slither down my spine. I narrowed my eyes and tried to make out his features, but he snapped the door shut before the moonbeams pummeled the darkness and lit the room up again.

Just as well.

I really only had my sights set on *one* shifter tonight. The one my team and I had been silently stalking for days. I returned my attention to my target, the criminal heading up the night's enterprise. A dangerous little fuck who'd gotten out of assault charges in the past and had slipped through our fingers because we lacked evidence.

Avin "El Fuego" Monterro, aka "The Fire," was a twenty-five-year-old mountain lion shifter who'd given himself his own nickname in order to appear more badass. *The punk.* He moved through the warehouse below like he owned the place, a glowing cigarette squeezed tightly in his fingers. Smoke curled

2

out and drifted up toward me, making the air almost as filthy as he was. I had to stifle the urge to cough or flap my wings to push the smoke away. Los Angeles had been a smoke-free city for years, but it wasn't like these gangsters gave a damn.

The 'fireman' dismissed his three lackeys with a wave of his hand, not even bothering to speak. He was an arrogant idiot, and kind of an asshole boss. Those lackeys had risked their skins breaking into a mage shipment for him. They at least deserved to watch him unwrap the prize, didn't they?

But shifters didn't operate on fairness or logic. They were pure instinct—*selfish* instinct—and because of that, they were tearing our city apart. We'd been at war with them for decades now, since before I was born. And now that I was a part of the cause, I was hoping I could help end the violence and suffering of my people... by ending the shifters entirely. They were out of control—on the verge of revealing us to humans and forcing all the magical races into enslavement again, just as things had been centuries ago.

I watched his lackeys trot out with resentful eyes. They might have been wolf shifters based on how they balanced on their toes when they walked. The door slammed behind them and 'hot stuff' rubbed his hands together in greedy glee.

He wanted to be alone? Fine by me. A single shifter was easier to take down. I had backup around the block, anyway, waiting for me to activate the silent

3

magical alarm button on my belt. My fellow enforcers would close in with guns and mage staffs blazing if I needed it.

But I didn't really want backup. My blood was pounding, my senses heightening. This was about to be the biggest bust of my career, the most important one since I'd become Chief Enforcer, and I wanted to handle the entire operation myself if I could help it. My fingers clenched and unclenched as I waited, ready to pounce.

I just needed to catch the little 'matchstick man' red-handed first. Once proven guilty, Mage Law encouraged execution instead of arrest. It was extreme, but I understood why it was necessary. It was either *them* or *us*, and if we didn't take them out immediately, they would kill even more innocent magic users. We couldn't allow that to happen. It was my *job* to ensure that it didn't.

I held my breath, heartbeat quickening as I stared down. I adjusted my bodycam so the feed focused directly on my target as he strolled along.

El Fuego used a crowbar to pry open a wooden crate. Sawdust and straw spilled out of the box and onto the jerk's expensive leather shoes. But I didn't notice the sawdust, other than the fact that the foot-prints in it would be another piece of evidence to tie the skinny shifter to the scene. I focused on the glowing jewel that the scraggly, couldn't-grow-a-beard-to-save-his-life shifter held up.

It was a mage jewel.

These shifters are going for the big guns. This war is getting worse.

My mouth dried out and my eyes grew wide, as the glowing lime green gem was lifted out of the box. Mage jewels came in all colors, shapes, and sizes, but there were two things they all had in common: they were all filled with otherworldly power, and because of that power, they all glowed.

For centuries, they'd been used to protect villages from floods and to end droughts; to stop wildfires, earthquakes, and tornadoes. They used to do a million different things. Once upon a time, the glowing jewels had even kept magical communities hidden from humans. But now... the damn shifters were trying to weaponize the magic.

This was, by far, the largest mage jewel I'd ever seen. It was nearly the size of 'sparky's' fist. His cigarette fell when his jaw dropped open at the sight of the jewel.

Yeah. You and me both. Holy mother of dragons, that jewel is huge.

I fought off the bile that rose in my stomach. If that jewel fell into shifter hands, it could do a lotta damage. It was more imperative than ever that I wrap up this arrest and execution in a pretty little bow, and hand El Fuego over to the Mage Council on a silver platter.

The burning end of his cig started to smolder in the

straw and he quickly jumped to stamp it out. That was when I made my move.

I leapt from the beam and spread my wings. Catching the air, I shifted my body weight, angling myself down and tucking my wings so that I gained speed and shot like a bullet toward my target. A wild smile spread across my face as I rode the adrenaline rush like a junkie rode a high.

El Fuego looked up a millisecond before I hit him.

SLAM.

I smacked into his torso and spun quickly, using my wings to hover, then kicked his cheek before we hit the floor. He gave a grunt as we crashed down, the impact of my body and my leg a double whammy. The jewel rolled across the floor, tinkling like a wind chime, but thankfully it hadn't broken.

As I pushed off him, I quickly grabbed a Lethal Protection Potion off my belt that would prevent him from killing me—for the next five minutes anyway. I smashed the little bottle into my chest and smeared the green goo around.

Licking my lips, I watched as the skinny little wet noodle scrambled to his knees.

I ached to kick him again as he pushed up, but I had protocols to follow. I couldn't completely ignore them. A couple hits, I could get away with, but no cheap-shots.

Stupid bodycams forcing me to follow the rules.

I hit the silent magical alarm on my belt, calling in

backup. Outside, a car alarm would go off on one of our undercover rides, alerting the team to close in. Technically, I needed at least one witness before making any moves, and definitely before making an execution—unless, of course, it was self-defense. And now that the fight had already started, maybe it would be?

The blood in my system pounded like the bass beat at a club. For a second, it was the only thing I could hear. Then, in a move that surprised the shit out of me, 'matchstick boy' grabbed me and flipped me over his head so I smacked to the floor, a broken piece of the wooden crate digging into my back.

Fuck!

My vision went white. Pain left me gasping as El Fuego shifted, transforming into a long, muscled, mountain lion. His tan fur looked almost grey in the moonlight, but his yellow eyes glowed furiously as he stalked toward me.

Part of me was pissed, but the other part of me was licking her lips and giving a sultry smile. *Yes.* This was exactly the kind of fight I wanted. After all those days my team spent tracking this asshole down, I was ready to see what he was made of. I wanted to ride the bull, so to speak. I wanted to feel that rush that I only got two places in life: in a fight or with violently hot sex.

I forced myself onto my knees before my vision had even fully righted itself. Black specks still swam around in my eyes as I lifted a palm and shot some fire at the asshole.

"Hola, El Fuego! I'd like you to meet my little flame!" My cheesy line didn't come out so great when I was still gasping from the literal fucking thorn in my side. But whatever. Fucker wasn't gonna live through this to mock me, anyway.

To my shock, El Fuego didn't start to smell like burnt fur or barbecue. His golden hair didn't even shrivel and blacken under my blaze.

What. The. Hell?

The mountain lion's amber eyes gleamed with satisfaction as he stalked right through my fire.

The impulse that had been driving me to fight suddenly stuttered.

El Fuego's mouth opened, showcasing huge yellow canines. His tongue flicked across those sharp points, drawing my eyes, before human words poured out of his lion mouth. "Did you think I got that nickname by accident, little fly?"

He used the shifter insult for fae to make me bristle, but I was too busy gaping.

Motherfucker was fireproof.

That's when he leapt.

My stomach lurched, and I watched in what felt like slow-motion as El Fuego's claws came unsheathed. His paws were the size of my face. Those claws were large enough to rake out my intestines with a single swipe.

He couldn't kill me thanks to the potion I'd applied, but that didn't mean he couldn't do unspeakable damage.

I shut my eyes and let my glamour wash over me a second before impact. Using his words against him, I transformed my body into a fly and buzzed right over his head as he came crashing down. I flipped around in the air and landed on his back, letting my glamour drop and my normal body return.

An insatiable itch immediately raced across my skin. *Fucking glamour...* it allowed all fae to transform their appearance but the aftereffects were brutal. It was worse than being swarmed by a herd of bloodthirsty mosquitoes.

El Fuego bucked wildly, but I latched on with one hand like he was a bronco. Then I pulled my gun from its holster and held it to the side of his head.

"El Fuego, you've been caught red-handed at the scene of a crime. I condemn you—"

His head moved wildly and one long tooth pierced my calf. A stinging pain shot up my leg and my vision went red as I yanked my limb away.

BAM.

The shot echoed through the room. I had to leap sideways off his body as it crashed to the floor. My heart trilled in my chest as I watched his body fall still.

Part of me felt a little sick to my stomach, like I always did after an execution. But the other part of me smacked that first part around, slammed down its cowboy hat, pulled up its chaps, and said, *"That's what happens when you mess around in my town, motha' fucka!"*

Because it was.

Moments later, my second in command burst through the warehouse's exterior door.

Tallulah Bell was a pixie with neon pink hair who was more piss and vinegar than pixie dust. She fluttered near my head. Only six inches tall, she was typically underestimated. But she was a total badass. I'd seen her wipe the floor with unsuspecting shifters more than once.

Tee glanced at the scene and her lip curled back in disgust. "*Ugh.* I prefer when you toast them."

"He was fireproof?" It came out as a question. Because that little golden nugget of info hadn't been written in his file. Someone in recon hadn't done a very good job.

Tee's face quirked in disbelief as she stared down at the shifter. "He was? Huh. Well then. Good thing the council passed that human weapons ordinance I guess. Why humans are so obsessed with loud, awful-smelling firearms though, I just don't understand."

I shrugged. My nose was not nearly as sensitive to the particles in the air as the little pixie's. She made a show of coughing and waving her hand in front of her face as she flew through the room.

Tee had argued endlessly when the ordinance passed about ten years ago. She'd wanted *citrus-scented* gunpowder, and approximately no one gave a damn. She was *still* complaining about it.

"Didn't save any baddies for me, did you?" she asked, longingly. Her pixie dust packed a buzzing black punch and burned up skin like road rash.

I shook my head and started scratching my itchy arms. "Did you catch the rest of the furries outside?"

I stepped forward gingerly on my injured leg. The puncture wound from his teeth immediately sent pain flaring up and down my limb. *Damn, that hurt.* But the pain also came with a sick, twisted sense of satisfaction. Because I'd won.

"Think we got them all," Tee responded, tilting her head to study my leg. "You injured, Princess?"

I glared at her mid-scratch. "Don't call me that."

She held up her hands. "Hey. It's not my fault you were born with a crown on your head and a silver spoon—"

I shot a bolt of fire at her, but I didn't put any real speed behind it. Tee flew to the side, dodging it easily.

"Someone's grumpy. Now I get why you went all Texas Chainsaw Massacre instead of a neat kill. Having a bad night?"

I rolled my eyes and pointed toward the mage jewel. "Think you could pick that up?"

Tee's eyes landed on the jewel and then went round as saucers. "Whoa, momma. Talk about a big one. I mean, I thought Aaron's cock was—"

"Tee, work talk." I didn't know how many times a

11

day I had to remind her not to talk about her mate. Too many. My annoyance seemed to make the itch intensify and I raked at my skin like mad.

"Oh, right. Yeah. That's one *big* mage jewel."

I shook my head in amusement, limping toward the door like some kind of allergic walking dead, but another squad member stepped inside just before I reached it.

Speak of the devil...

Aaron—Tee's mate—was a siren with a voice that could make you stop, turn, and drop your pants from a block away. Literally. Siren song could make people into puppets. So, while their mind might fight a siren, their body couldn't. Not that anyone would want to resist dropping their pants for Aaron. His smile wasn't anything to scoff at. Before I'd learned he and Tee were an item, I might have had a little bit of a crush on him.

He gave me a smile and Tee an even wider one. Then he pulled off his black police hat and ran a hand through his silky sable hair. "Hey, we got the others. Clean up crew is on the way. You all ready to go?"

I nodded as the itchy, prickling sensation spread out across my neck and back. I undid the top button of my collar and reached around so I could dig my nails in and ease the sensation. "Yeah, let's get out of here before I end up scratching my skin off."

"You had to use glamour?" Aaron asked.

"Yeah, and it feels like fucking poison ivy now." The

itch came on stronger as the adrenaline from the fight wore off.

Aaron shook his head. "Nothing I can do about that one. But..."

As he bent down and sang a little ditty, I had to turn my head away. Siren songs were seductive, and I did *not* want to get all hot and bothered by Tee's man. But the song did the trick. The wounds on my leg and back healed instantly.

For some reason, sirens could heal *bleeding* wounds. But internal injuries, rashes, anything else? Nope. Their power cut off. I'd always wondered if it was an evolutionary adaptation, a protection from underwater predators such as sharks who could sense blood in the water. I suspected as much, but asking people about their powers in detail was rude. Asking *employees* when you were the *boss* was twice as bad. So, I kept my theories in theory-land.

"Thanks," I said to Aaron, even as I scratched under my armpits like an ape.

Damn, this was turning into a full body tingle. I'd never glamoured into an animal before. That shit was for shifters. I was even more sure of it now.

I glanced between him and Tee. "Can I meet you guys back at the station for debrief and reports? Think you can tell the press I'll hold a conference in an hour to announce this takedown? I gotta—"

I scratched my chest and rubbed my thighs together so hard they chafed. After a glamour, clothes were a fucking nuisance. I could end this itch so much faster if I was naked. And showered.

"Go. Get outta here." Tee waved me off and turned to Aaron. "You take the dead shifter over to the council morgue. I'll take the jewel."

I practically sprinted out of the place. As soon as I was outside, I had no choice but to glamour myself again, so that the humans couldn't see me flying home.

Well, not *no choice*. But sitting in an uber and not scratching my cooch in public for the fifty-minute car ride just wasn't much of a choice at all.

Luckily, in L.A., most people didn't look past the tips of their surgically altered noses. Or, if they did, it was only to scan their phones. Hopefully that meant no one would see me as I altered my appearance to look more like a shadow, just a barely discernible silhouette against the nighttime sky.

I leapt into the air and flew through the light-polluted night back to my apartment, a small box of a living space on the other side of town. I landed on the front porch and walked easily through the wards my best friend had set up to protect me, unlocking the door and relocking it behind me.

As soon as I was inside, I shucked off my shirt and bra, not even bothering to turn on the light. I had zero shame, and once my back was free to the air, I rubbed up against my couch like a fucking bear, crushing my wings and not even caring. I struggled to safely remove my gun and my magical sleep grenades without setting one off and putting myself into a three-hour coma. Finally, I set the belt aside and slid down my pants until they got stuck on my ankles, tangled up in my work boots.

But even that was sweet relief.

The cool air kissed my irritated skin and made the awful itching recede a bit. I took a breath and just let my tense muscles relax, trying to meditate the itch away. If I could do that, I wouldn't have to take an hour-long ice-cold shower, standing there as the frigid drops pelted my skin.

You fucking nailed it tonight, I told myself.

Affirmation mantras were good for the soul. My soul liked them with a side of swear words. Somehow it made them more impactful.

A blissed-out smile came over my face when the air conditioner flipped on and shot cold air right at my ass from the vent next to my couch. I sat down on the floor, enjoying the chill before yanking off my boots.

That was when the door to my apartment slammed open. I nearly jumped out of my skin when a backlit silhouette appeared in my doorway. I scrambled for my utility belt, tits smacking my arms and getting in the way.

A woman's voice rang out. "Aubry, you fucked up big time."

AUBRY

THERE WERE ONLY FOUR PEOPLE WHO HAD A KEY TO THIS apartment. My parents, my ex, and me. So, unless my ex had undergone a sex-change to match his pussy-assed attitude, or some random chick had picked the lock, then that could mean only one thing—it was my mother. And based on the condescension in the intruder's tone, I had a bad feeling I was right on the money.

I sighed in annoyance and got right back to scratching, not bothering to dress or greet her at the door. "What do you want, Mother?"

The queen of the summer fae stormed into my living room and tore off her sunglasses, fluffing the furry red boa draped around her scrawny little neck. Her tiara twinkled in the nightlight I always kept on in the bathroom. I kinda wished mom would have caught her damn boa on something and strangled herself when she was marching her pompous ass through my front hall.

"What do *I* want?" she cried theatrically. "You just ruined the bust of the year, and you're worried about what *I* want? Darling, you should be asking what *the council* wants. And they want *you*—preferably on a skewer and roasting over the flames."

I rolled my eyes at her dramatic antics. "Well, call me Wilber and put an apple in my mouth," I snapped. "I got the fire; I can roast myself. But honestly, when they hear it was *El Fuego* that I took out tonight, I'm sure they'll be singing a different tune."

"They *know* it was El Fuego," she deadpanned. "It's *The Shadow* that they're angry about. Why must you always piss the mages off? Just like your grandfather."

I froze, mid-scratch. "The Shadow wasn't there. I would have known if he was."

"Would you?" she asked haughtily, tapping her stilettoed toes on the stone tiles of my floor. "Just get dressed, Aubry. And wear your damned tiara for once. This is a formal fucking hearing. The council is waiting."

I stood, the itch suppressed by worry as a wave of cold sweat moved across my body. I crossed my arms to appear more aloof, but deep down, her words had gotten to me. I'd caught El Fuego. But had I missed someone even bigger? Thoughts of the man who had stood in the doorway crossed my mind and I shook my head. No. This couldn't be happening. This was my biggest success, not my greatest failure. I couldn't have possibly fucked it up like that.

"Now? As in, *now* now?" I asked with a raised brow.

"Yes!" she cried in exasperation, tossing the ends of her boa. "I got called away from the Annual Imp Fundraiser for this! So unless you want me to drag you in there buck-ass naked, I suggest you *get. Fucking. Dressed*."

"Okay, hold your saggy tits!" I threw my hands up and spun out of the room, all but dashing to my closet.

"No, you hold *yours*!" she shouted after me. "They're on display for the whole god-forsaken world to see... what kind of fae royal..."

I rolled my eyes and ignored her, quickly skimming through my clothes.

This is not happening. This is not *happening!*

But it was.

I inhaled deeply through my nose, and exhaled slowly through my mouth, mentally commanding my body and brain to calm down. There was no way The Shadow—enemy number one on the mage's shit list— had been there. This was obviously just a test. Maybe even just a cover: bring me in on false pretenses, then congratulate me and give me a raise? Yeah, that must've been it. I took a deep breath and cracked my neck, trying to calm down. I needed to chill the fuck out.

Pulling a dark training outfit off the hanger, I struggled to hop into it quickly. I wanted something nice-ish, but also practical. You never knew what to expect with the council. They were like the Tyler Durdens of our little mage fight-club—half insane, half genius, but completely in control. Even though Dad had a seat on the council, it was a minor seat. Everyone knew that the senior mages held all the cards, and the deck was loaded against anyone they decided to beat.

I had to be ready for anything.

I grabbed a duffel and a change of clothes—tossing my tiara in, just in case—but I refused to wear the damn thing on principle. I was Chief-fucking-Enforcer, a title I'd *earned*. Princess Aubry was just a title I'd been born with. It wasn't who I was. And if I was going in front of the council, I wanted to feel like myself, not a damn facade.

I strolled back into the living room, grabbing my belt and reequipping my weapons, then added extra ammo from a stash I kept hidden behind my hall mirror.

My mother's face turned chartreuse when she saw that I still wore my combat boots and she clenched her fists. But we'd had the same damn argument for too many years for her to actually believe she'd win.

"We taking your town car?" I asked, shoving past her on my way to the door, duffel in hand. I was kinda hoping she'd lose her balance on those skinny high heels and land face first in my sweaty pile of work clothes. But she didn't, because apparently fate preferred to fuck snarky fae like me instead of stuck up brunettes.

She scoffed and followed me down the hall, reapplying her shades as I locked up. "Please, Darling. We could have, if *someone* hadn't taken so long to get ready. Now we'll be forced to glamour and fly."

"Are you fucking serious? Do you have any idea how long it takes you to get ready for *anything*?" My mother was the queen of primping. If it had been a sport, she would have won every trophy.

"Of course, I do. Which is why I always allot at least two hours for my beauty regimen, and why I'm never caught dead looking less than perfect. One must always be prepared."

I felt like slapping her sunglasses right off her perfect face and drawing a massive cock on her forehead in red lipstick. *Your beauty regimen can suck a big red dick, Katrina.* She'd always been a hardass on me. She was probably glad that she'd been the one to deliver this bad news. Sometimes I thought she took a sick, twisted sort of satisfaction in my failures.

"Whatever." I glamoured quickly and took to the sky, not even bothering to check if she'd followed me. We whizzed through the clouds, keeping to the shadows, our wings and bodies glamoured to look like nothing more than a patch of darkness. We flew so fast that if humans looked up and blinked, we'd be gone from their line of sight.

Touching down on the sidewalk directly in front of my precinct headquarters, I marched determinedly toward the seven-story building made of tinted glass and steel. I went up the exterior steps and through the front doors before dropping my glamour. The annoying, prickling sensation raced across my body like a herd of ants, biting me as they went. It took every ounce of control I had to keep from stripping and scratching right in the lobby.

If I turned left, I'd enter my home away from home, the precinct. I could hear the buzz of work, phones, arguments, and chatter drifting from the precinct's open doors. But I didn't turn left. I took the stairs to the lobby on the second floor. That lobby had much nicer carpet than ours, a plush grey. And the secretary's desk wasn't scratched up like ours. It was polished for the Mage Council's posh guests.

"Good evening, Chief Summerset. The council members are expecting you in chamber five." Lana, a squat gnome with straw blonde hair told me. Her job was coordinating the meeting rooms above for mages who portaled in from around the world.

I nodded in the secretary's general direction and kept moving, bypassing the elevators to take the emergency stairs instead. As a faerie, I preferred to get places fast via flying—though, having to use glamour to hide my wings sucked big time—so there was nothing quite as tedious and annoying as waiting for a slow-motion box to creep up the levels. I'd rather be winded and in motion. Besides, it helped keep me in top shape, a necessity in my line of work.

Side bonus, I could make pissed off faces and curse

my mother as I trudged upstairs because there were no cameras in the stairwells anymore. Not after it had been determined that they were the source of too many Mage Police Gone Wild leaks to social media.

I got to the fifth floor and passed a few mages, sirens, and pixies in the dimly lit hall, each of us ignoring the other. We went about our business as if our individual tasks were the most important in the world and only *we* were qualified to complete them. For me, that was actually true. For everyone else, they were just arrogant dicks. I liked it though. They were my kind of people.

Pausing outside of chamber five, I took a moment to catch my breath and collect my racing thoughts.

No matter what goes on in there, you are strong. You're a badass bitch. And you're going to take whatever bullshit they dish out like the fucking champ that you are. No tears. No hurt feelings. Just cold-hard confidence and cold-hearted determination.

I'd barely taken a single step inside the doorway when Citrine Pierce's voice assaulted me from her high and mighty pedestal in the apex of the circular council room.

"Aubry Summerset." Her voice was like a whip, cracking over my head when she asked, "Do you have any idea what you've done?"

Two council members perched on Citrine's right, one on her left, all of which looking like bloodthirsty vultures.

Grinding my teeth, I kept walking until I neared the circular inlay in the middle of the marble floor. The room was mostly dark, save for a single white light shining directly above Citrine's head, showcasing her silvery hair. It was an intimidation tactic, one that I hated to be on the receiving end of. Despite the low light, the circle in the middle of the council room floor was easy enough to find because it glowed with undulating turquoise magic. I loathed these damn circles. But I had no choice, they were a part of every council hearing.

At least today's trial didn't appear to have the full council. On Citrine's right, sat Indigo Summerset, King of the Summer Fae, a man I was unfortunate enough to call Dad. His black-lined wings spread out on either side of his seat, his face like carved marble, showcasing disapproval, an expression I was incredibly familiar with from him. Next to him was Obidiah Jenson, a man with dark brown skin and a beautiful South African accent. On Citrine's left, sat Lotus Mao, the woman who spoke on behalf of the Asian mages.

I took a deep breath and stepped inside the circle. As soon as both my boots were in, they were rooted there, the Movement Restriction Spell tying the magic within my body to the magic in the floor like an electromagnet. My feet could no longer move. I hated feeling like a bleeding rat at their buzzard-like feet, but I was in no position to fight back. I would literally be held hostage until my impromptu work evaluation aka

trial aka witch hunt was officially complete and they
let me walk out of here.

Lucky me.

"I asked you a question, Chief Enforcer Summerset,"
Citrine snarled. Her silver hair gleamed, but it was the
only part of her face even remotely attractive. Her
brows overhung her eyes so that they just looked like
dark pits and no amount of botox could remove the
sneer her face was constantly set in. I couldn't read her
expression, but her tone said enough. She was furious.

Beside her, my dad's stiffened posture said the
same. Which was absolutely, one-hundred and ten
percent ridiculous. My nostrils flared and I took a deep
breath so that I didn't mouth off.

In a carefully controlled tone, the kind I used for
press releases, I said, "I saved an invaluable mage jewel
from falling into the clawed, criminal hands of the
shifters, while simultaneously eliminating Public
Threat Number Nineteen who goes by the name of—"

"El Fuego," one of the other council members said
in a nasally voice, cutting me off. Lotus Mao watched
me stoically. "Yes, we are aware."

Then what's the damned problem? I wanted to ask, but
I was supposed to wait to speak unless spoken to.
Fucking bullshit chamber regulations.

"You are decisive, Miss Summerset," Lotus said. "But
also, impulsive. When you follow your gut, instead of
protocol, there are always repercussions."

My cheeks flamed. I was by-the-book most of the

damn time, and only went off-book on unimportant shit. I wanted to argue with her, but she hadn't asked a question, so I couldn't respond or deny. I simply nodded curtly and waited for the next council member to speak.

I can't wait to hear what other bullshit they've come up with.

My father opened his mouth, but then a puff of orange and yellow smoke appeared in the corner of the room. The British member of the Mage Council, John Daggler, brushed off his grey suit and strode up to the podium, taking a seat beside my father.

"Sorry I'm late," he offered to the other council members before turning to address me. I stared at his weak jawline with disinterest. "I've reviewed your body cam live feed. Not only did you act before you called for backup—a direct violation of protocol—but, you also acted before you were certain you had the proper suspect, which is just plain sloppy."

Bullshit! I wanted to scream. I'd properly identified him as El Fuego, the mountain lion shifter from my file, and I'd caught him red-handed with a mage jewel. What more did they want? I smelled a set-up.

"El Fuego was there, yes," Councilwoman Lotus conceded, as if reading my mind. "But you jumped the gun and missed the opportunity to take down none other than the infamous Shadow. Your recklessness has officially kept us from a massive win against the shifter gangs threatening this region."

"Do you deny these charges?" my father asked.

Finally, a question.

"Of course I do." My fists clenched tight and my nails dug into the skin of my palms. I wanted to say more but I held back.

"Under what circumstances?" He leaned forward and rested his chin on his clasped hands, waiting with the imaginary patience of a saint.

I knew better. That expression was the same one Dad had used when he'd found out I was dating a shifter when I was sixteen. It was the same expression he'd used when I'd failed one of the physical tests at the Mage Police Academy on my first try. It was his 'long-suffering patience with my ineptitude' expression. I couldn't fucking stand it.

I looked away from him and focused on Citrine, biting my tongue as I contemplated. If I didn't choose my words carefully here, they could be my last as an Enforcer. *How the hell did I go from hero to zero in a matter of hours?* It was like I was choking on my own kryptonite.

"Insufficient reconnaissance," I decided. "Whoever handled this case file either did an immaculately shitty job, or they left out invaluable information on purpose to set me up."

"Explain," Council leader Citrine said.

"Not only was Drake, *The Shadow*, Guerra left completely out of the file, but Avin, *El Fuego*, Monterro's information was incomplete and/or intentionally tampered with."

"Explain further," Citrine snapped, moving so I could finally see her eyes.

"He was apparently immune to fire. This was written *nowhere* in the file. Had I not used my *decisiveness* and *gut instincts*—" Oh hell yeah, I was totally using their own words against them, those arrogant bumble-bees. "—Then we could have lost far more than The Shadow. We could have lost El Fuego *and* a rare mage jewel as well. Considering my options, I think I did quite well."

Councilwoman Citrine stared at me with stern disinterest. "The council will convene for just a moment."

Again, I nodded, because I was physically unable to do much else. It wasn't like I could sit or pace.

They huddled together near the podium, exchanging harsh whispers, while I stood there with my heart racing.

Breathe, you badass, you. This might not have been the surprise raise you were hoping for, but you can bounce back from this. You just have to show those stuffy council members what you're made of. Though, how I planned to do that while I was stuck in place like a punching bag for their pleasure, was anyone's guess.

The council dispersed and took their seats once more.

Councilwoman Lotus, the nasally mage whose face

held more wrinkles than a map from 1982, laced her fingers and held her head high. "Miss Summerset, the council finds this evidence intriguing. But, while we will be conducting a full-scale investigation on your behalf, we do not believe it to be sufficient circumstances for an acquittal."

What the ever-loving fuck? I wanted to scream and lash out at them. I wanted to smack their heads together and swab the cum out of their ears. I mean, were they not even listening? I just saved our asses! The Shadow always eluded us—*always*. Even more experienced enforcers had been met with a cold trail and a dead end from that man. They should have seen that coming. But taking out El Fuego? Saving a mage jewel? That shit should have counted for something.

My father glared down at me with hard emerald eyes and he spoke next. Of course, the council would make him issue their ruling. I wondered if he got some kind of twisted pleasure out of it. "You will be demoted from your position as chief and watched like a hawk during any and all future missions until further notice. One wrong move, and your enforcer career is over."

Black rage pulsed through me, and they were goddamned lucky I was immobilized. If I could have reached out and crushed Dad's windpipe with nothing more than *the force* like fucking Darth Vader, then I totally would have. How could he do this to his own daughter? How could he embarrass and humiliate me like that?

He looked like he was about to dismiss me, but right before he did, he paused. Maybe he'd actually caught sight of the laser beams I was trying to shoot from my eyes. Because he finally sighed and asked, "Does this seem an adequate punishment to you, ex-chief enforcer?"

Mother of god, I wanted an anvil to fall from the sky and crush his dumb ass. "No, Councilman Indigo, it does not."

He spread his long, willowy hands out and shrugged. "And what would you suggest?"

This earned him a couple sharp glares from his fellow councilmembers, but he ignored them for the moment. He was giving me, quite possibly, my very last chance to turn this around. I yanked my imaginary anvil back from where it hovered over his head.

I huffed out a frustrated sigh. "Give me a week to take down The Shadow. Now that I know he's resurfaced in L.A., I'm sure I'll be able to track him."

"Out of the question," Councilman Daggler stated, his pompous British tone burning my ears like hot tea. "Her sentence has already been determined."

My father nodded. "This is true. But, perhaps, if another council member argued the matter on her behalf..."

Triton! I wished I could scream my best friend's name out loud. He'd stick up for me. He'd make sure these old bastards saw some sense.

He was the youngest council member to ever grace

the chamber floor. A minor council member, like my father, but still; any council member could speak for me. Citrine was his mentor, but he and I had been friends since college. Would he speak for me? I *needed* him to, because this job was everything to me.

I pressed my lips together in a thin determined line. I was just going to have to convince him that standing up to his mentor was the right thing to do.

How the hell I was gonna pull that off, I had no idea.

DRAKE

THE FLAME DANCED FROM MY LIPS OVER TO THE METAL bars, heating them to a bright hot-white. I gave a low hum of satisfaction as I watched the metal soften, then used my claws to bend it to my will. When the bar was firmly welded to the frame, I turned to Easton. A puff of smoke escaped my lips as I said, "Another."

Easton smiled and shook his tawny head. He'd kept his human form for this job because we needed at least one set of hands. My claws were good for swiping and slicing things, but not holding up prison bars. That took a bit more finesse than my dragon form could manage.

He easily hoisted up the next iron bar and held it in place for me.

Easton had crafted the bars himself in his shop, the same place he'd built almost all of our illegal weapons. Selling arms on the black market was one of the few ways for a shifter to make a decent living anymore. And we were damned efficient at it.

Of course, we weren't fabricating *guns* at the moment. No, our intentions were far more sinister...

I wedged my tail farther into the hollowed-out earthen hallway so I could get a better angle. My dragon could shift into a variety of sizes, depending on the space, but that tended to change the strength of my flame. For welding, I needed to be a little bigger than this underground passage was meant to hold. It made things awkward.

But Easton waited patiently in his welding gear, mask down, as I craned my neck and huffed out a jet of fire. My black scales reflected the light as I melted the last bar into place.

I took a second to watch the entrancing sight of the metal cooling—the soft fade from white to orange was beautiful. My claws clenched and my stomach tightened. The fire held me riveted. But I rarely allowed myself to see it.

Fire was dangerous when you loved it.

And I loved it.

Next to me, Easton coughed, snapping me out of my daze. I'd tried to keep the flames hot enough to minimize the smoke, but we didn't have a ton of ventilation underground.

I shifted, my limbs contorting, heat sizzling through my veins as my body changed shape, and turned back into a six-foot plus human. I was dressed in a grey collared shirt and slacks, looking exactly as I had before I'd turned into my dragon.

I ran a hand through my black hair as I eyed the welds. "Not bad for a fly trap, huh?" I said, admiring my work.

Easton removed his welding hood and flicked on a work light. The blond man tested the door to the prison cell, ensuring that the bars could still slide to the side smoothly. The iron shafts closed off the front of a dark, concrete box with a dirt floor. The spot used to be just another storage space in our underground lair. But now, it was gonna play host to an annoying little gnat.

Easton ran his gloved hands over the welds near the food flap. If anyone else had double checked my work that thoroughly, I would have been insulted. But Easton just couldn't help himself. He was a perfectionist.

"Come on, Goldilocks. You know it's *just right*," I goaded.

"Shut up with that already," he tossed back, punching my bicep. He hated that nickname. But his golden hair and his animal made it all too easy. Bodie and I loved to rile him up with it.

I didn't respond, just walked down the short earthen tunnel away from our newly created prison cell and took the stairs. About halfway up, the steps flattened off into a landing with a single door. If I continued climbing, they'd lead me to an intersecting hallway full of storage rooms and random shit. But I didn't continue upward. Instead, I took the door and entered our main meeting area.

Two hard plastic tables had been pushed together with a trio of folding chairs surrounding them. A flatscreen TV was mounted on a sidewall and another random-ass table and chairs—pub style this time—sat squashed in the back. Not lush accommodations, but we'd had to sneak everything down here under the noses of those damn MPs.

The Mage Police, or MPs as we liked to call them, cranked up the heat on this part of the city until even innocent shifters and humans were left sweating their every move. Skid Row always had their evil attention. We could have moved our ops elsewhere, but most packs were here. And what was a shifter without his pack?

Nothing. I knew that all too well...

Lorena, a wolf shifter who was the plump happy grandma everybody wanted—until they realized she was packing heat—hurried over to help Easton slip out of his welding overalls. Her glock peaked out of her waistband as she did.

"You poor thing—must be burning up!" she clucked as she helped him step out of the pants so he was in street clothes, a red t-shirt and dark blue jeans. "Let me get you a Gatorade."

She bustled over to the fridge and grabbed him one.

"Thanks." Easton always had an easy grin for people.

Unlike me. My face didn't work that way. Neither did the rest of me, really. There was nothing happy or easy-going about me.

I kept moving until I reached a locked filing cabinet in the corner. Using the key I'd stashed in my pocket earlier, I unlocked the drawer.

"Lorena?" I said. "We need the room."

She turned to look at me, Easton's gear filling her hands. "I'll just wash—"

"*Now*." I cut her off. "And send Bodie down."

She gave me a curt nod and hurried away, up the staircase to the tenement-like apartment complex that hid our lair.

"Dude, the word is please. Or thank you. Either one would work." Easton rolled his eyes.

I didn't bother to respond to that.

I shoved my hand into the cabinet and pulled out the file we needed. Easton's lectures on manners were far less important than the next job we had to pull. This wasn't just some under-the-radar gig. We were gonna go head-to-head with the MPs and show those mage fucks we were serious.

We needed every detail to be perfect.

I sat down at the head of the table. Easton took his spot at my right-hand side as I flipped open the file and ran my finger down the edge of the photograph paper clipped to the first page.

Aubry Summerset.

Fucking summer fae princess.

Head of the Los Angeles MP.

My lip curled into a snarl. *Look at that snobbish stare,* I thought. It ruined what might have otherwise been a beautiful face.

In the background, Easton pulled a bag of Fritos out of nowhere and started eating. The guy was a bottomless pit. It seemed like his bear instincts to put on weight for the winter couldn't be suppressed, though he never actually put on weight. He worked out so much that he simply bulked up.

I couldn't deny Aubry was attractive in a way that made heads turn. At least, for a fae, that is. Not a *real* woman. Real women didn't have lithe figures with legs for days or wings sprouting out of their backs. *Real* women had meaty thighs that I could dig my fingers into while I fucked them raw.

"Dude, careful, you look like you're about to flame," Easton warned as he licked his fingers.

I glared down at the photo one last time. "I'm just imagining how much she's gonna *love* being locked up and at my mercy."

The words came out harsh, but my dick hardened at the thought. The mental image of Aubry kneeling in front of me, her lips parted suggestively, her eyes wide and wanting, suddenly infiltrated my mind. I sucked in a deep breath and quickly shoved the image away.

We knew she belonged to a BDSM club from our research. One of my aliases belonged to the same club.

Syn. Too bad I'd never crossed paths with her there. I would have whipped her raw...

Jesus, I needed to fuck and clear my head before we pulled this job. But there was just no goddamned time. Princess Bitch had ruined our last one. We needed her out before she ruined another.

I slammed her picture onto the table. "She fucking ONE-S.K.'ed El Fuego," I growled. Her *one shot kill* was just another night on duty for her. But for me? Months and months of planning, subterfuge, bribes, and spying had gone to waste.

We'd lost another mage jewel.

And one of Easton's friends.

Easton set down his bag of chips and stopped eating. He put his one clean hand on the table, not touching me, because he knew I'd hate it, but just... getting close. "I know."

His eyes became slushy and I looked away. Out of the three of us, Easton was the softest.

Me? I couldn't afford to be. Not when every alpha in town came to me with questions, issues, problems. Not when I was constantly trying to keep one step ahead of the stupid wasps and stick-wielding magic men.

I took a deep breath, staring at the subtle lines in the plastic tabletop, seeking calm. The anger that I worked so hard to restrain bubbled up despite my efforts. *Damn it.* I tried to suppress it, but my nostrils still flared, sending out a couple smoke rings.

I wanted to end her.

My fingers twitched at the thought of snapping her neck, like they could almost feel her soft skin underneath them as they squeezed her life away.

Bodie walked in, then. His light green eyes settled on me and he gave a nod of acknowledgement as he walked to his seat on my left side. *The kid.* Twenty-fucking-two and he already had a seat at my table. I didn't know if that said great things about him or terrible things about how this war was going for us.

We'd lost so many good shifters...

I swallowed.

Bodie sat down and ran a hand through his ebony hair. He didn't even comb it half the time, just did that finger thing. But the rest of him was neat and meticulous. Which was good, otherwise I'd have been on his ass. I didn't do sloppy.

People watched the three of us. Bodie, because he was an alpha. Easton, because he should have been an alpha, and if people weren't so fucked up, he would have been. Me... because I was *The Shadow*. And somehow, that gave the shifters hope. Which was stupid. I dealt in weapons, not hope. I wasn't the hero they were looking for. And yet, I strived for it anyway. It didn't make any fucking sense.

Bodie might have been better at it than me, if he weren't the alpha of one of the largest wolf packs in the state. He spent every spare second hunting down fuckers who were looking to hurt or had already hurt his pack members, yet somehow, the kid had managed to stay off the MP's radar.

I was a little envious of that.

Bodie adjusted his wide-rimmed rectangular glasses and then reached for the map inside the file. He carefully unfolded it, smoothing out the creasing. Kid was almost as particular as I was. He traced his eyes over the routes we'd marked out.

"Too many tents here." He pointed at Carlos Avenue.

"There weren't any last week." Easton leaned forward, crunching on another chip.

"L.A. cops made the homeless camps move," Bodie responded. "Guess the Museum of Death a little ways down the street complained about the homeless scaring off patrons."

I shook my head. "Goddamned walking sticks, they're ruining shit all over the place."

This was the *mages'* fault. They were the ones constantly starting fires. Causing earthquakes. Buying up properties and driving up the prices so decent shifters couldn't afford homes anymore.

They were trying to starve us out of existence.

That wasn't gonna happen. I wouldn't let it.

We'd tried the indirect approach. We'd tried to lay low and stay out of their way, forming our own tight-knit communities. We'd tried to fly under the radar. But those fuckers were hunting us down like sheep. They didn't see us as anything more than a fun meal.

We'd show them. We'd steal their damned princess, then I'd slaughter her and the entire rescue squad they sent after her. I'd be a dead man, but it would be worth it. Because every shifter in the state would know what had happened, and they'd realize it was time to stop eating the mages' shit.

It was time to bite back.

I pointed to another route on the map. "We can go left here," I said, my finger tracing over the thin pink line that marked the road.

Bodie shook his head. "Too crowded."

"Not as crowded as a street lined with tents," I argued.

Easton scratched the golden stubble on his chin. "We could always push back a week. You know how the cops are. Hard core for a week then they ease up. Those camps will be moved again in no time."

I shook my head. "We're not waiting."

Easton sighed heavily. "I know you want—"

"We're *not* waiting." I cut through whatever bullshit he was gonna say. Sometimes, Easton was too mellow for his own good. Bears weren't always as aggressive as dragons. I knew that. He knew that. And he generally deferred to me.

He will *defer to me in this case. I won't let his heart ruin my plans.*

I looked back at Bodie. He was harder than Easton. More ruthless. He might be a kid, but he'd caused his share of death. Maybe even more than I had.

Bodie's green eyes stared back at me. He gave a solemn nod.

I swallowed my smile as I turned back to the file.

"Easton, you might wanna go get changed. You're the bait."

"I really don't think I'm the best choice," Easton started to argue.

I cut him off, holding up a hand. "You're the perfect choice."

He sighed and grumbled, but went upstairs to get his appearance magicked.

"Why him and not me?" Bodie asked, pulling a knife from his belt and testing the edge on his fingertip.

"Because you do shit like that."

"He's gonna fumble around, you know it," Bodie snapped.

"I do know it," I shot right back. "It will make him *believable*."

That was a lie. It would make Easton look *suspicious*. Which would trigger the little fly's investigative tendencies. Which was exactly what we wanted.

Bodie rolled his eyes and shoved his knife back into its sheath. Then he pulled the file toward himself. "Fine. He's the lure. Then what?"

I grinned, leaning back in my chair.

When Bodie and I had agreed on the next steps, we broke up the meeting and headed upstairs, to the surface streets of Skid Row. Tents lined the road like a sad, fallen rainbow. Homeless people and homeless shifters wandered and fought and mingled in this concrete jungle.

Bodie spotted a destitute shifter on the street, identifiable because of his gold eyes as he dug through a trash bag. My wolf friend shrugged off the suit jacket that made him look professional and handed it to the shifter. "Hundred bucks for you to take care of this. Better be in mint condition when I come back for it later tonight."

The skinny man nodded his head and clutched Bodie's suit coat like it was precious.

Bodie mussed his hair again and grabbed some leather strips out of his pockets. He wrapped them around his wrists. He yanked on his shirt and untucked it. Then he slouched, transforming himself into a pouty teen instead of the shifter world's best assassin.

He gave me a nod before making his way down the street. No one, not even the gang members down here, touched Bodie.

My mouth quirked up in a small grin as I turned and walked in the opposite direction.

It was time to set up our honeytrap and catch ourselves a fly.

4

AUBRY

I slammed a fist into Triton's side, his muscles flexing to try and soften the blow. My best friend's sandy brown hair became disheveled. It was a good look for the pompous, always-perfect prick. I smiled.

Every time I made contact, a little bit of anger escaped me, cleansing me. My muscles burned. My bones ached. It was fucking revitalizing. Who needed juice cleanses when you could just bash the shit out of someone? That was the way to reset.

Luckily, Trite knew me well enough to know that this wasn't personal, it was just what I needed. He grunted but grinned through the pain. "My ninety-year-old grandmother can hit harder than that. Stop being a bloody pussy."

Gross. He knew I hated when he used that curse combo. *Oh, it's on, Mage-boy.*

We circled each other on the mat, deep in the lower levels of the precinct.

As soon as the meeting with the council had concluded, I'd immediately come here. Nothing soothed an angered spirit quite like beating the shit out of something. Originally, I'd planned on decimating a punching bag, but when I'd passed Triton along the way, I'd dragged him downstairs to spar with me... and talk some sense into him.

The mat flexed gently beneath my bare feet as I circled my friend. Trite's light blue gaze was steady, his knees bent, his arms at the ready. He looked calm, collected, and totally ready for any move I made. It kinda pissed me off.

"Your mentor, Citrine, was fucking with me," I growled, trying to throw him off with conversation.

Lunging, I jabbed at his ribs with one hand before striking out at his jaw with the other. He dodged both hits like he was Neo in *The Matrix*, practically blurring due to his speed. His feet remained planted on the mat, though, so I dropped down and swung my leg out, trying to knock him off balance. But the mage was ready for me—again. He latched onto my thigh and dragged me straight towards him, resting a foot on my chest just under my throat.

"Come on, Aubs. You're better than this. Don't let the council's words bring you down; let them take you higher. Citrine's good at using anger to inspire others."

I growled in frustration, punching the side of his calf before rolling out from beneath him.

The council thinks I'm too impulsive? Damn it, I'll show them impulsive.

I ran at Trite like a freaking linebacker, tackling him to the mat with enough force to knock the wind right out of him. *That* was a move I didn't typically use.

Trite tucked his legs like springs and catapulted me over his head. I hit the mat hard, but I rolled quickly and jumped to my feet. He did the same, and once more, we were circling one another.

"Your head's not in the game, Aubs," he said, eyeing me carefully as we ringed around the mat. "You need to prove to the council—"

"I know!" I cried, launching into another attack. My fists hammered down like hundreds of bullets assaulting his arms as he tried to block.

But just like in the movie, he remained unaffected. As soon as my blows slowed and he found a tiny window of opportunity, he struck, jabbing my jaw hard enough to make me see stars. I blinked and shook out my head, ducking as another fist went sailing above me. My fist found his ribs with a *crack*, and he grunted as he stumbled back.

Take that, Neo!

"Better," Trite said, rubbing his side tenderly as he circled and assessed me. "But not nearly good enough. You usually kick my ass on the mats, *Princess*. Come on! Kick my ass!"

Princess? Oh, he was really fucking with the bull now. *Prepare to meet the horns.*

He didn't wait for my attack—he launched one of his own, coming at me like a hurricane, hellbent on pure annihilation. I brought my arms up to guard my face as he rained down blows on my forearms. Those fuckers were going to be bruised for days.

I needed to channel some energy and rage of my own; needed to counterattack like a *summer fae* would. Like a freaking wildfire consuming everything in my path, leaving nothing but charcoaled ash in my wake.

While Trite jabbed at my arms, trying to reach my face beyond, I brought my leg up and kicked him hard in the gut. His abs were solid and tight, prepared to guard him from any such assault, but it was enough of a jolt to slow his blows and allow me an opportunity of my own.

"I've gotten more arrests," I said in the brief gap, "and executed more shifters in the past year than any of my predecessors. What the hell do they want from me?"

I jumped, roundhouse kicking him in the shoulder hard enough to drop his ass straight to the floor, but he barrel-rolled away before I could pin him, my knee missing his chest and sinking down into the foam of the mat instead.

"Compliance," he answered.

I lurched to my feet, about to attack again, when his foot hit the side of my face and dropped me. My head throbbed, my vision blurry and blackening around the edges. Trite's features suddenly swam into view, wavering before me as if one of us was underwater.

"Are you all right, Aubry?" he asked, reaching out to offer me a hand up.

His voice echoed, as if he were at the end of a long cavern, and I had to squint against the pain it caused as it ricocheted around my skull.

"Yeah, I'm fine," I said as casually as I could, taking his hand and allowing him to heft me up. "Let's go again."

I hadn't even come close to venting enough ire— especially since he kept beating me. My anger was only stacking higher and higher like a precarious tower of rocks. I needed to knock that shit down before it collapsed on its own and crushed me.

"I don't think that's—" Trite began to protest, but suddenly the door flung open and Tallulah fluttered in.

She had both hands resting on her narrow pixie hips, a magically shrunken tablet wedged in between her fist and hip on one side in a little hip holster. "I've been looking all over for you, Triton. Councilwoman Citrine would like to have a word."

Oh, I have a word *for her, all right. The fucking cum-guzzling-thunder-cunt.* Okay, so maybe that was four words all strung together, but whatever. That old mage could go suck a dick. Maybe the red one I still needed to draw on my mother's forehead.

"Please," I looked at Trite. I begged with my eyes.

49

And I never begged. But his word could change everything.

His brow furrowed. "Aubry, you said your terms were taking down The Shadow. He's too dangerous. The very essence of *cold-hearted*. I don't think that it's—"

"Please," I repeated. I needed this. I needed him to put a word in for me.

Trite sighed and looked me over, making sure I wasn't dizzy before letting go of my hand and arm. Then he turned to Tee. "Did she mention the specifics of the conversation?"

Tallulah shrugged. "Just normal business, I think. Intel thinks they found a lead on a meth-toting shark shifter a few miles down the coast. She probably just wants some of your tracking expertise."

Trite nodded and tugged off his sweaty shirt, wiping away the glistening beads on his perfect face. His black stone necklace, the one he never took off, the one that came from his parents, hung around his neck. "Go home and get some rest, Aubs. Maybe a solid night's sleep will do you some good."

I frowned. "You're not coming back to spar with me after you talk to the…"—*arrogant, pig-headed douche-nozzle, nope don't say it aloud*—"… councilwoman?"

Trite grinned and rubbed his short beard, which somehow managed to showcase his physique. It seriously wasn't fair that he was strictly friend-zoned. I knew he'd be happy to break our friendship for some action on the side, but Trite was about to be engaged for one—though it was going to be an arranged marriage, he was still finalizing negotiations—and a manwhore for two. It would also just be way too weird. I didn't feel that *zing* with him.

There was a moment of silence as Trite decided what he was going to do.

Eventually, he sighed and gritted his teeth. "Everyone misses *The Shadow*. The council knows this. These goddamned shifters need to be wiped off the map like dogshit off a shoe. They're a menace. A fucking liability to supernaturals everywhere! How many times this week did you have to stop a shifter from revealing us to humans?"

Tee answered for me. "Thirteen arrests, twenty-two executions."

He snapped and pointed a finger. "Exactly!" He took a deep breath and closed his eyes, apparently trying to find his zen once more or some shit. Trite tended to get extra worked up over shifters. He ran both hands through his sandy blond hair. "Fuck. All right, listen. I'm going to go speak with them. I don't know what good it'll do, but I can try."

I scoffed. It was almost a damned laugh. "Are you kidding me? You don't know what good it'll do? You'll try?"

"Yes, Aubry, it's the best I can do."

"You sound just like my father," I accused, taking a healthy step back.

51

Trite's features softened and he didn't defend himself, which only frustrated me further. He was a minor councilor, yes. So was my dad. The only major councilors were mages who were centuries old. Trite and I used to jokingly call them the Cryptkeepers. But now that I was living out a horror story they'd created, for no good reason, I didn't find that name as funny.

I stared hard at Trite, shoving down any tears and trying to keep my voice level. "Both you and my father have the power to speak on my behalf. You could convince them to reinstate my position immediately."

If they combined forces, the other council members would listen. My heart felt like it had been stung. From Dad I'd learned not to expect much. But from Trite...

Triton sighed. "I'm not a siren. It's not that simple, Princess."

"Don't *Princess* me," I snapped, crossing my arms.

Calm down, Aubry. It's not his fault. He really is just trying to help.

I forced my brows to unfurrow, my frown to loosen its hold on my lips. "I'm sorry. Thank you for offering to help."

Maybe there was still hope. Triton was the youngest council member. He had a lot of respect. I should trust that. Trust him. I took a deep breath and tried to release some of the frustration still clunking around in my chest.

My best friend smiled gently and backed away toward the door. "We'll get this figured out, okay? Just give me a few minutes to talk to them. Maybe we can grab a drink and shoot some darts after? I know how you love kicking my ass in front of god and country. Pretty certain you demanded a rematch after last time, anyway."

The cheeky bastard still remembered the close loss I'd suffered previously. I gave a reluctant grin. "You cheated. You don't tempt a woman by mentioning Pho, then allow her own hunger and excitement to throw her off her game. That's like, don't-be-a-dick 101."

Obviously, he missed that class back when we were in college together.

He chuckled and I continued. "I *do* still want a rematch, but I have to talk to someone first. I'll text you and let you know for sure."

He nodded, not bothering to ask who or about what. *Thank fuck.* The last thing I wanted to do was get into the darker details of my sexual desires with my male best friend. No, not with Trite, not with anyone. That shit stayed on lockdown.

He disappeared and, suddenly, I was alone with a scrunch-nosed Tallulah. She stared after Trite like he'd left a bad smell behind, instead of just sweat and what-ever cologne he was wearing.

I sighed. "What's on your mind, Tee? I know you're gonna tell me anyway."

"I don't like him," she said, crossing her arms as she fluttered before me. "He's a fucking snake, Aubs. Cunning and manipulative and venomous."

I rolled my eyes. Tee and I had been over this a thousand times. Yes, Triton could be a royal dick at times, but he was my oldest friend; the only one who'd made it all the way from Mag-Sorgin University to the precinct, and that meant something to me. Six years of friendship was no joke in my book. Most people couldn't last six months.

I knew my workaholic tendencies were at the root of the problem—the root of all my fucking problems, really—but I couldn't change that. It was who I was. I was driven, and no one and nothing was going to stand in my way. Not friends, not lovers, *nothing*.

Never again, anyway...

Trite was the same. In fact, I'd only seen him once this month, the time he'd beaten me at darts. And I loved that.

Regardless, Tee and I had been putting up with each other just fine for a little over a year now since she and her husband Aaron had transferred up from San Diego. So, I guess it was safe to say we were officially friends at this point, which made her opinion on Triton that much more problematic. I couldn't just dismiss it, but I wouldn't stand for it either.

"He's a council member, Tee. It comes with the job description. *Must look like Nagini and speak fluent Parseltongue.* It's in the fine print."

I shrugged and she jabbed her little finger in my face. "You just compared council members to Death

54

Eaters. That alone should make you leery about them, don't you think?"

"Hey, Harry could speak Parseltongue, okay? And he was the hero, so…"

Tee sighed. "Where are you going with this analogy?"

"I don't remember."

The two of us busted up laughing before I glanced at the clock. If I wanted to reach a dom in time for a little punishment and reward session, I needed to get cleaned up and get the hell out of there.

"See ya later, Tee." I waved over my head and retreated to the showers. The steam released my muscles and tension in a way that even fighting hadn't been able to. I came out of the shower with almost a smile.

Then I changed into a conservative but sleeveless little black dress. The skirt hit just below mid thigh. It had a straight neck, but the ruffled straps hung down on my shoulders. Just a little hint of naughty to go with the nice.

I tossed on a choker with my favorite pendant—an amethyst. It'd been a gift from the mother of the most unfortunate, mentally decrepit asshole who ever lived. But I didn't blame *her* for my ex's flaws, and the stone was pretty. So I kept it.

Once I was dressed and had my duffle bag slung over my shoulder, I pulled out my cell and scrolled through my options. *Who will it be today?*

Mr. Steel. A man of few words, but many orgasms. He was always promising.

Or perhaps the Gov'na? A delicious hunk of British meat who insisted I scream his name in an English accent every time I came.

Ooh! Or maybe Captain Long Schlong? No, that was totally not his real stage name, and he'd probably whip me raw if he knew I referred to him as such. But holy hell the naughty pirate was hung.

You know what? Getting flogged while tied to a ship mast sounds pretty damn good right now.

Bypassing the elevator, I took the stairs as I made my call. Straight to voicemail. *Fuck.* Whatever. Getting spanked by the Gov'na sounded delicious as well. I dialed his number—and just like the Captain—it went to voicemail. I hiked even further up the stairs, starting to get winded. Don't fail me, Mr. Steel. I hit the call button and... *Son of a bitch!* No answer.

I glared as I sprinted the rest of the way up the stairs, taking them two-by-two. What were the fucking odds that all three of my favorite doms would be unavailable on the same night? I mean seriously. I could always just show up at Syn and see who was there. Maybe play with a new guy for a bit? But it just didn't sound as appealing for some reason. *Ugh.*

Guess I was in for a long hard session with my dinodick—I loved my dildos shaped like dinosaurs with dicks for heads. They were so cute I thought about setting them around my apartment as décor, but ultimately my cunt won that particular argument—she wanted them right next to my bedside at all times. They might've been cute, but they delivered a screaming good orgasm.

At the top of the stairs, I pushed through the doors and into the lobby, surprised to find Triton waiting near the desk.

"Aubry, there you are!" He smiled and strolled over to me, his hands shoved casually into his slacks.

He'd showered, changed, and met with Citrine already? Damn, he was either efficient or unsuccessful. My stomach tightened as I walked up to him. A faint waft of smoke drifted behind him, invisible on the breeze. Surely he hadn't picked up smoking?

"You spoke to the council already?" I didn't mean to sound brash, but I probably did anyway.

"I did," Triton replied with a smile. "They're conducting an investigation on your behalf."

"Yes, I already knew that."

He nodded. "Their ruling still stands, and they want you by the book. However, if you somehow manage to catch The Shadow they've agreed to reinstate your title of Chief."

Well, that was... good. At least there was *hope*. I supposed I should take my small victories when they came.

I leaned forward and wrapped my arms around Triton's neck. "Thank you, Trite. Thank you for talking to them and for sticking up for me. You put your neck on the line, and I really owe you one."

He pulled back and waggled his brows. "You know I won't let you forget that."

I laughed and shook my head, feeling lighter than I had all night. "So, how about that game of darts?"

"I thought you'd never ask."

We took his sleek black car with the dark tinted windows down to The Brickyard Pub. I loved the place, the smoky atmosphere and the cool vibe; Triton hated it. It wasn't nearly as posh as his lifestyle demanded, but it had alcohol and darts, and that was good enough for me.

We walked in and meandered around the ruby carpeted pool tables, careful not to bump anyone's cue stick, and approached the bar.

The tender, a man with a gold tooth and a crooked smile, came over immediately, drying a glass mug with a white cloth. "What can I get ya?"

"Access to the underground," Triton murmured.

The bartender glanced left, then right, before leaning in close. "ID?"

Triton smirked and withdrew his driver's license. All supernaturals were issued special identification cards. To the human eye, they were exactly the same as normal ones, but if you added a gentle pulse of magic and shifted it just slightly, you could see the insignia of the Mage High Council written in shimmering text.

The bartender nodded and allowed us to go

through a red side door that led down a dark flight of stairs. Music pumped and pulsed through the air, a sound you could feel through the floorboards and handrail, and voices chattered above the *clank* of pool balls and the *thunk* of darts.

The underground was buzzing tonight.

It wasn't just a Brickyard Pub thing, though. Almost every establishment worth their salt had an "underground" level that catered to supernaturals. Anything we could want or need. Need a supernatural lawyer? Ask for the underground at a law firm. Need a supernatural banker? Ask for the underground at your local credit union. Need a supernatural grocery store? You guessed it.

I let out my wings as soon as we reached the bottom steps, dropping the glamour. Trite knew the drill. He scratched his nails down my back and soothed the itch without me even having to ask.

Downstairs, the pool tables were clothed in royal purple and the dartboards glowed against the backdrop of a blacklight. Two of the four boards were unoccupied, so while Triton grabbed us each a set of darts, I moseyed up to the bar, which was manned by an ogre whose hands were the size of hubcaps, and ordered us some drinks—him, a dirty martini, and me, a galaxy cocktail.

I sipped at the blue, violet, and magenta colored liquid as I made my way over to our board. Triton handed me a set of torpedo barreled darts with dark blue flights. They were easiest to throw, so naturally, they were my least favorite. I liked a challenge, so I preferred the narrow cylindrical darts that had a center of gravity closer to the back.

But that's all The Brickyard Pub had in stock. I usually liked to bring my own darts when we played, but there just wasn't time for it tonight. Besides, even if I had to use plastic freaking darts, I was totally ready to kick Triton's ass.

"Around the Clock?" I asked, already eyeing the glowing wood board expectantly.

"Of course," he replied smoothly. "Losers first?"

I jutted out my chin. "*Ladies* first."

He grinned. "Whichever you prefer, Princess."

He soon regretted that decision when I mopped the floor with his ass twenty-to-twelve.

"Alright, alright." He finished off his drink and plucked our darts from the board. "Another round? For real, this time. No more letting you win."

"Ha!" As if he would ever just let me win anything. "I beat you fair and square, buddy, but if you're really feeling masochistic tonight, then who am I to deny you a good time?"

He raised a brow, quirked his lips, and shook his head. "You come out with the strangest shit sometimes, you know that?"

You have no idea...

He set our darts down on a nearby table and

handed me his glass. "I need to use the restroom real quick. Mind refilling our drinks?"

"Yeah, no problem. But you better watch it… breaking the seal and all."

He rolled his eyes and walked away, muttering under his breath. "Yes, yes."

Grinning wide, I practically skipped to the bar. Trite was right—a couple drinks and a few rounds of darts really were helping me feel better. Well, that and his chat with the council that saved my ass. I really did owe him for all he'd done.

I flopped down on a stool and bent forward, gazing down the shiny bar to where the tender was busy serving a group of siren girls who seemed to be having a bachelorette party. *Shit*. Hopefully it wouldn't take too long. I retreated to a nearby table, toying with my glass and eavesdropping as I waited.

"Did you hear?" a man's voice said quietly from the bar where I just stood a moment ago. "The Shadow was around these parts earlier."

"The Shadow?" his buddy asked in surprise.

I froze but didn't let my posture stiffen. My ears went into overdrive, honing in on the two men like no one else in the room existed. Other sounds faded.

"Yeah," the first man replied in a thoughtful tone. "He usually doesn't stick around for long, though. And the MPs can *never* seem to catch him."

"I wonder what the shifter scum was up to this time?" his friend replied.

The first guy just grunted his agreement. Clearly, he knew something he wasn't saying. Something about my missed target.

"Holy shit." My words came out as a breathless whisper.

Had I just found a potential lead on Drake "the *motherfucking* Shadow" Guerra?

5

AUBRY

THERE WAS NO WAY FATE WAS HANDING ME WHAT I needed on a platter. No fucking way.

I eyed the guy who'd spoken. He stood about three feet away, one hand on the wooden bartop, another holding a drink that looked like whiskey on the rocks. Or scotch. Or bourbon. All that shit looked the same. Like soda gone flat and turned into liquid flame.

The guy was a huge mass of muscle, probably one of those meatheads who worked out on Venice Beach, tanning and roiding it up at the same time. His neck was thicker than both my palms stacked side by side. His bicep was probably as big as my face as he moved and it flexed under his tight red t-shirt.

I subtly tried to glance over, to see if I could tell what kind of supe he was by looking at him. I couldn't. He wasn't fae though, he was far too bulky for that.

Sometimes I wished I had Aaron's siren nose. The

guy could smell a supe from a mile away. He could also smell pheromones, which was embarrassing once in a while. I'd learned not to have lunchtime sessions with a dom and staff meetings after.

Normally, I loved my summer fae flames. But right now, it was so inconvenient.

The hulking male noticed me looking and grinned.

Damn, he had a good smile.

He raised his glass in a toast. He had bright red hair, and eyes that looked too blue to be natural. Was he wearing colored contacts? The vanity in L.A. never ceased to amaze me. The guy was already hot. Why'd he need to go and fake it up? Was he an actor?

That thought immediately set off my spidey senses. If he was an actor, he might have been hired to mess with me.

But who would do that, hmm? Only the Mage Council knew that my target was The Shadow. Had they sent this guy? Was this a test? It was far too convenient that I'd randomly overheard something right after my meeting with them.

Another suspect came to mind as I took a sip of my cocktail to buy myself a moment. I knew my Aunt Meadow from the Autumn Court really wanted her daughter to take over in Los Angeles. As one of the larger territories, it was a prestigious position. Was *she* screwing with me?

Only one way to tell. Get 'Big Bird' to sing.

I set down my drink on the pub table next to me

and gave him a wide grin, the grin I used at nightclubs when I was willing to put up with mediocre vanilla sex for a night. He took the bait and left the bar, walking over to me.

That's right, Bruiser. Gotcha right in the dick, didn't I?

I followed up the smile with some sultry seduction, licking my lower lip and looking down his entire body, before glancing back up through my lashes. That was a combo punch on the dating scene. My second swing hit the mark. Beach bod's hand went into his jean pocket and not so subtly adjusted the enormous package there.

My throat grew dry for a second as I thought about how good a dick that big would hurt.

But that thought only crossed my mind because I'd been too busy with work lately to take care of other needs. That and my fucking doms didn't answer their phones. I shoved my irritated thoughts away and played with my hair, popping a hip to the side and letting my black dress ride up a bit as the stud set his drink down next to mine. He was way more clean cut than I'd normally go for, but he had a magnetism, that was for sure.

"So, what's your name?" I asked.

"E… Ethan," 'Tarzan' lied.

I hoped whoever was paying him hadn't paid too much. He was a shit actor.

"Ethan, I'm Candace," I lied right back, using my cousin's name to see if that triggered any recognition.

His fake eyes just traveled down to my breasts. This dress didn't reveal that much, because I'd come here for darts, not a hookup. But guys were guys. The boob check told me all I needed to know. Either "Ethan" was *that* dumb or he didn't know my cousin. Just to be sure, I tried one more time. "Candace Wintern." I used my cousin's last name.

His eyebrows rose mockingly—but in disbelief of my *lie*, not recognition of the *name*. "Oh? That's a cool last name."

So, he knew I was lying. He somehow knew my name wasn't Candace Wintern. But he didn't seem to know exactly who Candace Wintern actually was.

He *had* to have been sent there to test me.

Adrenaline pumped through me, just like it had earlier during my spar with Trite. This was sparring too. But a different kind.

I liked this kind just as much.

Beef cake swallowed hard and I scooted closer. If he was already nervous and uncomfortable, I wanted to press my advantage and interrogate him until he broke. A little thrill ran through me when I got close to him. The energy between us intensified.

I was pretty certain my aunt and cousin hadn't sent him. But, just to check one last time, before I accused the Mage Council of something that would infuriate them, I ran my fingers over the back of his hand flirta- tiously. His hand was very, very warm. And rough, like he worked outside.

I got distracted for a millisecond as I traced a small scar on his skin. It was jagged and curved. But part of a successful interrogation was to make the other person feel like it was just a conversation. So, I let my moment of distraction guide me.

"How'd you get this?" I asked. The scar looked deep. I was tempted to flip E-Ethan's hand over to see if it went all the way through. But I didn't.

He cleared his throat and replied softly, "I'm a machinist. Get a lot of little scars when you work with metal all day. I couldn't tell you what that particular one is from." His words said one thing but when I glanced up at his handsome face, it said another. His eyes tightened for a second before he gave me a half smile to go with his half truth.

I believed the first part of his statement, but his acting was really atrocious. He knew exactly where that scar had come from. And it hadn't been from a damn machine.

Part of me pitied him because I could tell that scar was traumatic. But another part of me shook my head. Would the council really send such an amateur? They'd sent actors to test us multiple times the first year out of the police academy. They wanted to ensure that noobs weren't subject to 'corruption.'

I'd been tested by supposed humans, a mage who offered to sell me an illegal Compulsion Spell, which was ironic, because then they'd approved Aaron's hire and he was allowed to sing. But really... their other testers had been decent. The guy in front of me was panty-melting hot. Part of me wondered if he had been a model first. That was always a mistake. A machinist slash actor? I mean, come on.

More importantly, why would the council feed me a fake lead and send me off on a snipe hunt? Did my aunt pay them off? Was she trying to pull strings behind the scenes? I knew she had been jealous when my family had been assigned Los Angeles. My parents were suspect too, there wasn't a lot of love lost between me and my mage-ass-kissing parents. Dad had proven more than once that his loyalties were with the council first. But Triton was on the Mage Council too. Would he sell me out?

I quickly dismissed that thought. Trite had just helped me keep my job. I shouldn't go all crazy para-noid on him. It wasn't fair. Besides, there'd been a time Triton had wanted to get into my pants. If he'd been going to do anything nasty, it would have been back then, when I'd told him I didn't feel the same way. Now, Trite was like my brother. He was family here when the rest of my real family was either scattered to the wind or too asshole-ish for me to want to spend time in their company.

The council, though... would they go behind *his* back?

I wondered, taking another sip of my multicolored cocktail and watching a couple shifters who'd let their zebra hair pop out for a night of clubbing. They eyed

"E-Ethan" and myself before tossing on their coats and making a quick exit. That made me curious about just who the couple was scared of, the huge dude or me? I was typically pretty recognizable in the magic community because of all the press conferences.

I glanced over at 'Rocky,' trying to keep my thoughts off his handsome face as I wondered if he was dangerous. He gave off nothing but giant marshmallow vibes as he ran a finger over his whiskey glass and gave me a shy smile.

Triton returned from the restroom just then. He sucked in his lower lip and evaluated the situation when he spotted 'Mr. Universe' looming over me like an oversized, cartoon superhero.

I almost felt bad about that, but Trite and I really had given it the old college try. We'd kissed, the way supes do when they're looking for their true mate. But it was a big, wet, sloppy no go. He wasn't my fated mate. I didn't think Paul Bunyan here was either, but he had an ax handle the size of the Mississippi, so I would make an exception.

I winked to let Trite know everything was okay; his posture eased up slightly. He didn't really like me dating. But, since he was a serial womanizer who hopped from girl to girl, and there was no zing between us, he couldn't really stop me. Luckily, he knew nothing of my secret proclivities. He just thought I was a workaholic with no time for a real relationship. That was what I'd told him to let him down gently. And it was mostly true. But I still made time for naughty play... if and when a dom that I could actually stand was available. I was still bitter about all the send-to-voicemail brush offs. *The fuckers.*

Trite straightened his shirt, as if he were some self-respecting British billionaire about to meet his daughter's suitor. *Idiot,* I thought fondly, knowing disaster was coming.

He gave me a big fake smile when he reached us, holding out a hand to 'Superman.' "I see you're picking up my best mate. I'll warn you right now, she packs a mean right hook and she will try at some point to scam you at darts. Don't be fooled."

"Hey!" I punched his arm as he and E-Ethan shook hands.

Trite then raised his arms in surrender. "Just the facts."

E-Ethan laughed. He had one of those contagious laughs that could set people off in fits of giggles. Or maybe that was the cocktail I drank. Or the night I'd had. But I ended up laughing until my ribs hurt.

The guys watched me for a second, but when Trite realized I was out of control, he turned to the BFG and said, "Sorry, man. She's not usually this giddy. But when she gets like this you kinda gotta just wait it out."

E-Ethan nodded. Trite started up a conversation with him, chatting about the weather, the Lakers game last weekend, boring guy shit. But all that reinforced my feeling that Triton was innocent. That he didn't know this guy had been planted there. Which begged the question... could my own parents do this to me?

How could I get The Beast to tell me? I watched E-Ethan down his beer as Trite wandered off and started talking up a cute fae in the corner. E-Ethan's overly bright eyes flickered to me. I saw desire there, with maybe an edge of desperation. Would something bad happen to him if he didn't get me to follow his bread-crumb? Had the Mage Council threatened him?

I knew no one on the council had clean hands.

I might have to suffer through some vanilla sex in order to find out what I want, I reasoned. I peered up at Brick House and decided I might be able to sacrifice myself for one night. I just hoped he was better at sex than he was at acting.

If all else failed, I was pretty sure he could pull my hair hard. And that monster dick...

"So... I was thinking about heading out," I glanced up at Big Sexy D-List Actor suggestively.

He grinned, picking up my non-verbal invite and RSVPing instantly. "I'll grab my coat. One sec." The big guy lumbered off to the coat rack by the stairs.

I turned and waved to Trite. "See you tomorrow," I called out.

Trite held up a finger to let the giggling winter fae with pale, snowflake-shaped wings know he'd be right back. Then he walked over and gave me an odd smile. One that showed far too many teeth. "Don't go home with him," he ground out. "Something's off about him."

"Yeah, he's a damn actor. Someone hired him to fuck with me." I rolled my eyes. "I know."

"Then what are you doing?"

"I'm gonna let him *fuck* with me." I grinned.

Triton's face grew dark. "Why the hell would you do that?"

"So I can figure out who hired him."

"I'll pay him double to just tell us. Don't—"

I held up a hand. "*I* could pay him double."

"Then why—"

"Because that's no fun."

Triton grabbed my shoulders and squeezed, stopping just before he made it painful. That was part of the problem with Trite. He could never push himself to be mean enough, to be what I needed. "Aubs, don't. Please. My gut says something's off."

I stared into his light blue eyes. He was worried. Really worried. And he never worried. Plus, he was begging. In that stupid, nearly irresistible British accent.

I rolled my eyes. "Fine. But you're ruining my fun."

He gave a sigh of relief. "Thank you." He took a step back toward the fae he was hitting on.

"I'm still gonna let him *think* I'm going home with him," I warned.

"What?" Trite stopped.

I couldn't stop my eyes from lighting up as I grinned. "The easiest way to pick a guy's pocket is to let him put his arm around you."

6

EASTON

MY NERVES TINGLED AND MY FINGERS SHOOK AS I hurried back over to Aubry after grabbing my coat from under twenty others on the rack—this acting thing had me on edge.

"One sec," I told her. "I gotta run to the restroom before we head out."

She slid an arm around my waist and smiled up suggestively. My skin heated where her fingers touched me. Other parts of me heated up too. But that was just a natural response to any woman rubbing up against me. *Nothing special,* I told myself, as I walked off.

I stepped into a rank bathroom stall and slipped my hand into my pocket so I could grab my phone—I had to tell Drake—but there was no phone.

That bitch!

I grinned. *Shit. Drake was right.* She'd picked my pocket just like he'd predicted.

I shook my head, half full of admiration, half full of envy. Give me a weapon and I could picture all its pieces. I could pull them apart and put them back together in my head. I could design extra pieces to see if they might fit.

But people?

Drake could do that with people. He could pull them apart and see what made them tick. He could predict what they were gonna do next. It was how he'd survived so long. It was why he was our leader.

It was fucking annoying.

He better not pull this shit on me, I mentally grumbled, even though, I knew, realistically, there was no chance in hell that Drake hadn't manipulated me at least once.

Next to me, a toilet flushed and the awful stench in the room doubled. I waited patiently, trying to hold my breath until the bathroom was empty, then I snuck out into the rear hallway of the bar. I glanced to the front of the room, trying to see if Aubry was still there. Yup. She waited smugly by the stairs, probably assuming I'd be back any minute now.

Who's playing who now, Tinkerbell?

I slinked down the hallway and up an emergency set of stairs before I snuck out the backdoor into the humid L.A. air. A homeless guy outside nodded at me and pointed left. His eyes flashed gold. Shifter.

I nodded and handed him a couple bucks from my

wallet before turning and walking toward the street. Drake was waiting behind the wheel of a black sedan. I didn't recognize the car, but then again, I never did. Drake's operations were smoother than my cock. And that was saying something.

I climbed into the passenger seat and said, "She took the bait."

Drake checked the clock on the dashboard.. After nodding, he shifted the car into drive. "Good. Time for phase two."

He pulled a cell out of his pocket and carefully hand-dialed each digit. He didn't say anything, but I knew he was calling Bodie.

"She'll be on the move soon."

"Yup. Ready to follow." I heard the monotone response from Fuzzball before Drake lowered his window and tossed the burner phone into the street. Some lucky, or *unlucky*, homeless chump would pick it up and use the ten minutes left on the prepaid plan.

My leg started to bounce when we got stuck at a red light. My hands turned clammy. I usually worked on the set up *behind* the scenes, not front and center during the actual jobs. I felt like I'd drunk three cups of coffee topped off with a couple shots of Redbull. "You sure she's not gonna fly—"

"She has to go back to the precinct first. She wouldn't carry around a magical tracer on her. Those things are too bulky. She'll have to go back and trace the phone's owner first. Then she'll fly out."

I nodded, feeling stupid and annoyed. I *knew* she'd trace the cell she'd stolen from me. That was why Drake had insisted I carry only a burner tonight. We'd registered it to a condemned apartment complex out in Santa Clarita. That was pretty far north of our normal territory, but Drake didn't want her getting suspicious of us. He didn't want her sniffing us out.

Could fae even sniff?

With those tiny little noses of theirs, barely a dot on their face, I doubted it.

My fingers twitched and I brought them up to my lips, chewing on my nails. "Got any snacks?"

"No."

Shit. My stomach grumbled and my foot started tapping. I really wished I had a spare gun to take apart right now. Or something to munch on. Anything to occupy my nervous hands.

I glanced over at Drake behind the wheel. He had a gun; but I didn't ask for it. You didn't take a man's weapon from him. "You got a pen?"

Drake cocked a dark brow in my direction but passed me one from inside his jacket nonetheless.

Sweet.

I twisted the tip and pulled out the cartridge of ink, carefully disconnecting the tube from the pointed nib to avoid spilling any of the dark fluid within. "What if she gets caught up with something else at the precinct?" I asked.

"She won't." Drake looked out the window. He was so calm. So collected.

Meanwhile, my pulse was racing like a horse at the Kentucky Derby. I blew out a breath and nodded to no one. Because no one was looking.

I unscrewed the other end and removed the pen's barrel. There was a spring inside to activate the clicker, so I plucked it out and set it meticulously next to the other disassembled pieces. I licked my bottom lip. Then I chewed it. What if Aubry *did* show up? Then what? We had a plan for her capture, but beyond that, we couldn't seem to agree.

I suddenly realized my scent was filling up the car. I'd put on a bit of cologne for my "date" with Aubry, and coupled with the heat of my current nerves, the spicy aroma was now intensifying. I took another calming breath and started putting the pen back together. It was too easy, though. It wasn't enough to hold my focus and keep my thoughts from straying.

Aubry's face kept popping up in my mind. That smile. The thick hair that trailed to her waist like a waterfall and made me wanna touch it. The way her voice tinkled like a bell when she laughed. There was just something about her.

Nope! Nope. That bitch had wings. She was a damned wasp, and I did *not* need to get stung to know that it was true. Honey bees, I'd dealt with—being a bear shifter it came with the territory—but wasps? They were real fucking dicks.

The light turned green and we were once more accelerating through the gilded streets of downtown L.A. After assembling and disassembling the pen at least five times, all I could do was stare out the window, not actually seeing anything. Traffic lights blurred and pedestrians smeared like oil paintings in the background. I was tired. It'd been a long night, and daylight crept toward us. Just a few more hours and the sun would be up, and we'd lose the protective cover of darkness.

We needed this to go down without a hitch.

But could we pull this off? Could we really go up against the Chief Enforcer and win? I didn't want to piss Drake off... but even a genius like him was bound to fail sometime.

I hoped it wouldn't be tonight.

Don't let it be tonight, I begged the universe. Then I tried to smack myself for visualizing defeat.

After a while, we crossed into Santa Clarita. Like most other cities, there was a bustling downtown area and some nice clean suburbs, but there were also the neglected outskirts. That's where our little apartment was located—right at the edge of an abandoned warehouse, across the street from an old railroad station that had long been overgrown with tall grass. The station's windows were busted out and graffiti covered every available wall space. Every once in a while, a couple of homeless shifters would shuffle in for a few days, but they never stayed. It was too far from the inner city where they could actually make a living off of begging. Out here, they'd starve to death in weeks.

Drake cranked a hard right and our car was thrust into the darkness of an old loading bay at a warehouse across from the apartment complex where everything would go down. He killed the engine and cut the lights, strolling around back to dig through the trunk. Taking a deep breath, I followed, helping him carry the ropes, chains, and medical kit. It wasn't for tending wounds, but for drugging the princess on the off chance the iron chains didn't do the dirty work for us.

We desperately needed this win, but it kinda made me sick to my stomach. Smuggling illegal drugs, weapons, and raw materials into the country was one thing. This was something else entirely.

Drake and I slipped from the warehouse over to our apartment and deposited the supplies on the table. A cell phone buzzed, and he pulled yet another burner phone from his pocket. "Yeah?"

I couldn't hear what Bodie was saying on the other end of the line, but based on Drake's, "Perfect. We'll be ready," response, I had to guess the fae was officially on her way.

Shit.

I'd never really cared for adrenaline spikes, and I definitely didn't love the rush that flooded me when Drake hung up the phone. It felt like spiders crawling under my skin.

Drake's eyes glowed yellow and scales crawled up

his forearm as he partially shifted and crushed the little phone into dust with a clawed hand. "Let's get to work."

About an hour later, after we'd set up every trap known to man, and about a hundred that *weren't* known, Bodie slipped in through a hidden trap door in the kitchen floor of my fake apartment.

"She's here," he whispered, before darting off to find his position.

Go time.

I ran into the pantry and cracked the door, then removed my handgun from my holster and ejected the mag, counting my ammunition one last time before slamming it shut and racking the slide. I slung some iron chains across my chest. Blood thundered in my ears. *Am I seriously prepared to shoot the girl I was just flirting with at the bar?* I guess I was about to find out.

I leaned back against the wall, glancing through the crack to try and peer out the kitchen window. I started to sweat bullets. I had to swipe a hand across my fore-head to stop the sweat from getting in my eyes. Then, suddenly, a salt-haired head bobbed just beneath the pane, assessing our perimeter. My eyes fell shut and I took a deep breath.

She really is here. Fuck. All right, Easton, you got this, I pep talked myself.

I mean, my hands weren't clean. I'd fought and killed before—more times than I cared to admit. I didn't exactly lose sleep over it, either. So why was my stomach churning?

It's for your three-man pack, I reminded myself. Together, Drake and Bodie meant more to me than the pack I'd been born into. And they wanted this. No, *we* wanted this. *It's for shifters everywhere.*

Minutes passed, and I started to worry that she'd only look around instead of coming in to inspect. Then a set of wings fluttered outside, hefting her up so she could peer in through the windows.

I'd hung the jacket I'd worn to the pub over one of the kitchen chairs, hoping she'd recognize it. Drake assured me she would, but what if she didn't? Would she still come inside and check things out? I rubbed my fingers over the textured grip of my gun and mentally tried to take it apart in my head.

What is taking so long, damn it?

A faint *click* sounded, and though it was soft, it practically echoed through the silent room. A hammer on a gun, preparing to open fire? A mage-made skeleton key in the lock, ready to illegally open that door and break in? A car door opening, signaling she'd called for backup? That sound could have been anything. I needed to be prepared.

The knob twisted quietly, quite a feat considering how old and rattly the damn thing was. The rusted hinges whined as the door crept open. Sweat dripped again from my hairline and snaked down my temple. The floorboards creaked as she took one delicate foot-step. My ears just barely caught the soft fluttering of wings as she took to the air and flew closer.

Then she was in my line of sight.

I watched as she moved soundlessly around the table, her fingers skimming across my jacket with the same seductive touch she'd used when sliding them around my waist. Goosebumps rose on my skin, tingling where she'd made contact earlier. It was goddamn ridiculous.

I needed to make a move before I said fuck it and walked away.

The pantry door opened at the push of my fingertips, slowly revealing me tucked into the shadows. "Hey, Candace. Fancy seeing you here."

She eyed me curiously, and I watched every muscle in her tiny frame clench. But her eyes narrowed when she saw me. "E-Ethan? What happened to the red hair and the bright blue contacts?"

Ah, shit. The mage's spell must've worn off. My gold hair and light blue eyes must have come back.

"Washed it out and removed them," I lied as smoothly as I could. Fuck, I sucked at this stuff. "How'd you find this place?" I asked like I didn't know.

She stared at me for a moment longer before completely ignoring my question. "You blew me off at the pub. Why?"

I chuckled. "Guess you weren't my type."

Total and complete lie. My eyes were drawn to the soft lines of her cleavage even though she was tastefully covered. She was the kind of beautiful that made a man nervous.

The sudden urge to bite my nails came over me again and I crossed my arms to keep from giving in. There was something decidedly *un*confident about nail biting. I couldn't let my bad habits give me away.

"You know..." She cocked her head and studied my blond hair and golden stubble. "I just *don't* believe you."

I smirked. "Then that's the first thing you got right, Princess."

She grinned almost malevolently. "See, I *knew* you knew who I was. I knew you were just an actor. Who sent you?"

Oh shit.

The moment she created a plump flame in the palm of her hand, Drake burst through the kitchen door on my right. He launched at her with the speed of his dragon and hit her hard. I had a bad feeling he was going to break a few bones; she was so dainty.

But I was dead wrong.

Drake went flying through the air a moment later, launched off her feet when she kicked him. He crashed into a chair, splintering the wooden thing to bits, before rolling across the floor.

Crap. I guess that meant I had to step in.

I bent down and grabbed a set of chains, wishing I didn't have to carry the deadly things, and stalked toward her. I didn't like the idea of her delicate skin burning underneath them. But she'd just hurt Drake. "That wasn't very nice, Princess."

"I don't give a flying fuck, you lying ape!" she shouted before charging me.

She—a tiny little faerie no more than a quarter of my size—attacked *me*—a bear shifter. It would have been comical if she hadn't packed such a serious punch. As soon as her fist made contact with my cheekbone, my skin split and the blood flew.

What the hell? I pushed away the pain and let fury tunnel my vision. I focused only on her as she flew through the air and then pushed off the kitchen wall, flipping over my head.

She landed on my back and lit another fire in her palm as I struggled to throw her off. She was so small, there was almost nothing to grab onto.

"Can't get past your own enormous muscles can you, Terminator?" she sneered. "You're a shit actor and a shit fighter."

I growled and reached for her again, but Drake was back in action, yanking her by her pretty hair until she was off of me. She grabbed her hair and kicked up so far she did a split and her foot went behind her head in a move so flexible only a fae could pull it off. She smashed Drake right in the nose.

"*Fuck!*" he cursed, grabbing his face as the blood streamed down. "You're going to pay for that, little fly."

"No, I don't think I will." Her wings spread out and she took to the air, buzzing around the shitty apartment in search of an exit.

Oh, no you don't.

I threw my iron chains across the door she'd entered through—the only exit that hadn't been booby-trapped. The chain caught on a nail we'd put in earlier and hung there. I strung it down the doorway from nail to nail until it looked like a Christmas garland.

The little royal was now officially trapped. Anywhere she tried to go, she was going to get a rude and painful awakening. After the blow she'd just given me, I decided I didn't mind if it was a really painful awakening.

Princess Aubry opened a window. That triggered the first trap. Before she could even think of flying through, a puff of iron dust rained down from above. The shriek that tore from her mouth was like nothing I'd ever heard.

My heart clenched, immediately backtracking from the cruel thoughts I'd just had. I regretted that trap in an instant.

This was so fucked up. I was so fucked up. But we'd already gone too far to turn back now. We had to finish it.

Aubry cut her screams off quickly, gritting her teeth as she thrashed around in the air trying to shake the dust off her sizzling skin. She flew upward. That's when her wings hit the flypaper we'd plastered to every ceiling.

One wing hit the ceiling and stuck. Her face contorted in horror when she realized what had happened. She turned and yanked on her own wing, ripping the delicate scales and tumbling to the linoleum floor. Outraged, she pulled out a gun with a silencer and aimed it right at me.

A bullet flew through the air like a ghost. No loud *bang* accompanied the blood that flooded my vision. But it wasn't me who went down. Aubry fell to the floor; Bodie had sniped her from the back room before she could kill me.

I should have felt relief.

I didn't.

My stomach twisted as I saw her writhe in pain, watched her blood gush from the wound.

At least he hadn't made it a fatal shot. I'd seen him shoot the eye out of a target from a mile away, so if he hit her wing joint instead of something more vital, then it was damn well intentional.

Aubry quickly rolled across the floor and stood back up. Legs wide and ready to move, she held one arm up protecting her face, the other arm swiveling her gun between Drake and me. Tears streamed down her cheeks, and she gritted her teeth so hard I thought they might shatter. But she still planned to fight.

Jesus fuck, she had tenacity.

Drake charged her, letting his head and tail shift into dragon form. His black tail swept forward, the spiked end lashing out at Aubry. But even though she was injured, she was fast. She ducked his tail and shot his foot.

"Fuck!" He tipped forward and face planted on the

floor. I ran to check on him, but he shoved me away. "Slow her down!" he shouted.

I turned just in time to see her disappear out the kitchen and into the living room. I ran forward and shoved the door open. A moment later, another quiet shot tore through the air, ripping through her calf muscle like fucking butter. She fell.

But it felt like *I* was the one who'd taken the bullet when a sob escaped her throat and her chin quivered, as she dragged herself across the carpet. The scent of her blood, that warm iron tang, made my stomach churn.

Oh, Princess, why are you doing this to me?

I was sick. A nervous fucking wreck for her. I needed to end this before she took any more damage, or worse, ended up dead. Apparently, I was softer than I'd thought. Something was wrong with me. I couldn't even handle an enemy—the woman who'd killed El Fuego, my fucking friend—getting hurt. Not if she cried.

"I'm sorry, Princess," I muttered before rearing back with my fist and jabbing the side of her head to knock her out. Her pretty brown eyes rolled shut and she slumped to the floor.

I wanted to vomit. They called me a warlord, but this? This wasn't who I was at all.

Drake came up beside me and patted my shoulder with a smile. "Nice hit, Goldie."

Bodie strode into the living room carrying a long

gray case that I knew was full of various weapons. His light green eyes gleamed like fire in the early morning sunlight. "Holy shit! We did it. We captured a fae royal!"

Yeah. We'd done it, alright.

Now, what the fuck were we going to do with her?

7

AUBRY

I came to with a single thought: I was gonna get out of this—and then torch these motherfuckers' feet, so that they couldn't run. Then I was gonna melt all the plastic in the room so their damn shifter noses were in agony while I slowly, painfully, killed them.

"I'm gonna nail you—" My threat trailed off as someone moved my body and iron chains slid along my skin. My teeth clenched involuntarily. The chain wrapped again and again and again, like a constricting snake. I writhed, trying to relieve my skin from the burn where the fucking evil iron touched it.

My movement backfired and just allowed the pain to spread more. I nearly blacked out. Again. I moaned.

"Stop moving," E-Ethan the giant lying shifter scum, tried to use a kind voice on me.

It hurt so badly I couldn't even spit at him. And that

was saying something. I knew pain. I loved pain, craved it even. But this? It was too damn much.

The chains weren't pure iron, otherwise my flesh would have burned off completely, but there was enough that my skin was immediately covered in horrid welts. The chains snaked up and down my torso and around my arms before I heard a lock click behind my back and smash into my tailbone.

Fuck.

I could hardly move. It made me feel claustrophobic. Which made no sense. But I felt as wrapped up and trapped as if I'd been shoved six feet under in a coffin. The pain devoured my rational thought; it made me see things.

Darkness. Shadows. Shifters. Nightmare things.

I faded in and out of consciousness, only barely aware as I was picked up by Sasquatch and transported in a car somewhere. *Monster,* I thought at E-Ethan, before I passed out.

When a bump made my head hit the car window and I found myself awake again, I tried not to let myself slip back under. I listened quietly for a minute, but the only sound other than the car and the air conditioner was breathing. These guys didn't speak.

We made a sharp turn, which triggered my training. I knew, as a kidnapping victim, that I should try to take note of my surroundings. I knew I should try to make a mental map of where we were going.

These guys hadn't even attempted to kill me. I

didn't know if that was because they'd realized I had used a lethal protection tablet on myself while I was flying around, inspecting the exterior of the building, or because they wanted me alive. But they'd shot me in the shoulder. And that asshole hadn't looked surprised —like he'd missed my heart. He must have been aiming for the shoulder then. They wanted me alive. For a reason.

I forced my eyelids open. They'd put a blindfold on me. Of course. These shifters might be criminals. But The Shadow was no amateur. And that's who the dragon was. The moment his tail had come out to whip me, I'd known. We didn't have his human photo on file at MP, but the word on the street that The Shadow was a dragon shifter had filtered up to us. And there weren't many dragons left.

I nearly screamed as I bent my head to my shoulder and swiped, nudging the blindfold—but causing the chains to slide across my back. It made me feel like I'd fallen backward into a pit of lava. It took all I had to breathe through that pain and keep moving.

Finally, I uncovered the tiniest sliver of vision by my right cheek.

Slowly, trying not to draw attention to myself, I leaned back in my seat and lifted my head. It was morning and light was threading through the buildings like a surfer through the waves. But the sun was behind the brick facades, throwing them into shadow. So, we were moving east. I tried to make out what area of the city we were in. Not Rodeo Drive, I could tell that much. But specifics? Good luck. That was, until I saw a mural on the side of a brick building.

The mural was peeling, but still distinguishable. It was of a solemn-faced Native American woman, staring defiantly out at the road, challenging those who walked by to ignore her and her pain.

Indian Alley.

One of the most famous alleys in Skid Row.

I didn't smile as I lowered my head, though part of me wanted to. That info was only useful if we stopped driving soon. If we didn't, I'd need to look again.

The car trundled over a pothole and I fell into the brute sitting next to me. I could feel my dress slide down and expose the top of my cleavage.

Some fucker chuckled. I didn't know which one.

Just wait, I thought. *Just you wait until I get out of here, Muscles.* I hurt so badly I couldn't even come up with a real insult. I couldn't right myself and spent the rest of the ride tipped over against the giant that I'd hoped would pillage me earlier. I hated the fact that his wide chest was a perfect pillow.

The car stopped not long after and someone grabbed me. Based on the size of his hands, I figured it was E-Ethan the liar who carried me down the stairs.

"She's in bad shape," he muttered.

"Her own fault."

I recognized the voice of the green-eyed man. The one who had an aura of cold around him. The one who'd shot me. He was nearly as frightening as The Shadow. I didn't get why E-Ethan was with them.

But lackeys weren't always the brightest crayons in the box. He wasn't a good actor. Maybe he was stupid, too. I hadn't gotten that impression. But, maybe he was the weak link.

When he turned sideways and started down yet another set of stairs, this last one descending into darkness, my chains moved yet again. I sucked in air through my teeth. I had to breathe through the pain, but it was hard not to fucking pant.

I didn't even realize I was sobbing until he set me gently down on a concrete floor.

"Shh, sweetheart, almost done." E-Ethan deserved a punch in the mouth for calling me that.

I heard some steps shuffle, like people entering. I wasn't sure.

I was rolled onto my stomach and I tensed, expecting all kinds of horrid things. But all I felt was a bite in the back of my arm, an injection from a needle.

The pain lessened and my head sagged forward onto the cool tile floor. They must have given me Elixir. Nothing else worked that fast to counteract the pain, though not the damage, of iron. My eyelashes fluttered.

I felt rough hands at my ass and my throat dried out. But the hands only lifted the lock, dragging my arms up behind me. A distinctive click told me the lock had released.

But whatever was in that Elixir was heady, good shit. I passed out before I felt them remove the chains.

When I came to, for the zillionth time, my throat was parched and every part of my body ached.

I felt something swipe softly across my neck and I stiffened. Someone was crouched over me. The shifter with dark skin and pale yellow-green eyes stared down at me. The asshole who'd shot me.

Immediately, I went into fight mode. I grabbed onto his wrists and lifted my legs to my torso. Then I kicked out, hitting him right in the chest with my feet. I shoved at his hands, but I was too weak to do the move properly—fucking iron—and he ended up falling forward onto me.

We grappled on the ground. I tried to bite his ear, but his forearm pressed against my neck.

So, instead, I wrapped a thigh around his torso, shoved his face toward my chest, and smacked my palm against his ear. I rolled us sideways so that I ended up on top. My eyes flashed with fire and so did my pussy when he dug his fingers into my arms and forced them to my sides.

He thought that would stop me? Stupid furry fuck.

I jerked forward and smashed my head into his and as I did, his lips dragged across my cheek.

Light burst behind my eyelids and red spots dotted my vision. But I also felt something else.

Something impossible.

My hands reached up to cradle my pounding skull as I skittered backward.

The dickwad shifter I'd been fighting propped himself up on an elbow. His green eyes found mine. And it was like I'd been sucked into a whirlpool.

My heart thumped hard.

With longing.

Holy fuck.

"What the hell did you do to me?" I snarled, scrambling up to my knees and finally taking in my surroundings. I was in a cell. From the looks of things, it was a cell underground. No windows. The hallway outside was walled in dirt. But everything paled in comparison to the feeling in my chest.

It was like faeries flying and sirens singing and mage magic swirling around me all at once.

"What the hell spell is this?" My voice came out as a rasp.

Green-eyes stared at me like I'd just slapped him. His face looked shocked, mouth hanging open in utter disbelief. It took a few seconds before he collected himself enough to speak. "I... brought you water."

"Is that how you drugged me?"

"I didn't drug—"

"Bullshit." I cringed when yelling made my skull feel like it was split in two. I closed my eyes and waited for the nausea to pass. When I opened my eyes, the stupid shifter was right in front of me, holding a water bottle to my lips.

"Drink," he said softly.

This close, his lips grabbed all of my attention. They were thick, his bottom lip the kind that was perfect for biting. Heat flared in my chest and traveled down my spine. It hovered between my thighs.

I saw his nostrils twitch. He closed his eyes and tilted his head back, a small smile on his lips. Then his eyes flew open and he shook his head once, as if jolting back to reality and telling himself no. Damn it. Could he smell my arousal?

No! This wasn't happening. It was a trick. There was magic involved.

"You evil bastard," I cursed.

"Yes," he agreed, his face solemn. "I'm a wolf-shifter who's killed more people than you've probably ever met."

He gave me a smile that I thought was meant to scare me. *It didn't.*

"How did you do this?" I gestured between us.

I hadn't wanted to drink the bastard's water, but my throat was too freaking dry. I grabbed the bottle and took a swig. Whatever spell he'd cast to make me horny —and therefore, potentially more compliant—was already done. But what the Big Bad Wolf didn't know was that this little girl had already strayed from the path. My tastes were so deep into the dark woods that they'd scare even him.

"Me? You did this," he growled. I could hear the edge of the wolf in his voice. His animal was close to the surface. Either he was just as pissed or just as horny as I was. Or both.

I backed away from him. That was a mistake. My wings, already damaged, smacked into the iron bars of the cell. I screeched and fell forward. He grabbed onto me and dragged me over to the cot in the corner, placing me on it more gently than I expected him to.

But then he grabbed my jaw. And his grip was hard. Just how I liked it.

Damn it.

"Don't touch me!" I snarled, furious that my body was responding to him. "And reverse this damn spell, whatever it is."

"It's not my spell, you magic-stick-loving hussy. Who'd you pay to get a spell this strong, huh?" His hands were back on me, shoving my chest down so I couldn't rise, and turning my head so that I had to look into his eyes.

I noticed flecks of gold in his irises, swirling inside the green.

I tried to shoot fire at him, but my power didn't work. I was too hurt. Too drained. "I'm going to kill you," I spat at him.

"Not if I kill you first." His teeth started to elongate.

A sick, twisted part of me wondered what it would feel like to have those teeth nip at my throat.

My panties grew wet.

Above me, my captor howled at the ceiling. When his face turned back down to look at me, his eyes had gone from green to golden. His irises had turned into slits.

And I was panting.

But not from fear. My nipples pebbled. My sex ached. And even though my body was utterly wrecked and ruined, my pulse throbbed for his touch.

His hand on my chest slid down to cup my breast through my torn dress.

Yes.

But another voice sounded and Wolf Man shoved away from me faster than a toddler touching a hot stove.

"What's all the damn yelling about, Bodie?" E-Ethan asked from outside the cell. His forehead wrinkled as he glanced between the two of us.

Bodie. That was his name.

My chest gave a little thrum of satisfaction, which I tried to suppress. But Bodie's golden eyes glanced my way and I knew he'd registered the change in my pulse. Stupid shifter hearing.

"Somehow, this bitch paid some mage to create a fake mate bond," Bodie said.

"You did that!" I rasped.

Bodie backed away from me. "Let me out of here," he demanded at the closed door of my cell.

"A fake mate bond..." E-Ethan really did seem slow on the uptake. "I don't think that's possible."

"It is!" we both yelled in unison.

It wasn't funny.

But E-Ethan laughed.

"Fuck you, Goldilocks. Let me out." Bodie said.

E-Ethan let him out of the cell and closed it with a clank behind him. Bodie walked away and I heard their hushed voices as they ascended the stairs.

My heart gave a little pout when Bodie didn't even glance back my way. If I could have, I would have punched my heart in the tit. Stupid organ. Couldn't tell magic from reality.

Once they were gone, I scrambled off the cot and across the cell to grab that bottle of water. I chugged it like I hadn't had water for a year. Then I glanced down the earthen hallway outside my cell. It petered out into darkness before I could see stairs.

I glanced toward the floor where I'd woken up and saw a little pile of bandages and a tube of Neosporin. I looked down at my arms and realized Bodie had been trying to fix me up.

I shoved down my heart, which started thumping happily like a dog's tail hitting the floor when master got home. No. No way. There was no way in hell I'd just felt a mate bond with a fucking shifter.

8

AUBRY

PAIN FLOODED MY HEAD AND MY WHOLE BODY ACHED. IT was like I was drowning in it.

I carefully cracked a bleary eye open and the dingy little room swam as I struggled to focus.

Where the hell am I?

My heart raced and suddenly all the memories came rushing back to me. A trap at the apartment I'd traced. A fight with shifters. A car ride in agonizing pain. Iron everywhere, my skin burning so maddeningly I passed out. Waking up in a cell. A mate bond with the wolfish asshole…

Fuck.

How much time had passed? Days? Weeks? I barely remembered the food and drink they'd set inside my cell, the bathroom breaks, the questions, the shots of Elixir they'd given me to keep me complacent.

My wings fluttered and helped steady me as I sat up

on the cot I'd been lying on. I blinked and fluttered them again. No pain. Glancing over my shoulder, I was terrified to find my wing had almost entirely healed. A tiny scar was all that remained of the nasty tear that had grounded me. That could only mean one thing— I'd been here for entirely too long.

Shit.

Fear crept down my spine at the idea I might have been here for weeks. I wondered what Trite thought. My heart clenched a little, thinking about how worried he would be. Then I wondered what my parents thought. We weren't close, but still. They were my parents. My throat dried up as I worried that I might be hard to find. Would anyone associate E-Ethan with my disappearance? Or would they think I'd crawled under a rock after the Mage Council had chewed my ass? Was anyone even looking for me?

I stood and strode over to my bars, clinging to them for a moment before my hands hissed and my skin burned. Iron. Of course. A snarl curled my upper lip as I peered up the dark tunnel beyond. The walls of the tunnel were made of dirt. A single lightbulb propped up on the floor attached to a long yellow extension cord, was the only light in the space.

"Where are you shifter assholes?" I whispered in frustration.

My gaze darted around the prison I was in, trying to figure a way out. Much like a typical jail cell, it was a box surrounded on all sides by thick concrete, with tall iron bars making up the front wall. The iron was unfortunate, but unsurprising. The concrete, however, was a welcome error on their part—I could melt that easily without messing with the iron at all. No risk of allowing dangerous particles to permeate the air.

I paced the cell as I thought. It'd probably be easiest to reach the tunnel through one of the side walls. From there, I'd have to play it by ear. Follow my instincts as best I could until I found a way out. Maybe I could fly and test the air for any currents that might lead to an outside opening?

I glanced up the tunnel one last time, ensuring I was alone before making my move.

These fucking furballs had no idea who they were messing with. I was a damn enforcer for a reason. I was gonna make sure that for every bit of fury I felt now, they paid for it in pain later.

I smirked and pushed both hands toward the concrete on my right, willing my summer fae flames to come out and play. But they didn't. They crackled and sparked, but no fire appeared. *Damn it!*

Suddenly a door cracked open at the top of the stairs. The hinges screeched. A thin line of light spread out across the steps and the tunnel floor before disappearing with another creak as the door shut. Voices sounded like whispers, eventually growing in volume as four men approached my cell.

God, I hate being outnumbered like this. Unlike the other night with El Fuego, I *wasn't* desperate for a fight.

I retreated to the back of my cage, eyeing them warily from a distance.

The wolf shifter I recognized immediately—if not by the tanned skin and pale green eyes, then definitely by the fact that my very blood was howling for him. My heart and soul soon joined in until I felt like I might burst. It was difficult to suppress those chaotic emotions, but I damn well fucking tried. He was my captor, nothing more.

E-Ethan, the redhead turned blond mountain man from the pub, was next to him carrying a tray of… food. Or something. It looked like crusty bread and a glass of milk. First of all, I hated milk. Second of all, if it wasn't Vietnamese takeout, then I didn't have the time of day for it.

As if on cue, my stomach freaking rumbled. I tightened my abs to keep the sound from spreading further, but I'm pretty sure the shifters heard it. Sensitive hearing and all. Well, apparently their noses weren't sensitive—otherwise they would have brought a better smelling meal.

I lifted my chin and cut straight to the chase. "You stemmed my fire powers. How?"

The tallest guy, the dragon shifter who'd swiped at me with his tail—*The Shadow*—was a dark-haired man with a mobster vibe. He merely smirked at my question and turned to the fourth guy, an older dude, the only guy I didn't recognize in the slightest. "What do you think, Larry? Another round?"

On instinct, my heart started hammering. But then my training kicked in, and I focused on taking slow deep breaths, in through the nose, out through the mouth. "*Larry?* Real badass name. Who are you other idiots? Curly and Moe?" I glanced from the dragon and wolf over to the ex-ginger. "Looks like you're the odd man out, E-Ethan." I stuttered over his name just like he had when we first met, mocking him. It was all I could do in my powerless state.

His eyes narrowed but a blush crept over his cheeks. He actually *didn't* look anything like the others. The dragon had dark hair and dark blue eyes. The wolf had dark tan skin. The fourth guy, Larry, had once-dark hair that was now more salt than pepper and frazzled like crazy, but still. This guy, E-Ethan, was blond. Like, ice blond, only a few shades more golden than my silvery white, and his eyes were a sweet baby blue. He gave off more of a surfer vibe than a dangerous one. Strange that the most muscular one of the whole group had the softest face.

The hulking blond heaved a heavy sigh. "My name's not Ethan."

"Ha! You think?"

He rolled his baby blues and gestured for his wolfish buddy to unlock my cage. "My name's *Easton.* I'm sure you remember Bodie."

Mm. Bodie. My insides hummed in delight, while my brain rebelled like some punk rock goth. *You'll never make me succumb to this bullshit mate magic.*

I glared at them as Easton-Ethan continued. "That's Drake." He pointed at the brooding dragon shifter. "And that's—"

"Larry," I answered curtly. "I know. Which brings us full-circle and back to my original question: how'd you stem my magic?"

Bodie unlocked the cage and Easton silently lowered my tray of scraps to the floor, oh so cleverly avoiding my question. Again. I thought about lurching past them and making a run for it. My wings were healed, if I could just get past all four of them...

Yeah, no. I wanted freedom, but I wasn't stupid. I'd have to bide my time until the perfect moment. Then I'd make like Houdini and *poof*!

Blondie stared at me expectantly, like he thought I'd clamber all over myself to get to the tray. I mean, my stomach may have been spasming, but I wasn't *that* desperate yet.

"What, *Goldilocks*?" I asked, recalling his nickname from the other day. "The porridge looks disgusting. Tell the three bears I only eat Vietnamese takeout. Pho, if they can manage."

"You're kidding me, right?" Easton asked with a confused half grin. His teeth sparkled as brightly as his eyes. "You're a hostage right now, Princess. You should be happy that we're feeding you at all."

I raised a brow. "Should I? You fuckers obviously want me alive. So, if you want me to eat, you're gonna have to bring the food I want."

I had a kitten once, a stray I'd taken in behind my parents' backs. It was so tiny and cute, but it refused to eat cat food. The only thing it wouldn't snub its nose at was tuna, fresh from the can. Spoiled little hairball. But I had wanted to keep it and take care of it, so I'd catered to the damn thing's whim. Everyday, I'd bring it the chicken of the sea. That is, until my parents found out about the kitten and disposed of it—permanently. "*You never know when an animal is real or actually a shifter in disguise,*" they'd told me. "*They aren't all criminals but the ones who are will stop at nothing. They don't have human morals.*"

I supposed they were right.

But the point was: I was the cute little kitten in this story. All I had to do was hold out long enough, and I'd soon have pho served to me on a silver platter on the daily. Or so I hoped.

"Fuck her, then," the dick-headed dragon shifter spat. "She doesn't need to eat."

"Of course she does," Bodie argued, coming to my aid. My mind loathed it and my stomach appreciated it all at the same time.

Easton stood and backed out of the cell, leaving the tray with me in case I changed my mind. Which I obviously wasn't going to do. I mean, hell, they could have poisoned it or hidden more Elixir in there somehow, maybe planted a tracer that'd stick to my stomach walls, or something equally fucked up.

I took a couple steps closer, bent down, and flipped

the whole tray over, crushing the bread into chunky crumbs and spilling the milk halfway out the door.

"I don't want your flea-infested gruel," I told them coldly.

Easton's blue eyes widened in surprise, while Bodie's yellow-green gaze shuttered in disappointment.

"Good," Drake growled through gritted teeth. He ripped the barred door open and stomped inside. "Maybe you don't want your *flea-infested* freedom, either?"

He reached for my wrist, but my instincts were faster. I yanked my left hand out of his grasp, and with the right, jabbed a fist into the side of his arrogant face. His head cocked just slightly to the side, not as far as I'd been hoping, but the look of malice that invaded his face was enough to make me grin. *Come on, Puff. Let your magic dragon out to play.*

Scales tore up his arms and a ring of smoke shot from his nostrils. His eyes flashed yellow, and when he came at me again, his hands were replaced by massive black claws. He'd only partially shifted into his dragon —just as he had the first time—but it was still enough to make me falter. I had no fire, no weapons. All I had left was my pride and my determination to retain a little dignity. He wanted to drag me out like a naughty child, then he had another thing coming.

"Just try and cuff me, you overgrown gecko," I gritted out.

More smoke flared and he charged at me. Leaping, I split my legs and flew just over his head, quickly smacking my wings into the concrete ceiling above.

You think you could have made my cage any smaller? I thought at him angrily.

He grabbed my leg and yanked down, throwing me onto the concrete floor hard enough to pop my shoulder out of place. Pain raced down my arm like a bolt of lightning and an involuntary whimper escaped my lips.

"Damn it, Drake," Bodie said, storming into the cell with us. "That's enough."

"It fucking better be," Drake huffed, snapping the cuffs into place on my wrists.

I wanted to lash out, but my skin hissed where the malevolent metal touched me, weakening me instantly. "Iron? Really? You couldn't have gone with standard steel? You had to go that extra mile to mar me and piss me off?"

Drake grinned maliciously. "If I had my way, Princess, you'd already be dead. So, yes."

"Are we ready to proceed, then?" a quirky voice asked, cutting through the tension. I glanced over and saw the frazzle-haired man, Larry, approach my cell. He held a wand in his hand. He was a mage?

"Fucking traitor," I spat at him. "Turning on your own kind to help the wrong side!"

The mage heaved a heavy sigh and shook his head

sympathetically. "No, Dear Princess. After nearly a century of wrongdoings, I'm finally on the *right* side."

Brainwashed. How long had they held him captive before his mind cracked? What sort of lies had they fed him? I had the sudden urge to help him, to bring him with me when I broke free, but I didn't know if that was gonna be possible.

"Hang on, Larry," Drake growled. "I have a few questions for her first." He rattled my cuffs so that the iron dug deep into my skin, making me wince.

Easton grabbed the bars from the outside and pressed his face in close. "Come on, man, she's already in enough pain. You don't need to push her around and make it worse."

Drake threw my hands away, knocking me onto my ass, as he stomped between the wolf and the blond—I didn't know what kind of shifter Easton was, yet.

"Are you two fucking kidding me right now? She's one of our biggest enemies! A fae royal. Chief Enforcer. She fucking murdered El Fuego in cold blood! She's murdered hundreds of us…" He trailed off and shook his head. "And you want to go easy on her because she's easy on your stupid blind eyes? Because her skinny fae ass somehow gets your dicks hard? Remember the goddamn plan."

"Excuse me, asshole," I hissed as I tried to right myself without the use of my hands. I felt like a fucking fish flopping around on a butcher block. "But I have a rather nice ass. With plenty of curves and an hourglass shape."

Drake ignored me, fisting a clump of my silvery white hair and dragging me closer to his face. "Where are the mages keeping the bodies?"

"What the fuck are you talking abo—"

"Where are they keeping the bones?"

"*Bones?*" I asked, astounded. "What bones?"

He quickly changed direction. "Where are they hiding the other mage jewels?"

I scoffed. "As if I'd tell you even if I—"

He yanked my hair again, making me snarl. "Who's responsible for the fires?"

"What fucking fires?" The normal every-summer wildfires that always plagued California? Was he serious? "The trees. The trees caused the fires," I said. An idiotic question deserved a stupid answer.

"You fucking wasp!" Drake bellowed, his voice echoing through the underground tunnel. "Stop playing stupid with me! You're the goddamned *Chief Enforcer*! I know you know what I'm talking about."

"Maybe she doesn't," Easton muttered, eyeing me carefully with those clear blue eyes.

"Why are you two doing this?" the dragon shifter roared in frustration, glancing back over at the other two shifters.

Bodie came forward and pried my hair out of his friend's grasp. Then he went nose to nose with him. "Because she's my *mate*."

111

"She is not!" Drake shouted.

At the same time I cried, "I am *not*!"

The wolf shifter didn't so much as roll his green eyes, just kept facing off against Drake in an epic battle to see who blinked first. I wanted to blow a big bratty raspberry at both of them and tell them to hurry this shit along. The sooner they got the hell out of here, the sooner I could come up with a viable escape plan. And the sooner I could figure out exactly what all my injuries were and try to treat them.

"Right, well, as invigorating as this is, I have other things to do, so…" the mage began, but Drake cut him off.

"You have *nothing* more important to do than this, Larry. Now get in here and get it done."

"This isn't fair to her," Bodie snarled, running a hand through his dark hair.

Drake pushed him, and Bodie stumbled out through my cell door into the hall. The dragon shifter bellowed, "I don't give a fuck what's fair and what isn't to a *fly*. And neither should you."

"Don't fucking push me! She's more than that. She's my—"

"So, help me god, if you say *mate* one more time," Drake threatened, stalking towards him as he too exited my cell.

For once, I agreed with the dragon. Bodie needed to shut the fuck up.

Drake shook his head. "It's bullshit fae magic.

Nothing more. The sooner we get rid of her, the sooner your damn brains will come back."

"Yeah," Bodie agreed, his features twisting in sarcasm, "about this *getting rid of her* plan. It's not gonna happen."

"What did you say to me, kid?"

They were back at each other's throats in an instant. Drake was taller, but Bodie's wife beater showed he had all the muscles necessary to back up his claims. My eyes flickered between the two alpha males. And, against my every conscious wish, my pussy flickered to life watching them about to fight.

Down, girl. We have to focus. I slid my eyes over to the Thor-wannabe instead. His eyes flickered gold when he inhaled.

Shit. Could he smell my arousal?

"Guys, why don't we take this… outside," Easton said, glancing warily between them and me.

"Fine," Bodie said, sounding a little too cocky.

The three shifters strode off down the hall and disappeared into the darkness.

I had a bad feeling Drake was going to knock Bodie out as soon as they got out of my sight. My stomach twisted into hundreds of tiny knots, making me sick with longing and worry for the wolf. *What the hell? No.* I tried to suppress the emotion, but it was like swallowing down knives—it fucking hurt.

The mage turned to me once they were gone. He sighed. "Let's just get this over with, shall we?"

I cocked my head arrogantly. "Get *what* over with, exactly?"

Larry smiled calmly, more of that strange sympathy shining through. "You asked how they'd stemmed your powers. I'm the reason. I've been using a Power Limiting Spell on you."

My mouth must've dropped open, because he quickly said, "Don't worry. The effects aren't permanent, and they'll cause no long-lasting damage. It's simply a necessary precaution."

My lips pursed and I rolled my eyes. "A necessary precaution," I mocked. "Because they *know* I'd kick their asses and escape in no time, otherwise."

"Actually, Princess, it's a precaution against *yourself*. I wouldn't want you doing something you'll regret."

I laughed right out loud. Poor brainwashed bastard. Maybe he was already too far gone. I might not have been able to rescue him, but I could damn sure *use* him.

I squeezed my fists against the iron handcuffs and smirked at the unknowing mage.

These stupid fucking shifters had thought of just about everything.

Everything *except* how far I would go to escape.

9

BODIE

Aubry's face invaded my mind, just like her sweet citrus scent invaded my nostrils.

I'd tried to fight the bond at first but there was no denying it. As she'd laid down there for days, I'd gradually come to accept this new reality. That I was intoxicated by her. Everything about her, from her white hair to her delicious, orange scent.

Wait. Her scent? I shouldn't be able to smell her this far away. Even a mate bond shouldn't extend—

I turned to see Larry striding up the stairs behind me, scratching the back of his grizzled head. Guess he was finished re-casting the spells to suppress her fire. Larry was a great mage, but also a good man. Sometimes, too good for the likes of us. He generally refused to use murdered people's bones in his spells, which meant he had to redo them more often. The magic just wasn't as strong without murder bones.

I watched our mage pass by the open doorway without looking my way. His posture was stiff, like he was trying not to acknowledge me. I knew he didn't agree with this plan to keep and use Aubry. I didn't even agree with it anymore. Not now that I knew the woman down there was my mate.

Fucking hell. My mate was hurt. I didn't have time for this shit. Her scent retreated as I stared at the doorway while I watched Drake and Easton argue out of the corner of my eye. They were fighting about me. *With* me, though I'd stopped responding.

"Bodie, I think you're overtired. You've been taking too many shifts watching her." Drake said something idiotic like that and I would have rolled my eyes but I was only half-listening. Quarter listening maybe.

This was wrong. So wrong.

How could this be happening? Was fate punishing me? The mate bond, a magical, spiritual connection that a wolf shifter only got once in a lifetime—and mine was with the enemy.

Fate had big fucking balls, that was for sure.

Asshole.

I growled and paced the room. Something felt off. Wrong in my chest. Was it because Drake didn't believe me? His frown said as much.

Or was it because I wasn't down there helping *her*? Was that how bad a mate bond was? Did her pain somehow extend to me? I'd never been annoyed by my magic before. But I sure as hell was now. What the fuck? Was I gonna be off on some sniper assignment and feel it if she stubbed her damn toe? I rubbed at my chest, where the feeling of panic increased.

I never fucking panicked. Not anymore. Not unless the stupid women in the pack brought up *babies*—I shook that thought off as a serrated knife sawed back and forth inside my chest. This feeling would not be ignored. I abandoned Drake and Easton, heading for the stairwell. And for some reason, I looked up, instead of down toward her cell.

Larry was emerging from the storage closet.

What the hell was he doing in the storage closet?

His hands were empty. So... a whole lot of nothing. Why would he go in there and not get anything out?

My feet started moving before I could stop them. I climbed the stairs. And as I did, that bright orange citrus scent hit my nostrils again.

My dick twitched in response. But the rest of me grew furious. *What the fuck?* I started taking the stairs two by two, my feet silent from years of practice sneaking out of my pack house.

I watched Larry scratch his lower back as he tried another door, one that led to yet another storage room. He didn't know where he was going. Because... that wasn't Larry.

I leapt, slamming into his back, both of us tumbling into the open door. I landed on top of the mage and straddled him. It smelled like I'd walked into an orange orchard.

That bitch!

Even as I cursed her, I could picture everything. She hadn't given up when she'd fought us back at that apartment, even when she'd known she was fighting three on one. Even when she was injured. My mate was a firecracker. She'd probably dropped Larry in two seconds flat. And obviously, his spells to limit her powers had worn off.

Shock overtook me as I realized... my mate was trying to run away from me. That's what that sensation had been. The pain quickly solidified into anger and determination.

There was no way that was happening. My mate was not going to leave me. I glared down at Larry's wrinkled face. *Fucking fae glamour.* I growled as I leaned down and put my hand on Larry's neck.

"What the hell are you doing, Bodie?" Easton's tone was alarmed.

"Told you he's losing his shit," Drake replied. He sounded annoyed more than anything.

I ignored them both as my eyes shifted to gold and I stared down at Larry, demanding submission. My fingertips dug into his throat as I leaned closer.

"Change back," I snarled.

Larry stared defiantly up at me before sliding on a pathetic, pleading expression for the guys behind my back. "Help me," his voice croaked.

Drake's hand slipped over my shoulder, but before

he could get a good grip and yank me back, I leaned down and smashed my lips into Larry's.

"What the—" Drake's shock ended his sentence before he finished it.

I felt the transformation before I opened my eyes. The lips underneath mine grew softer. I nipped at the plush lower lip. The scent of orange grew more pronounced and I noticed it was tinged with the slightest hint of honeysuckle.

My wolf howled in approval. He loved honeysuckle.

I felt Aubry's breasts press against me and her hips shrink as I pinned her down. She fit me perfectly.

"Holy fuck!" Easton's shock filled the room.

When I opened my eyes, I stared down into the gorgeous brown glare of my mate. She was pissed.

"Hey there, Butterfly," I cooed.

She lifted a hand to hit me, but I wrapped my hand over both her wrists then pinned them down by her shoulders, careful not to hurt her silky wings. She wasn't wearing handcuffs. Had she picked the lock? What a resourceful little thing.

"My mate was trying to sneak off," I told the guys.

"How... how did you know?" Easton sounded awed.

"Mates can tell," I smiled down at Aubry's look of fury.

"We aren't mates!" she screeched and spat at me. She tried to roll her hips to move me off her, but that only got me hard. For a second, that fact seemed to alarm her.

As if she needed to worry. We were mates. Whether either of us wanted it or not, there would come a time when she begged me for it.

She knew it.

I knew it.

And I'd wait until then. Because, while I *was* a killer, I definitely had limits—and *that* was way beyond them. Besides, I was gonna take so much pleasure in watching her beg.

She turned her face aside, refusing to look at me, staring at the racks of paper towels and cleaning supplies. It wasn't quite the submission I wanted. I wanted her to tilt her head back and expose her neck so that I could nip it gently then nuzzle it before I started to explore it with my lips. But it wasn't outright defiance either.

Which meant, given her history, it was a trick.

"Check on Larry," I ordered. I didn't normally give the orders. Drake did. He was good at it. But, right now, I didn't trust Aubry not to flame the guys if I let go of her.

"Yup. On it," Easton replied.

I heard his footsteps retreat as I watched Aubry's pulse thundering through her gorgeous neck. I stared at the shadows created by her muscles and tendons. I'd never looked at a woman's neck before. I'd always focused on *other* areas. But my mate had an exquisite neck.

I had to resist leaning down and dragging my nose

over her pulse. But I did resist. Because she wasn't ready for that. Not yet. But she would be.

A small rumble escaped me. Aubry's eyes flicked up, then quickly glanced away. I made the sound again and her eyes came my way once more.

A grin spread across my face. Interesting. Apparently, my mate was drawn to my little noises.

She must have realized what I was doing, because suddenly her knee was at my groin. "Shut up or I'll make sure you walk with a limp for the rest of your life, Fuzzball."

Behind me, Drake groaned. "You told her your nickname?"

"Fuck off," I told him. "Get outta here." I didn't need him hovering over me and my mate. And of course I hadn't told her the idiotic nickname they'd given me.

"Fuzzball? They actually call you that?" she scoffed.

"Like it, Butterfly?" I asked.

Her knee dug into my crotch, but just hard enough to be a warning.

"Careful, now," I told her. "You're messing with your future children too, if you hurt my dick, Princess."

BAM.

I fell sideways onto the floor, my vision going red from the pain.

Probably a little too soon to make baby jokes. Not exactly sure why I'd done that, considering I was nowhere near ready to have a baby. But I'd wanted to get a reaction out of her.

You certainly did, asshole! Now, we're dead! My balls screamed up at me.

I was faintly aware of Aubry scrambling around on the ground. Then there was fire. I wasn't sure who shot it, her or Drake. But suddenly, his wings were out, one of them shielding me. It was like a thick black curtain going up between me and the fight.

I heard a rough thump and a high-pitched scream. I yanked on his wing, not caring if I got hurt by the flames. Because I had to get to her. I had to see my mate.

She was curled up into a ball on the floor, her beautiful wings pulled in toward her back. I threw myself on top of her, shielding her from Drake.

"Are you hurt?" I whispered.

She flipped around and latched onto my neck, using me as a human shield—which was exactly what I'd thrown myself to the floor to do, anyway—but the princess had used our mate bond to manipulate me. I didn't know if I was pissed or proud. My aching balls told me to go with pissed.

"You aren't gonna get away, Princess," I said, as she struggled to stand up and maintain her grip on me. I let her, slowly rising to my knees for reasons beyond my own comprehension. I guess I wanted to see what she would do.

"Just watch me," Aubry hissed in my ear.

"We're mates. If you leave, you'll hate it."

"You're fucking delusional," she snapped. "Wouldn't

expect anything less from an assassin."

"So, you've heard of me?" I asked.

"Shut up," she edged around Drake, toward the door.

"I'm disappointed. I thought I'd kept a low profile."

"My team is good."

"Yeah? Really? Why don't we test them? See if they're good enough to find you." I let her back me up instead of twisting away like I knew Drake wanted me to do. But if I shoved myself to the side, he'd hurt her. I could see the dragon rising in his eyes when I glanced over my shoulder.

Drake's fury was no small thing. It was an inferno. I'd seen him burn down entire buildings. I'd seen him beat a mage, and those spell-toting fuckers were harder to kill than roaches.

I only got one mate. Good or bad, wolf shifters only got one, and I wasn't giving her up. So when my hands reached back to touch her hips, I didn't grab on and then smash her back into the wall like I could have. I just lifted her up and wrapped her legs around my waist.

Nothing had ever felt more right.

Aubry's hands tightened around my neck and squeezed in warning. "Don't."

I let her squeeze as I backed out of the storage room and started down the stairs. Immediately, her hands started to flame. But as soon as I felt the slightest pain on my neck, she stopped with a gasp.

I grinned. "Can't hurt me, can you, *mate*?" I emphasized the words as I grabbed her willowy legs and pulled her tighter into me. I glanced down. Her legs were perfection. My thumbs traced little circles on the tops of her thighs. I was tempted to touch her ass, but I resisted.

Soon.

One of her hands reached down and smacked my arm. "We are not mates. That wasn't even a kiss."

I chuckled. "Oh, I agree. We aren't counting that as our first kiss."

"We won't ever have a first kiss."

I arched a brow and turned my head sideways to glance at her. "Really? So, you won't mind if I bring one of my shifter friends with benefits around the next time I've got guard duty?"

Her eyes darkened and her uninjured wing flared out, filling the stairwell. I stopped walking, not wanting her gorgeous wing to get torn on the earthen walls.

After a second, she controlled her emotions and retracted her wing. She stared over my shoulder, refusing to make eye contact. But her body had spoken.

She knew.

I knew.

It was only a matter of time.

This mate bond had blown us both apart. And the only way we could be put back together... was to be together.

10

AUBRY

It had been nine days since my escape attempt—I'd started counting by scratching notches into the cot— and still, no one had tried to break me out.

Was my team really that incompetent? What about Trite? My parents? Where the fuck was everybody?

The door opened at the other end of the tunnel and voices immediately filled the air along with the scent of Bun Cha. I inhaled deeply, my mouth watering over the smoky pork and tangy sauce.

"Uncle Bodie, we still wanna play!" a child's voice drifted down the stairs.

"Don't go!"

"Can we come with you?"

"We've never met a real-life bad guy before!"

Bodie chuckled, the rich sound of his voice echoing down the earthen tunnel walls and making my heart jump. "Stay upstairs, guys. I'll be right back."

Oh yes, children. I'm the Wicked Witch of the West. I'll get you and your little...

Huh. Guess some of them already *were* little dogs.

The door shut with a click, and tiny little fists that I imagined belonged to those tiny little voices began pounding on the door. They didn't open it and try to follow, though, so at least they'd listened to him. Kinda surprising, considering shifters never listened to anyone. They were too lawless and wild, a liability to society in every way.

"They sure love you," Larry commented. His tone was light and warm, like the sunshine I hadn't seen in weeks. It annoyed me.

"Yeah, they're good kids," Bodie agreed. Unlike Larry, Bodie's voice was a deep growl.

My ears liked his voice better.

When they appeared in front of my cell, the wolf shifter had four styrofoam boxes balanced in his arms, each piece of my dinner ensemble kept in separate compartments—even though I was just going to mix it all, anyway. It was a sympathy offering; an attempt to keep me on his good side, despite the spelling that was about to go down. I knew, because Larry was there with his wand. It seemed necessary for him to spell me about every couple days. *Such a joy.*

The smile that lit up the wolf's tanned, handsome face when he got close to me was freaking contagious. I smiled back for a fraction of a second before I realized what the hell I was doing. Idiotic polite reflexes. I was his prisoner. I was being manipulated with a fake mate bond. I was not attracted to him in his tight black t-shirt in the slightest.

Or Easton. The delicious blond lumberjack…

Definitely not Drake—and I actually meant that one for real. He might've been hot, but his abysmal personality more than took away from any good looks he might've had. The bastard.

"Evening, Beautiful," Bodie said with a lopsided grin. "I hope you're hungry, because I brought—"

"Bun Cha?" I guessed, smirking a bit as I raised a single brow.

His lips parted. "How'd you know?"

I rolled my eyes. "I might not have a keen sense of smell like a shifter, but I know my Vietnamese takeout."

Larry chuckled from Bodie's side, mussing his already frizz-tastic hair. If he'd let it grow a little longer, he could gel it and look like a cartoon troll. "I'm afraid it's that time again, Miss Summerset."

I sighed dramatically and placed my book face down on the cot, awaiting their entry.

Bodie had pulled some serious strings with Mr. Stick Up His Ass. The way Larry talked, Easton had helped, too. The deal was, as long as I received my spell treatments every other day to keep my fire and glamour in check, and as long as I was handcuffed, then I was allowed outside of my cell under strict supervision. My faux freedom usually only lasted about an hour or so, but it was better than sitting in that iron-infested cell all fucking day and night. Plus, it allowed me to scope out my terrain, creating a mental map for use in future escape attempts.

If my people weren't gonna come for me, then I'd bust my own ass out of here.

Bodie moved all the takeout boxes over to his left arm, and unlocked my cell with his right, shutting the three of us in as soon as Larry was through. Moving the book aside, he sat down at the edge of my bed and passed me my boxes of dinner.

The wolf shifter read the book title and his dark brows furrowed over those bright yellow-green eyes. I tried not to be mesmerized by them, I really did, but he was so damn beautiful… and this mate magic bullshit was seriously strong. I could feel a tingle between my legs just from how close he was sitting.

"Where'd you get this?" he asked, nodding toward the book.

In the background, Larry rolled up the sleeves of his robe and got to work, chanting in another tongue and waving his wand while I did my best to ignore him and the tickle of uneasiness that flowed through me as his magic entered my system.

"Easton dropped that book off," I said, opening the first box and plucking out a small chunk of grilled pork. The book wasn't too horrible. It was about the mechanics of ships. Dry at first, but with nothing else to read... I'd slowly become fascinated by the ingenuity of the builders.

"*Easton?*" Bodie asked, surprise clear in his tone.

I opened the second box in search of the dipping sauce. *Come to mama.* "Yeah, you know, Goldilocks? Ethan? Whatever other stupid nicknames he goes by."

Bodie pursed his lips. "Yeah, I know the guy. I just don't understand why he was anywhere near your cell."

I shrugged, finally finding my sauce in the third box. I dipped the meat and took a bite, my eyes practically rolling back in delight as I savored the tangy flavor. "I guess he feels bad for me. I mean, playing me at the pub, then locking me up like an animal."

"I'm an animal," Bodie deadpanned, letting his pinkie finger brush against my skin.

Immediately, his naughty implications sent a flurry of pictures through my mind. Him pressing me into the bars, my shoulders burning as he pumped into me. Damn it. I shifted away from him and shoveled more food into my mouth.

"You all are fucked up."

His eyes narrowed. "No more than the mages, Princess."

"Don't call me Princess," I reiterated for what felt like the millionth time in my life. I tucked my legs beneath my butt, trying to get comfortable during this uncomfortable affair—Larry's magic slowly moved from annoying tingles to irritating pinpricks, almost like a tattoo.

"Whatever you say, Butterfly," he teased.

"That either."

Bodie rolled his eyes before watching me take another bite. His gaze was rapt, as if he were imagining me putting an entirely different piece of meat in my mouth... I licked my lips, then each individual finger, taking pleasure in driving him crazy. The mate-bond-faking-liar-fuck. He deserved to suffer for this mess he'd made.

"When was Easton down here?" he asked.

I pursed my lips and smiled smugly. "Wouldn't you like to know?"

Somehow the gold flicker that came into Bodie's eyes gave me a rush. Defiance. *That's what it is,* I told myself.

The door opened at the top of the steps and Bodie turned sideways to yell. "I said stay upstairs! I'll be back in a minute!"

"Nah, bro, it's me."

The deep voice coaxed an evil grin onto my lips.

"Speak of the devil..." I muttered to Bodie, who was tense and glowering, looking pissed as hell.

"Drake said he needs you for..." Easton trailed off as he approached, eyeing me hesitantly. "For a job."

Bodie sighed and ran his hands through his dark brown hair. "Now? I'm literally on babysitting duty for the pack tonight."

Easton nodded, a sympathetic half smile tugging at his soft lips. "Yeah, man, I know. I've been ordered to take over for you while you're gone, so…"

Bodie stared at him for a moment with a suspicious glare.

Ohh, he was jealous. Interesting. I'd have to figure out a way to use that someday. But seriously, what did he think? That his friend had made the whole thing up just to separate us and get some extra time with me? I wasn't *that* great of a catch. Especially not while I was rocking unwashed, knotty hair, overgrown leg hairs, and week-old pho-breath. What I wouldn't give for a toothbrush and a razor…

Actually, I could use those to help me escape. Probably why they hadn't offered them to me. Butt-licking fuckers.

Bodie stood and set the book back down on my cot, kneeling off to my left side so as not to interfere with Larry's work. "I'll be back soon, Buttercup."

"Oh, I'm Buttercup now? Butter*cup*, Butter*fly*… I'm just some chunk of heart-attack-inducing lard that gets stuck in your arteries?"

"What the fuck? No," he protested, shaking his head.

"What'll it be next? Buttercream? Butterfinger? Butterscotch?"

Bodie's exasperated expression quickly turned smoldering as his eyes hooded and he bit his lip. "I gotta say, I like the sounds of each and every one of those. Maybe I *will* use one of those next time."

I groaned at how epically my plan had just back-fired. Especially the look in his eyes when I said fingers. He definitely wasn't thinking about candy. He better not lay a finger on my...

"Keep a close eye on her," Bodie patted Easton's shoulder as he entered the cell and my *supposed* mate made his exit. "But not too close."

He backed out into the tunnel, flipping two fingers between his eyes and Easton's. On anyone else, that gesture would have looked stupid. But Bodie radiated menace.

Easton hesitated, shooting me a curious glance before laughing at Bodie's comment and his weird-ass behavior, as if any attraction to me was a huge joke. "Yeah, man, no worries."

I glared at him. I might not think of myself as a catch, but fuck him and his stupid claws.

Bodie opened the door at the top of the stairs, and immediately the sound of rambunctious children saturated the air.

"Uncle Bodie's back!" they cried, followed closely by, "Aww, where's he going?"

I almost felt bad for the little shits. They wouldn't have anyone to teach them to scoot across the carpet now.

As soon as the door was shut, Easton took a seat on the floor, his muscular frame sprawling out over half of my damn cell.

"You look comfortable," I goaded him.

He chuckled and leaned back on his elbows. "Yeah, so do you." His eyes traveled over me with an interest that stated his prior laughter was a lie.

My cheeks heated but I had other things to focus on. I gritted my teeth as Larry continued chanting, his magic transforming from irritating to borderline painful. It was a familiar sensation, one that triggered a reflexive response of arousal in me, but also one of disgust, considering I had zero desire to get my rocks off with Einstein's doppelganger.

Other present company, though...

I bit my bottom lip and *tried* not to imagine Easton inflicting this delicious pain on me just before he ravaged me senseless. As my nipples hardened, heat pooled between my thighs, and my breaths grew short, it was clear I'd failed miserably. I knew his cock was just as thick as the rest of him, from the bulge I'd seen at the club, and I bet it was excruciatingly orgasmic.

I crossed my legs, hoping his damned shifter nose couldn't somehow smell my arousal. Judging by the way his pale blue eyes suddenly swirled with golden streaks, I had a feeling he'd done exactly that.

"What kind of shifter are you?" I asked, trying to change the subject while numbly rubbing my arms after the old mage finally finished his spells. My whole body held a dull ache that seeped through skin, muscle, and bone like the frigid cold of deep Pacific waters. I felt frail. Human. I didn't like it.

Easton grinned and sat up, draping both arms over

his bent knees. "I'll give you a hint. Why do you think they call me Goldilocks?"

I grabbed my box of takeout and took another bite. "Because of your blond hair?"

He rolled his eyes but cocked his head, silently admitting that I had a point. "Try again."

I hummed as I chewed. "Because you're so pretty it's almost feminine?"

Easton's jaw dropped open, snapped shut, ticked a bit like he might speak, then popped open again. "I don't know whether to take that as a compliment or a burn."

I snorted, dipping a bite of noodles into my sauce before slipping it into my mouth. "You can take it however you want, pretty boy." I couldn't help myself. I had a few more shinies and I couldn't hold back, even though maybe I should have. "Arm candy. Flower boy. Trophy wife. One Direction." I spat them out, rapid fire.

He raised a brow at me, and somehow managed to look even more enticing than my meal. "You know I'm, like, three times your size, right? There's nothing *feminine* about me." He flexed his bicep and I dropped a little bit of noodle.

Damn it. There was no way to hide that. I tried anyway.

"Please." I rolled my eyes.

"I can smell that you're lying."

"Vietnamese food turns me on," I countered.

It was weak as hell. But whatever. I was more comfortable bantering with Easton than Bodie, because at least with Easton, the attraction was real—albeit, a bit fucked up, but still—*real*. We'd genuinely hit it off at the pub. I'd honestly been attracted to him—more so as a blond, but even as a redhead. I'd truly been looking forward to getting my world rocked by his anaconda all night long.

Now that he was an accomplice to my kidnapping, that'd obviously put a damper on things, but clearly not enough. It irritated the hell out of me that I was attracted to him. What kind of Stockholm Criminal Minds shit was this?

"Okay, final guess," he said, pushing up onto his feet and withdrawing a set of handcuffs from his back pocket. God, I wished this whole thing had happened under different circumstances. Like, tie me down and fuck me up, circumstances. The sight of him holding handcuffs and sporting wood sent a shiver racing across my skin, giving me goosebumps.

It's just Stockholm Syndrome, you crazy bitch! I told my panting pussy. *Get it together!*

I didn't miss the way Easton's eyes drifted down to my pebbled nipples, barely covered beneath the wife-beater Bodie had lent me. I would've said no to the wolf's offer of clothing, but I'd been too tired of parading around in that ratty dress to argue. The shorts he'd lent me fit perfectly—for a cheerleader or a playboy bunny. I was pretty sure my ass-cheeks would have been spilling out the bottom if the spandex material hadn't been clinging on for dear life.

I held out my hands and waited impatiently for him to cuff me. "They call you Goldilocks because... you're a bear shifter?"

"Ding, ding, ding!" he sang with a grin as he snapped the cuffs in place.

My wrists didn't immediately burn and sting. "Ooh, not iron this time?"

Easton shook his head and led us out into the tunnel. "Nope. It took some convincing, but Drake eventually gave in."

"Why would you do that?" I asked, staring at our feet as we shuffled forward through the dirt that led to the stairs. Mine: bare, Easton's: in sneakers, and Larry's: in some curly-toed elfin getup. Jesus.

Easton sighed. "I don't know. I guess... we kidnapped you to prove a point. That point isn't to prove that we're savage monsters. It's that things need to change. We shouldn't have to treat you badly because of that."

I didn't answer. I wasn't even sure if I believed him. *We* never gave *shifters* any leeway; in fact, most shifters didn't even make it past the initial arrest. So why would *they* give *us* any? It had to be a trick. A ploy to make me lower my guard and then really hammer it home. I wasn't about to be caught with my pants down around these pricks—at least, metaphorically.

Physically... maybe.

Fuck, I was horny. I wondered if I could request a dino dildo? For some reason, I didn't imagine Bodie going for it. Not unless he got to watch. Which would only encourage this mate bullshit. But Easton... no, he probably wouldn't either.

"I have other things to attend to now, Mr. Beretta," Larry said, placing a gentle hand on Easton's shoulder.

"Yeah, man, no worries. We'll just be in the conference room keeping an eye on the munchkins."

Ha! Munchkins. That totally made my wicked witch reference all the richer.

Larry waved goodbye, slowly heaving himself even further up the stairs, while I followed Easton to the door. Muffled shouts and giggles filled the room beyond. Sounds of objects clanging and banging together. If I didn't know there were kids on the other side, I might be tempted to think an arrest was going on.

Easton cracked the door open, and immediately, they started.

"Uncle Easton!" one of them shouted, running over and jumping on him.

I took a step back. There were at least twelve kids in here. I hadn't spent a day with little people since I was one myself. There were a couple Chinese boys on one side, a kid with a wild afro in the middle, and several brunettes and blondies sprinkled around. One shifter kid was even sporting some porcupine quills instead of hair. Ouch.

"Are you here to play?" one boy asked.

"Can I be Elsa and you be Marshmallow?" a little girl with blonde pigtails ran up and begged, lacing her fingers together.

Porcupine head noticed me and his eyes flashed wide. "Oh em gee, you brought the prisoner up! Can we play shifters and mages?"

Next to him a little girl's nose morphed into a wolf nose and she sniffed at me. So... they had a mix of shifter kids in here. Interesting.

Easton shook off the kid that was hanging on him and held up both hands for silence. To my amazement, the menagerie actually quieted down a bit. "Aubry's here because I have to look after *all* of you at the same time and I can't be in two places at once. And no, we're not playing shifters and mages. I don't think she'd understand the rules."

I scoffed and raised a brow, settling down at a pub table off to the side of the room. Though the room didn't look like it was typically used for kids, folding chairs and whatnot had been moved to the sides to create a makeshift playspace in the center of the room, it didn't look like that bad of a spot. Easton sat in the remaining chair, while the children all gathered around like it was fucking story time or something.

"I don't know. I'm pretty smart. I'm sure I can figure the rules out," I deadpanned.

"See?" the kids argued. "She likes playing the prisoner! Please, Uncle Easton!"

Ha. Those kids were right. But I only liked playing prisoner with a consenting dom. One who would unlock me and let me go at the end of a scene. Not this way.

Easton sighed and shook his blond head, grinning all the while. "Sorry, guys. Not tonight."

They moaned and groaned, and a few of them wandered off to play with blocks. Porcupine head pulled out a little pouch that looked like it might hold marbles. But he started to pull out toy car after toy car, until he and his buddies all had two each. His pouch must have had an Expansion Spell on it. I briefly wondered if the spell would be big enough for me to sneak inside and escape. But, he'd probably still have to be able to carry whatever weight the bag held. So, maybe not.

While the other kids wandered off, one fierce little girl with wild black curls stared at me inquisitively. I was about to ask her what she wanted, when she blurted out her question. "Why'd you kill my cousin?"

Shock slapped me across the face like a flyswatter, momentarily stunning me. "Excuse me?"

"El Fuego," she explained. "He was my cousin. Why did you kill him?"

"Uh…" I half chuckled as I wondered how to get out of this precarious conversation.

There was nothing I could say that she'd understand. Nothing she'd agree with, anyway. Plus, she didn't look more than eight. She didn't need to be thinking about shit like that. Even shifter kids deserved a carefree childhood.

"It's alright," Easton encouraged me. "You can tell Mariana your truth. There are multiple angles to every story, and neither side is definitively right or wrong, just different."

As I stared at him, my brows furrowed. Where the hell had the awkward actor gone, and who the hell was this confident philosopher?

"*Right…*" I directed my attention back to the little girl, my tongue suddenly dry. "Well, your cousin broke the law. He stole something that didn't belong to him, and he tried to use it to hurt thousands of people."

Her nose scrunched in confusion. "Hiding the shifters from the mages wouldn't hurt anybody," she replied uncertainly.

Is that what they'd been telling the kids? Feeding them lies to ensure they had new generations of adamant soldiers lined up? For fuck's sake.

"That's right, sweetheart, hiding wouldn't hurt anyone. But that's not what they're using them for. That's a lie." I said softly.

"No, it isn't." Mariana shook her brunette head defiantly. "My daddy told me."

I rolled my eyes and crossed my arms. Fine. I'd give her the eight-year-old level reasoning. "Plus," I added, "he tried to kill me first." Why the hell I couldn't just let it go was beyond me. I just felt this ridiculous need to prove myself to the girl. "It was technically self-defense."

"He was definitely tough," she agreed with me in a roundabout way.

The little girl with pigtails looked up from her blocks and eyed me intently. "Why did the mages set my friend's house on fire? She wasn't doing anything wrong."

Oh fuck, the friend hadn't died, had she? My stomach twisted at the thought. Killing adult criminals was one thing, but murdering innocent children was another altogether.

"Mages don't set fires, sweetie," I explained. "Summer fae can, but we don't go around burning down shifter neighborhoods, either. It must have been an accidental fire."

"It wasn't." She stuck her little nose in the air, channeling a pretty solid Elsa as she gave me the cold shoulder. I was mildly impressed, but mostly annoyed.

"Did your friend live?" I couldn't help but ask.

"Yeah, but she had to get a new haircut because her long hair burned off. Her mom died, though. And her dad—"

Easton sighed and interrupted. "Her dad is upset, as any father would be."

141

Pigtail girl nodded and got back to building her block tower.

I glanced across the table at Easton. "Take me back to the cell?"

"What? Why?"

Seriously? He was cute, but apparently a little slow in the uptake. The muscle, not the brains, clearly.

"Because I'd rather sit in mind-numbing silence than suffer another round of the Spanish Inquisition led by ill-informed and incredibly stubborn children."

He blinked, his blue eyes flashing with what looked like amusement.

"What?" I snapped.

He chuckled. "I'm not taking you back to your cell, Princess. I think this could be good for you. Open your eyes to the other side of the story."

"This is not *another side of the story*," I hissed. "These are blatant lies that you're feeding your own youth to fuel a pointless war. If shifters could control themselves and *not* risk exposing supernaturals to humans on a daily basis, then maybe they'd have a case. But they can't, and they don't."

Easton glared at me before looking away and scratching the golden stubble along his jaw. "So… what? All shifters just need to die? It doesn't matter if it's El Fuego or his baby cousin Mariana—kill them all? It doesn't matter if it's Suzie's friend's mom, or Suzie herself—let them all burn?"

Suzie must've been the pig-tailed girl, aka Elsa. And

Mariana must've been El Fuego's argumentative cousin with the ebony ringlets. Got it.

Anger built in my chest like flames, fanning through my blood. But not flames that would kill a fucking child. "No, that's not *at all* what I said."

"Oh, but it was absolutely *dripping* off the words you didn't say," he bit back. "You want to eliminate all shifters. Why not start with the kids?"

He gestured to the room full of shifter children, some of whom had been eavesdropping and now held terrified expressions on their little faces.

"That's enough!" I whisper-shouted at him. "You're freaking them out."

"Who cares?" he mocked. "They're just shifters. They need to die, anyway, according to you. And better sooner than later, right? That way they can't make any teensy tiny mistakes and fuck everything up. God knows, mages and other magic users are perfect and never make mistakes."

My nostrils flared as I glared at him.

Okay, scratch my earlier thoughts. Easton had officially moved down into Drake's camp. Which only left Bodie to be attracted to, and I hated that more than anything since it went beyond the scope of reality and took away my free will.

Basically, I was back to square one—hating these assholes.

Still, a strange emotion swirled through me, making my internal fire die down. I couldn't pinpoint exactly what it was, but I knew I hated the way it made me feel. Almost like… guilt or shame.

From the corner of my eye, I saw Easton reach his hand across the table and brush fingers with mine. "I'm not trying to hurt you, Tinkerbell. I'm just trying to make you *see*."

On instinct, I pulled away, and for some reason, that strange, painful emotion intensified into near sadness. Heat burned across my cheeks and water welled along the rim of my eyes, but I'd be damned if I fucking cried in front of this whole room of shifters.

I took a deep breath and reiterated my previous request. "Take me back to my cell."

"Why are so many shifters homeless?" another child asked, a small boy with bowl-cut brown hair. God, I thought that style had gone out back in the nineties.

As much as I hated the question, I was actually glad for a slight change in subject. "Probably because they can't afford to pay their rent," I explained, keeping my voice carefully neutral. "Just like humans and mages, if we can't pay, we can't stay."

"Yeah, but I never saw a homeless mage," the boy argued.

Me either, kid.

Mages were far too important—and therefore *wealthy*—to be destitute. But money was a difficult subject to broach with full-grown adults. I certainly didn't want to discuss it with a child.

"Can I see your wings?" another kid asked, I couldn't tell which.

I nodded, and a small smile crept onto my lips. I stole a glance at Easton who smiled encouragingly. His pearly teeth and his baby blue eyes practically sparkled, cooling that aching burn in my chest—yet *another* weird sensation I didn't appreciate this shifter making me feel.

I stood and slowly turned around, allowing my wings to slip out from two slits in the back of the white tank top and spread to their full potential. Light filtered through the gossamer material and sparkled like prisms on the floor. I loved my wings.

"Whoa!" some of the kids cried, and almost all of them moved closer.

"So, you can really fly?" a boy asked.

I glanced over my shoulder and nodded.

"Just like a bird shifter?" another clarified.

I shrugged. "I suppose so, yeah."

"Can you carry someone and fly?" a different kid asked; there were so many of them, it was impossible to keep track of who was who.

Easton chuckled, his deep voice filling the room with warmth. "No, she's not giving you a ride, Pip."

Okay, well *almost* impossible. Apparently, the muscled marshmallow could tell them apart.

"Can we watch *Frozen*, Uncle Easton?" the pig-tailed Suzie asked sweetly.

145

"Again?" he groaned, scrubbing a broad hand across his face.

Suzie ran over and bounced into his lap. "Yes! I love it so so much. Please?"

"*Ah*. Fine," Easton grumbled as he stood and lifted her high in the air. She giggled as some of the other kids gathered around Easton's feet, very much like puppies at the feet of their owner. Shuffling carefully, he deposited the girl on the floor near the flatscreen TV and grabbed the remote.

A low whine touched the air as the screen lit up and came to life, black at first, but quickly morphing into the scene of another house fire. Local news channel eight was on the scene—human news.

Easton frowned and turned up the volume.

"There seems to be yet another accidental house fire here in Skid Row. Authorities believe it started with a backyard grill due to the extreme drought California has suffered this summer. They advise using caution when handling matches and lighters, and—"

Easton flicked the channel over to the shifter magical news, channel two. Mages owned channel one.

"Uncle Easton!" the kids cried in frustration. "We want *Frozen*!"

He held out his hand and shushed them. "Hang on. Just give me a minute."

When I saw the image on the screen, my throat clogged like a wad of toilet paper stuffed in a drainpipe. My *goddamned parents* sat regally behind a long desk opposite a popular newscaster named Sharon Streamer conducting an interview of some sort. Their postures were stick straight. Their button noses were high in the air.

What the actual fuck?

"Do shifters usually get mage news?" I asked Easton cautiously. My heart pumped in my chest, like a plunger trying to dislodge that freaking wad of soggy toilet paper.

He turned to me, his expression worried and confused. "No."

The cameraman got a closeup of Sharon for a moment, all snazzed up in a pink skirt suit, her big brown hair riding her heavily made up face like a wave. "King Indigo and Queen Katrina are here today with a very important announcement for supernaturals across Los Angeles and all of California. Your Majesties?"

The camera panned over to my parents once more who stared straight ahead with perfectly practiced smiles.

"Good evening." Dad addressed the magical world with a casual calm he never directed at me. "We would like to announce that our daughter, Princess Aubry of the Summer Fae Court, has officially stepped down from her position as Chief Enforcer of the Mage Police to pursue other opportunities."

My fucking heart stopped dead.

Other opportunities?

What the hell did they think this was? A vacation? A

job opportunity? I'd been kidnapped for fuck's sake! Their only daughter, abducted and held hostage by the enemy, and they acted like it meant *nothing* to them. Like *I* meant nothing…

"We wish her all the best in her future endeavors," Dad continued. "And we are delighted to announce that Candace Wintern, Princess of the Winter Fae Court, has stepped in to take her place."

11

AUBRY

I TURNED AND FLED, NOT TOWARD AN EXIT, BUT TOWARD my cell.

So many painful thoughts rushed through my mind at once. I tried to escape them, but it was like trying to dodge machine-gun fire.

Memories of my parents flooded my brain. Training with my father. Getting my ass beat on the practice mats, every bone in my body aching from the strain. Him kicking my ribs and telling me, "A shifter won't have mercy. Neither can I. Get up."

The memories shuffled as I ran down the stairs, each step rattling my legs like my mother's tight-lipped frown used to rattle my heart. "Come on, Aubry. Candace would do whatever she needed to get this position. You can't even muster up the courage to go on one little date—"

A new memory flashed and my ex-fiance's face darted into my mind, making me stumble on the stairs.

Matthew was a mage with dark brown curls, cold blue eyes, and a bleach-white smile. I'd dated him at my mother's urging, hoping it would get me a promotion that would put me in line for the chief enforcer position. But somehow, that snake charmer had cast a little spell that had *his* snake dancing in my basket two seconds later.

Everything snowballed and went downhill after that. Engagement rings and a tiny apartment... all before my mother could swoop in and tell me no.

She wanted to, I could see it in every broken blood vessel in her angry eyes, but it was too late. Even if she *had* said no, I wouldn't have listened to her, especially when Dad encouraged the arrangement. But I should have. It would have been one of the few times that ice-cold social climber had been right.

Because one asshole could always spot another.

It took less than six months for Matthew to cheat. Less than a year for him to get promoted and leave me. And over five years for me to get over it. I still wasn't over it. I hated him, and the pain he'd caused would haunt me for a lifetime.

The ache of that betrayal throbbed in my chest next to the new, freshly opened wound. I was surprised I wasn't bleeding out. With the way my emotions poured like a hot, crimson river, it felt like I should be.

My parents just turned their backs on me.

I repeated that mantra in my head, trying to rationalize what I just witnessed.

They turned their backs on their only child.

But I couldn't rationalize shit. I was too angry and confused. I was drowning in emotion and couldn't breathe much less think clearly.

"Aubry," Easton called out behind me.

I ignored him

"Aubry!" he yelled.

Still, I didn't respond. I flew instead, down the tunnel until I saw the iron bars. *Closed* iron bars. Some idiot had shut the door to my cell. And I couldn't open it myself without scalding my hand on that putrid, godawful metal.

Whoever had invented iron deserved to be drawn and quartered slowly while the Spongebob Squarepants theme song played over and over.

I sank down into a crouch in the tunnel, leaning against the packed dirt wall for support.

Tears didn't stream down my face, though I expected that they should. I just felt empty. Hollow. My head got that floating feeling, like this wasn't reality and I was in a dream. Or a nightmare.

Easton stopped just beside me, his heavy feet like bricks. The guy didn't know how to walk softly. He didn't know how to sneak up on someone. There wasn't a true deceptive bone in his body. Which made the fact that they'd sent him out to lure me in all the more insulting.

151

The fact that I'd fallen for it?

I shook my head and pressed my cheek against the dirt, turning away from him. Maybe my family was right to be disappointed in me. To leave me behind.

"Tell me what's wrong."

I heard him sit down on the step behind me, then clasp his hands together. I could picture him doing it. Easton was always wringing his hands like some damn worried mother. Better than my own. *She* only wrung her hands over what other people would think when I messed up. Mom would have made the perfect Hollywood starlet.

I dug a finger into the wall, wondering if I could dig my own grave by hand, crawl inside and just die. That sounded more appealing than talking to Easton. Or breaking out and facing the family that had just publicly fucking forsaken me.

I wasn't even worth a ransom? A trade?

The tears started then. I tried to keep them silent, but a tiny sob escaped.

Easton immediately stood from his step, came forward, and put his hand on my shoulder. When I didn't move to stop him, the giant sat down next to me and wrapped an arm around me.

The last person to hug me when I cried was Tee. And her hug was nothing compared to the strong, security-laced feeling I got when Easton wrapped me up like he was trying to shield me from all the world's spitballs and soul-shredding hatred.

Despite myself, I ended up leaning into him and crying harder.

"You can't be nice to me," I sobbed into the front of his cotton shirt. It was soft as hell and it smelled like Irish Spring soap. I dug my face into his pecs shamelessly. It wasn't fair. It wasn't right that these criminal jerkwads could be nice when my own parents...

Easton's arms came around my back. He was careful not to bend my wings as he stroked down my spine. "*Shh, shh.*"

Eventually, my cries grew softer.

That's when Easton spoke.

"My dad always hated me." His voice was soft, tentative. "I'm a golden bear, and a blond kid. My dad's a brown bear, and a brown-haired guy. It didn't matter to him that my mom's grandmother was fair. He never believed I was his."

I paused, frozen where I clutched at him. Why the hell was he telling me this? Wonder, confusion, and downright panic filled me. What was I supposed to say?

"Goldilocks is the name the guys call me now, and I can stand it because I know they're just yanking my chain, trying to toughen me up. They're trying to erase what it used to mean. But that's what my dad used to call me when he'd beat me. He'd tell me I wasn't man enough, wasn't bear enough. He'd tell me he hoped I didn't make it through the winter."

There was a hitch in Easton's voice and I looked up.

Even with only a single light bulb down here, I could see his gaze was glassy. His blue eyes were focused on the end of the tunnel in front of us where the earth floor gave way to cement stairs. His eyes traced the yellow extension cord that trailed down those stairs until they came to the tunnel we sat in.

"Parents say shit and do shit," he muttered, dragging his fingers up and down my spine once more. But this time, I wasn't sure if he was touching me to comfort me, or to comfort himself. "They don't realize the power they have to do good. Or evil. They don't realize that we remember every damn time they say shit to us." He shook his head. Then he finally adjusted his gaze and looked at me.

I didn't know what to say. Because it was true, what he'd said. Parents held so much power over their children. Every glance, every word, every action. Praise was as rare and precious as a diamond in my family. It sounded like it had been the same, maybe even worse, for Easton.

But awful family members? That wasn't something fae discussed. You didn't mention your weaknesses. He'd just handed me a way to manipulate him. A way to hurt him. Why?

Because he sees you're hurt, idiot, my heart snapped.

But he shouldn't care if I was hurt.

I was his prisoner.

Nothing more.

No amount of feeding me Pho or taking me to

babysit pack members could change the fact that we were mortal enemies.

Could it?

Easton must have been okay with my lack of a response, because he kept on talking. "I left my family years ago and haven't looked back."

"Left your family?" I leaned back and studied his face. Who could leave their family and still have honor? Among the fae, if you abandoned your family—like my cousin Kira in Russia—you were spurned by all fae. You were a traitor.

My question must have registered in my expression. Easton reached out and gently smudged away a tear that remained on my left cheek. "If they're not good for you, they're not good for you. There's another family out there, waiting. Other people who will have your back and make you whole."

I swallowed the giant, sour, garlic shaped knot that rose in my throat.

Not true. Not true. He's trying to turn me.

I took a deep breath and faced the bars of my cage. I tried to remind myself that these men only wanted to use me… just like my parents. I was just a stepping stone for their own prestige.

"You're wrong." My voice came out scratchier and weaker than I would have liked. I scooted away from Easton then.

"Maybe," he said. "Maybe I'm wrong. Maybe they'll betray me. But, for seven years I've been right about them. Ever since... the night Drake found me... he's had my back."

Easton's voice broke on that last statement and I knew something about that night had haunted him. I could see the shadows of ghosts lingering in his eyes. The hollowness in his features, like a graveyard.

"What—" I cut myself off from asking what happened. He wouldn't tell me. I stared down at my hands, interlocking my fingers.

The silence drew on until I felt it like a thick blanket over my head, making me hot and claustrophobic, making it hard to breathe.

"I tried to kill myself," Easton admitted quietly.

My eyes flew to his beautiful, pain-carved face.

He stared at the dirt wall. "Stupid, I know. But I did. Drake stopped me."

"I bet you hated him." I didn't know what else to say. 'I'm sorry' didn't sound right, it just sounded idiotic. There was no good response. So, against my better judgement, I reached out and rubbed the top of Easton's hand. Unlike I had done upstairs, he didn't pull away.

"Yeah, I fought him that night." Easton gave a small chuckle. "He clipped me with his wing." He lifted my hand and traced my fingertips over a small scar on the bottom of his chin. The subtle touch flooded my body with heat and confusion.

"I'm sure you got in a couple good hits yourself," I said, trying not to focus on the stubble that scraped over my finger. I tried to think of anything except for the sharp line of his jaw or how his hard pecs moved when he sucked in a breath just before he laughed.

"Yeah, I did," he said, grinning. "It was a pretty epic fight."

"Does he have any weaknesses?" I asked, too casually.

That only made Easton laugh harder. "Yup. Tons. Try stabbing his pinkie toe on the full moon."

I rolled my eyes. "Fine. That was too obvious. But I had to try."

"I'm glad to see you trying."

"Why?" I furrowed my brow.

"Because it means we haven't broken you." His words came out breathy.

I leaned back, feeling the tension between us amp up.

"Isn't the *point* to break me?" I asked, my voice catching.

He tilted his head and considered his words before he answered. "Maybe before I knew you."

"But now?"

"Now, I think it would be a shame for the woman who took on three shifters to crack." He jabbed a thumb over his shoulder, gesturing up the stairs. "Don't think about those assholes on the TV."

And just like that, the thoughts and feelings came rushing back.

"Don't remind me about them, then," I snapped.

"They only want to use you."

"And you're so different?"

"No." Easton's reply was so curt that I didn't even have a retort ready.

I was so shocked, my jaw dropped. Who answered a question like that honestly?

"I'm not different," he agreed. "But I wanna be."

I stood. This was too much for me to handle. Too much for me to take in. Emotions were punching me, making my chest feel like a speed bag.

"Can you open the door, please?" I asked quietly.

"Yeah. Uh. Sure," Easton stood, awkwardly rubbing his hands down his pants, as if his palms had grown sweaty. He leaned around me and gently pushed the cell door open. But as he did, I realized just how huge he was.

We'd flirted at the bar, and I'd mentally mocked him then. He'd held me in the tunnel, and I'd accepted his soothing touch. But standing in front of him, I felt so tiny. My head reached his ribcage. His fingers were probably as thick as most of the dicks I'd ever had. His chest... one of his pecs could be my pillow. He could tuck me into his left side and I'd be all but invisible to people on the right.

Standing in front of him and realizing how powerful he was... triggered the submissive in me. I licked my lips as my nipples pebbled.

Easton had just confessed a shit ton of emasculating stuff to me. I shouldn't be turned on. I hated that emotional bullcrap, that Eeyore-like *'poor me'* shit that everyone pulled. I should be disgusted right now. Annoyed. I wasn't thinking clearly. That was the only explanation for the heat that was forming between my thighs.

"Um... thanks," I muttered. I didn't even have to duck under his arm to go into my cell, he was that big.

I stopped when I was in the middle and just stared at the wall, suddenly aware that Easton was about to leave, and I didn't want to be alone.

Fuck me.

I turned, clearing my throat. "Will you stay?"

The stupid question came out so soft even I could hardly hear it.

But Easton's shifter ears didn't have any problems. "Sure."

He walked in and sat down gingerly on my cot, testing it to ensure it would hold his weight before he relaxed and leaned back against the concrete wall.

I felt weird just standing there in front of him while he watched me, so I made my way over and sat beside him on the half-assed bed. He was so huge that our legs touched.

I stared down at the ground instead of at our point of contact. "My parents suck, obviously."

"Obviously." I could hear a smile in his reply, even though I didn't glance up to see it.

I shrugged, trying to remain nonchalant, though both of us already knew otherwise. But I refused to break down again. "Comes with the territory. Fae aren't known for being snuggly soft."

"Too bad, most bears are." His shoulder brushed mine. *Accidentally*, I was sure.

"Only that stupid detergent one," I retorted.

"Hey! The Snuggle Bear is my hero. He's the only TV representation shifters get."

I snorted. "Talking stuffed animals are not shifter equivalents."

I turned to face him, a skeptical expression on my face. But inside, I was glad I'd asked him to stay. Happy he was here, almost. Banter was better than the bitter thoughts I'd be having by myself.

He grinned and shrugged one of his massive shoulders. "To Hollywood, stuffed animals might as well be shifters for all they get it right."

"What about all those animal movies?" I asked. "*Air Bud* or whatever?"

"Those were dogs. Not bear shifters."

"Well... they're closer. There are movies with *actual* shifter characters, too." I point out.

"So help me, if you say *Twilight*, I will leave and you will not get Pho for a month," Easton threatened.

I burst into laughter, then he laughed, too. I made the mistake of looking up at him. Easton laughing, *really* laughing, not fake laughing like he had when we'd met at the bar, was just—was just—I couldn't think. I didn't have words for what his laughter was. Pure joy, maybe? Light streaming from a person instead of a bulb? Energy—kinetic, powerful movement that radiated so that the very air around him rippled with mirth.

It was entrancing.

I froze and stared... until the laughter died on his lips and his eyes flickered down to my mouth.

My tongue darted out and wet my lips. That hussy. Stupid tongue.

I wasn't going to kiss my captor.

I wouldn't...

But when Easton leaned forward, I didn't stop him.

My chest lightened, anticipation filled me, and when he leaned down, I tilted my head back.

"WHAT THE FUCK? THAT'S MY MATE!" Bodie thundered behind us.

I whirled around, heart thumping like a rabbit darting away from a predator.

Bodie stalked into my cell, his green eyes poisonous. Fixed on Easton. His eyes morphed to pure gold in front of my eyes and his torso rippled, shirt disappearing and fur sprouting from his back as he started to shift.

"We were just talkin—"

"Bullshit!" Bodie snarled, as his upper body transformed into a giant black werewolf. He grabbed me by the upper arm and hid me behind him. His move put my poor wings too close to the iron bars. One wingtip touched the heathen metal and I shoved forward into Bodie, hissing in pain. He wrapped an arm around my waist, tugging me closer. He didn't stop until my front was plastered to his very taut rear.

"Sorry." His apology was clipped short and he immediately refocused all his attention on Easton, who stood holding his hands up, trying to pacify the growling wolf shifter.

"Look, she was just upset after that announcement," Easton supplied.

"You tried to take advantage of my mate when she was hurting?" Bodie yelled. He took a step closer to Easton.

"No! *No!* It wasn't..." Easton trailed off.

"I will fucking end you," Bodie growled.

My stomach tightened and I stiffened against him. Oh shit, was Easton gonna try to shift in here to fight back? If Easton shifted, there'd be no room.

"Bodie, stop," I told him, hands going to his shoulders and pulling him back.

"No," the voice that responded was furious. Almost possessed. He yanked away from me and took a swing at his friend.

Easton didn't even try to defend himself. He just took the punch.

Fucking shit. That was the worst thing he could possibly do. I knew, because it was the same thing my asshole father had done to me. Taken the punch when we sparred and acted like it was nothing. It made me feel powerless and my anger worthless. Bodie was gonna explode.

Unless...

I darted through the open doorway of the cell and bolted up the stairs as fast as I could. Not two seconds later, I felt paws on my back. I stumbled and fell onto the stairs, my knees screaming in pain.

Right above my ear, I heard the low, threatening growl of a wolf.

I knew he'd follow me.

I stilled, waiting for Bodie to grow calm. It felt like forever, lying there as the corners of the steps dug into my chest, stomach, and legs. The cold of the stone and the darkness of the stairwell pressed against me just as hard as Bodie's paws.

Eventually, the wolf climbed off my back and I felt *hands* on my shoulders turning me over. Bodie's yellow-green eyes still didn't have normal human pupils. His wolf was still lingering, just under the surface. He scrubbed a hand down his face. Then he leaned in, nose right next to my neck, and inhaled deeply.

I opened my mouth, ready to tell him to fuck off, when I felt his teeth close over my pulse. Not biting down, but literally holding my life in his jaws. I froze.

I was terrified and fucking turned on more than I'd ever been in my entire life.

Bodie relented and pulled away, staring down at me with a knowing look. "Mate," he growled, pressing down on me, showing me how hard he was.

I shoved him off me.

He let me, we both knew it, and it pissed me off just as much as Easton taking the hit had enraged him earlier.

"No," I denied him, marching down the stairs. He could go fuck himself. I was not listening to some idiotic supernatural hallucination. I was going to choose a fucking life partner myself. And it would not be some hot under the collar junkyard dog.

"I'm gonna make it so that you never wanna leave." Bodie called down after me.

I skirted around Easton, avoiding eye contact, avoiding how Bodie's words made me feel. Those words inflated my chest like a life raft, they kept me floating when I felt like sinking.

But the practical side of me shook her head. I'd heard words like those before. My ex-fiance had been full of pretty words. They were lies.

And this mate thing?

I could probably thank that asshole Larry for it. Apparently, not all of his magic wore off as quickly as stemming my powers.

If I gave it a little time, this mate bond shit would fade.

The bond in question suddenly tugged at my heart like a little kid tugging on a shirt. It got on its tiptoes and whispered at me, "You know that's not true." But I shoved it down, not caring when it scraped its knee and cried.

I was alone.

I'd always been alone.

I had deluded myself with the ideas of family and friends and colleagues. But the reality was, at the end of the day, when I became inconvenient for people, they'd shove me aside. My parents had just proven it. Bodie wouldn't be any different. Neither would Easton. No matter how much I wanted them to be.

My heart gave one painful throb of longing.

My heart was an idiot.

DRAKE

WE NEEDED TO KILL HER. IT WAS THE BEST OPTION WE
had left.

I ran a hand through my black hair and paced
through the meeting room, waiting for Bodie to come
back upstairs. I'd sent him down to collect Easton,
who'd abandoned babysitting duty and let the cubs
completely wreck our meeting room.

Idiot.

Thank god Lorena had shown up and hauled the
kids off or I would have scared the little shits to death.
I turned around and paced in the opposite direction.

The mages hadn't even responded to the ransom
letter we'd sent regarding Aubry.

I mean, she was their fucking princess. She'd been
on the news every other goddamned night with
announcements about arrests and fucking shifter

murders. She was the L.A. figurehead. And they didn't even care? What the fuck?

After that bullshit press conference her parents held this afternoon, I doubted an offer was ever coming. We'd wanted the mage jewel back—the one that El Fuego had given his life for. But those stick swingers weren't coming up to bat. Hell, they weren't even stepping into the box.

So it was up to me to get what we needed in some other way.

And the girl was a distraction.

Bodie hadn't been focused since that fake mate bullshit she'd pulled, and we needed our best assassin to stay sharp if we hoped to keep making progress in this war. Even Easton had a soft spot for her, and while he wasn't as active on the front lines as us, he was still a huge asset behind the scenes due to his skill in armor and weapon making.

Which meant the worthless faerie princess was now a fucking liability—for *us*.

I shook my head at the goddamned irony.

She was supposed to be a liability for *them*, the mages. It just went to show, you couldn't trust a magic user. They only cared about themselves. They had no sense of loyalty or pack whatsoever.

I righted an overturned chair. It had a couple deep claw marks on the seat, but it was salvageable. The same couldn't be said for the table. I didn't know what the pint-sized shifters had done to it once Easton had left, but it didn't have legs anymore, just flattened hunks of twisted metal and splintered wood.

I grabbed the other chair, but they'd somehow managed to make a hole right through the middle of the seat.

Jesus fucking...

Pinching the bridge of my nose, I allowed my eyes to fall shut. I loved Bodie like a brother—he and Easton were literally my three-man pack—but these babysitting escapades needed to stop. We were too busy to watch the cubs and pups. Case in point with Aubry tonight. As per usual, the pretty fae had fucked us over.

I stared around at the disaster. We were not mentally equipped for kids. There had to have been at least a thousand other people more capable than us. But there was nowhere safer than wherever we were, and most shifter parents had shift work and barely an hour to themselves without our help, which is why I'd agreed to let the kids come stay on the weekends.

I was a bleeding fucking heart.

I just hoped everything I was doing was actually going to help. I didn't think I could live with myself otherwise. All the blood on my hands, and the blood I'd yet to spill, it haunted me. It plagued my thoughts and memories. It woke me in a cold sweat after nightmares where I watched faces screaming as they burned.

If we lost the war, and this was all for nothing...

My legs gave out and I flopped into the only remaining chair, burying my face in my hands. I was going to go to hell for my sins. But as long as the mages went down with me, then so be it.

"Hey, Boss," Bodie said. His tone was clipped and it instantly got my attention.

"You find him?" I asked.

"Yep."

Easton entered the room a moment later, sporting a shiny gray cheekbone and half a swollen eye. He wasn't smiling, nor was he looking at either of us. He kept his eyes carefully trained on the conference room floor. Though, now that he saw the mess he'd left behind, I'd bet he didn't want to look there, either.

I held out both arms, willing either of them to give me some sort of explanation. "Well, where was he?"

Fuzzball glared at Goldilocks with the heat of a flaming sun.

Oh for fuck's sake. Please tell me this doesn't have anything to do with—

"Making out with Aubry," Bodie accused.

"I was not!" Easton shouted back in defense.

Before it came to blows—AGAIN—I interrupted the argument. "Enough, boys. There will be no more fighting over this fae princess, because, quite frankly, there will be no more fae princess."

Bodie paused and turned toward me. "What did you just say?"

I sighed and gestured to the entire room. "Help me pick up, will ya?"

Easton immediately got to work scooping up wood

chips, while Bodie glared at me. I found the magic expandable bag hanging over the TV, so I grabbed it and started chucking shit in—blocks, dolls, controllers, a fucking lost shoe.

I grabbed a snowman toy and sighed, just staring at it.

Come on, Drake. Man up and just do what needs to be done.

"*I said…*" I shoved the snowman into the bag like the bastard had just insulted me. "The fly—fae—has to go. We tried ransoming her but, obviously, that fell through. We tried questioning her, but she's either an idiot or she's refusing to talk. So now it's time we try to make an example—"

Bodie dropped his entire armful of toys and clenched his fists. "*No.*"

My nostrils flared, and the faint scent of smoke trailed through the air. A warning. "Don't you tell me *no.*" I let my wings come out and with them, a burst of alpha pheromones. I didn't like to pull that bullshit, the three of us were friends, not a goddamned dragon valor with ranks and shit, but if I had to…

Bodie swallowed hard, clearly fighting the dueling urges to submit and attack. Among the wolves in his own pack, he was the alpha. Hell, even Easton could have been an alpha if he'd ever returned to his family to tell them where to stick it. But here, right now, in this moment, *I* was the alpha. If I didn't lead us away from this fucking wasp, then we'd be at each other's throats,

171

constantly fighting for dominance. Those two idiots had already started. The only solution was for me to take the lead and keep it, so I couldn't back down now.

"She's a waste of our resources, Bodie." I tried the soft approach first, trying to reason with him. "The mages have us clawing for scraps. We can't afford to house a prisoner, buy her takeout every day, and allow her to distract two of my main assets to this war—that would be you idiots, by the way. I need you two to stay focused. And as long as that dollface is around, I don't see that happening."

Bodie took a deep breath, regathered the toys at his feet, and dropped them into the bag I was holding. "She's my *mate*, Drake. You can't just... get rid of her." He couldn't even say it. He'd killed a hundred-odd people point blank. And he couldn't say the word.

Apparently, he needed the hard approach.

I took a deep breath and felt my fingers shaking slightly as nervous tingles spread through my entire body.

Buck up, Shadow. Time to channel the heartless asshole again.

I cinched the bag shut and tossed it onto the clawed-up chair. "A public humiliation and assassination is the final play we have left."

I didn't even have a chance to finish my speech before the Fuzzball's fist connected with my jaw. A low growl escaped my throat. I felt the heat of a shift passing over my eyes as they flashed to gold and jet-black scales started crawling up my arms.

"If we show the shifters that we kidnapped her," I continued, trying not to fight or fully shift before I finished my lecture, "and then we kill her right in front of their very eyes, it will give them confidence and determination; it will create the kind of momentum we need in order to win this thing."

His fist flew through the air once more, but I caught it in my steely grasp.

"The shifters need this, Bodie," I pleaded, though it came out as more of a snarl. "It's not about *her*, or even *us*, it's about the survival of our kind! If we don't make this last stand, then shifters are as good as extinct."

He bared his teeth at me, his own eyes flashing gold. "If I have to kill my mate in order to prove shifters are worthy of survival, then maybe we're *not* fucking worthy."

My lip curled and my teeth elongated into razor-sharp points. "She is *not* your mate! It's a trick! It's bull-shit fae magic fucking with your head!"

Fur raced along Bodie's spine, splitting open his shirt, and claws burst out from beneath his fingernails. "It's not a trick!" he growled, his voice deep and husky. "Larry told me the truth: no magic user—not a fae, not even a mage—no one has the power to fake a mate bond. This connection I have with her, it's fucking real, and you are not going to take her from me!"

He lurched forward, snapping his half-human, half-canine teeth at my throat.

I stumbled back, caught completely off guard by that little Larry-bomb.

The mate bond's real? How the fuck could that be possible? She isn't even a shifter. There's no way she could be right for him.

He snapped his teeth at me again and swiped a clawed paw at my gut. Luckily, I jerked back before he made contact, but damn it, that was way too fucking close.

Embracing my shifter magic, I allowed it to consume me. My bones snapped and popped, lengthening and rearranging into the spine of my dragon. My skin stretched and hardened, thick black scales replacing soft human flesh. It was painful, but familiar, and right then, I relished the agonizing ache as it spread through my body, giving me strength. I was sure to control my shift so that I could fit inside and move around the meeting room but I still ended up with my horns scraping the ceiling.

By the time I was in full-dragon mode, Bodie had completely shifted as well—into a full wolf the size of a horse, not his werewolf—and to my astonishment, so had Easton. His golden bear prowled from side to side in the back of the room, in the tiny space not occupied by me or the furious wolf. Easton was trying to stay out of the fight, but ready to join in at a moment's notice. Usually, he was the middleman, the one who made Bodie and I see sense when we butted heads over stupid shit; but whose side would he take over this?

I thought I knew, but I didn't want to admit it.

This can't be happening. No way in hell is some fae cunt going to waltz in here and break up our pack. It felt like she was a bowling ball and we were a couple of pins teetering at the end of a waxy lane. Fuck no. We weren't that easy to knock down.

I'd fight for this, for *us*, because we were more than a pack—we were family.

Bodie leapt at me, but I caught him in my teeth and threw him off to the side, his wolf hair sticking to my tongue. He quickly scrambled to his feet and attacked again, this time coming at me from the side. With a quick flap, I opened my wing to protect me, and his claws raked over my leathery skin like white-hot coals. A screech tore from my throat as I tucked my wing back in and struck at him like a viper.

Easton growled from the back, a threatening warning. I glared at him, watching Bodie from the corner of my eye.

"You'd allow a girl—*a fae fly*—to come between us?" I snarled.

Easton's scowl dropped right off his face and his golden eyes shined with what looked to be sadness and confusion. Bodie, on the other hand, was not so easily swayed.

"She's my mate!" he cried, launching once more at my wounded side. My wing was just a bit too slow that

175

time, allowing him to sink his canines into the meaty flesh of my shoulder.

I roared, incidentally spraying a wave of fire around the room. The walls and furniture turned black with soot; they smoked but thankfully didn't catch fire. I needed to be more careful. But how could I, when my world was crumbling in front of my eyes?

I craned my neck, latching onto the scruff of Bodie's neck and whipping him off of me. He hit a charcoaled wall and slid to the floor, smearing a line of black down with him. He was up again before I could blink, glaring as he circled me, searching for a way to bring me down.

I was lucky he'd shifted into his wolf. If he'd attacked with a gun as Bodie-the-assassin, my brains would have been splattered across the wall like that soot.

"I don't want to hurt you," I assured him. And honestly, I didn't. If I let another accidental wave of fire out and he was in the way... God, the burns would be atrocious.

"You don't want to hurt my *flesh*," he corrected through a snarl. I'd never seen him look so fierce and wild. "You just want to rip my heart and soul from my chest and pretend it would somehow damage me *less*."

Another roar shook out of me as anger and frustration built inside. I *didn't* want to hurt him at all—flesh, bone, heart, soul, or whatever. I didn't want to murder his mate! I didn't even hate the annoying fly as much as I let on.

But we had to kill her.

Couldn't they see that? It was the only way to save the shifters of Los Angeles from going out like a candle, blown into nothingness by the nasty breath of the mages. We needed a victory, and this was the last one we were going to get, unless it served its purpose and rallied our forces. Otherwise, the mages may as well sing *happy birthday* right now and make a fucking wish, because we were about to go out like a light, nothing more than a fading stream of smoke whispering on the breeze to remind them we'd ever existed at all.

Easton suddenly shifted back into human shape. "Someone's coming."

Reluctantly, Bodie and I did the same, but we stayed all up in each other's shit, neither of us daring to back down.

"This isn't over," I promised him.

"Oh, but it is," Fuzzball threatened, making me feel small. I held firm, though, not allowing myself to shrink back by so much as a hair. "You kill her, you kill me. Then I kill you."

"Stop it," Easton hissed, his eyes glowing gold once more as he snarled in our direction. "This is fucking stupid. There are other options besides murder, murder, and more murder! Get your fucking heads out of your asses."

177

Huh. Back to playing middleman and peacemaker. I had to admit, I was pleasantly surprised.

A moment later a shifter soldier burst through the door of the conference room, out of breath, and in a panic. He didn't scan the torn-up room or assess our tattered clothing; his eyes locked right on mine.

"The Amara apartment complex, it's on fire!"

AUBRY

ALL OF A SUDDEN, THE GUYS BARGED DOWNSTAIRS.

"Get some clothes on," Bodie demanded. He had a cut on his forehead that definitely hadn't been there before, though it was already healing.

"*What?*" I asked, staring at him like he'd completely lost his shit. I was still in the white wife beater and tiny black cheer shorts he'd given me. What the fuck else was I supposed wear?

He unlocked my cell and tossed a black t-shirt and a crumpled pair of jeans at me. "I said get fucking dressed! We gotta go."

I scrambled into them, dragging the shirt over my head, grateful for the pre-cut wing slits in the back, and hopping around on one foot as I shimmied the soft denim material up my thighs and hips. Before I could even zip or button the pants, he yanked me out of my cell, and dragged me up to the surface following Easton and Drake.

My freaking head spun as I tried to make sense of what they were doing. Had they lost their furry little minds? Were they setting me free? Or were they about to end me?

It was a moonlit night and the polluted haze above the roofline was broken up by the scent of smoke. Ash billowed down over the street like black snowflakes from the pits of hell.

It looked like the apocalypse. Or, you know, every other fall in Los Angeles when brush fires swept through different parts of the city.

I watched as thick orange flames licked up the side of a blackened building just a couple blocks down. *Shit.* That was close.

"Why did you bring me up for this?" I asked.

They could have left me wallowing in the cell. Or did they worry that the fire would spread that far? That I'd be trapped under all that smoke while the oxygen was slowly sucked out of my tunnel and cell and their precious negotiation ended? Did they even have a negotiation? Had they seen that fucking press conference?

I didn't particularly want to die. Death by fire would be a pretty stupid way for a summer fae to go. But I didn't understand why the hell they'd brought me with them.

Drake glanced down at me, gaze scathing. "I don't trust you to be left alone."

His eyes flickered to Bodie and Easton like he wanted to say something else. But he didn't. His look put them in their place though, before his eyes flickered to gold, the color of his dragon's eyes. They both lowered their gazes, showing just the slightest hint of submission.

My throat went dry. But that was just from the fire leaching all the moisture out of the air. Nothing else. *Definitely* not from Godzilla staking his claim to dominance.

Drake bolted toward the flames before the others, shifting in the middle of the street, making panicked humans scream as his black dragon emerged above people's heads and flew through the grey shadows toward the fire. Damn. His dragon was enormous. His wings definitely hadn't been that big the last time I'd seen him shift.

But shifting in public, that was an idiotic move that would make life harder on the L.A. Mage Police. I knew the protocol for shit like that. Someone would explain it all away as mass hysteria. And then the containment division would go out and give memory wipe potions to any human who stuck with the 'I saw a real dragon' line.

His actions annoyed me, but at the same time, had me enraptured.

His beast was epicly beautiful in a fearsome way. He had long twisted black horns, a hooked mouth, and his scales glittered like black jewels in the flame. Drake headed straight for the danger. And while dragons were fireproof, they were also completely smitten by fire. They reacted to it like kittens to catnip, or pigs to mud. He'd have to be hella confident that he could ignore his primal instincts in order to save some people.

That kind of self denial and self control was admirable. *Not hot*; I'd never use that description for Drake. Despite his looks, he was a pure egotistical evil maniac. Plain and simple.

Bodie tugged on my hand, interrupting my open-mouthed gaping. "Come on," he urged.

He pulled me off the overcrowded sidewalk and into the road. We followed Drake, but on foot, weaving through a mass of shifters and people and abandoned cars that still had headlights on and doors left wide open. Easton parted the crowd racing towards us with his bulk. Once we made headway, people started to veer around us naturally. They were all heading in the opposite direction through the trash-strewn streets, fleeing the fire.

A small herd of zebras thundered past us, their hooves echoing against the cracked concrete streets. A couple of parrots soared above us, one of them squawking, "Run for your lives! Mage fire! Mage fire!" A set of gorillas hopped from car to car, landing on the hoods, denting them irreversibly.

"Goddamned fire at the fucking zoo or something?" I heard one human guy say as he sheltered a girl under his shoulder and ran past us.

"Must be!" she responded.

It *was* as wild as a zoo. Shifter panic triggered their animal instincts. I shook my head and fought the urge to show my wings and fly. I'd typically float above this fray. Normally, when there was a fire, I'd arrive at the scene and wait for the winter water fae to do their thing. Then I'd investigate the smoking ruins to figure out if a shifter gang had started the fire. Nine times out of ten, they had.

It was strange and unnatural to *not* do that now. But I was no longer the chief enforcer. I was… on permanent vacation or some shit. "Pursuing other ventures" I think my parents had said. Those lying dicks.

A hulking human openly carrying a rifle charged down the street, knocking into Easton's shoulder and growling, "Watch it, motherfucker!"

What a shit-eating idiot. Freaking people out even more with his gun and then being all hostile and aggressive? I hoped that prick tripped and blew off his own arm. Or better yet, maybe I could teach this bitch-assed punk a lesson?

My heart thumped faster as my mind and body flooded with adrenaline. It had been awhile since I'd had a good fight, and this dunce looked like my brand of crazy. I took an anxious step toward him, raising a cocky brow.

But Bodie's grip on my hand grew stronger and he shoved me away behind him.

Spoilsport.

That giant piece of scrotum lint just laughed at me and walked on. He wouldn't have been laughing if Bodie hadn't stopped me. I flexed my fingers, wishing I could just lift a hand and flame him. But Larry had gotten better at stemming my fire power, and I couldn't so much as conjure a spark.

Bodie tugged on my arm, switching my attention back to him. He leaned down and murmured softly, "We gotta hurry. There are still people in that building, and Drake's gonna fucking give himself a heart attack trying to get them all out by himself. Old fuck."

I dropped all thoughts about the rifle-toting dick-weed then, and instead focused on keeping up with Bodie and Easton's long legs. The closer we got to the flames, the hotter it got. Like those horrid, dry, blazing hot summer days in Death Valley. I had to blink more to keep my eyes from drying out. I had to shield my face from the ash that rained down on us.

The fire raged, roaring out the doors and windows like an angry demon trying to break free. Glass shattered and beams broke, crashing to the ground somewhere deep beyond the wavering orange curtain before us. Flames reached and stretched, licking a nearby building before suddenly engulfing it in a blaze.

"Go!" Bodie shouted, gesturing for Easton to head toward the new burning building. But the big golden bear hesitated for a moment, glancing back at me with longing eyes.

My throat tightened but I didn't say anything, just held his gaze for as long as I could before he turned and disappeared into a tenement apartment building.

"We need to find somewhere safe for you to stay," Bodie said, leading me down the street.

"How about my apartment?" I joked. But inside, my heart started to beat faster. Was he actually going to tie me up and leave me somewhere? Was I going to have a real chance to escape? I tried to keep a poker face. But I couldn't look directly at him. I was worried I might give myself away. I stared out at the street ahead of us, watching him in my peripheral vision.

"Wish I could say yes, Princess," Bodie responded as he led me over to an old-school fire hydrant. "Maybe I should just wait with you."

"Maybe," I nodded. "I'm sure Drake will be fine."

I casually pushed his buttons. Like a good little robot, he responded.

"Ah, shit. You know I'll feel it if you try and leave, right?" Bodie stepped into my personal space, his chest bumping against my chin.

I looked up. Ash had landed in his hair like snow. I had the sudden urge to dust it off. Maybe run my fingers through those luscious brown locks. Instead, I balled my hands into fists. "Yeah, I know."

"Good. Don't be stupid."

He reached into a pouch on his waistband and

pulled out a chain. I watched in awe as this tiny pouch, one that looked no bigger than a pepper spray container, coughed up twenty feet of chain. Damn it all! I was hoping they'd just put my fucking cuffs around a tree.

Bodie gestured toward the fire hydrant like we were at some fucking five-star restaurant. "Sit, please."

I widened my eyes and gave him my what-the-fuck stare.

It had cowed many people in its time, but apparently not my cocky-ass ma—I let that evil fated word die, and tried again. *Not on* Bodie, *that cocky-ass, dingleberry wolf shifter.*

He just grinned, completely unfazed by my stare. "I can help you sit, if you want. But I've got iron chains in my hand. You'd get burned."

"*So sweet,*" I mocked, placing a hand over my heart. "You don't want me to get burned by the chains *now*, you want me to get burned by them *after* you've wrapped them around me multiple times."

The grin fell right off his face and I smirked.

"Besides…" I gestured to the thirty-foot flames destroying the building right behind us. "I'll probably literally get burned by those."

"I'll be back before they get to you," Bodie promised. "I just need to help Drake."

"Chain me up farther down the street," I bargained.

He rolled his green and gold eyes. "Fine."

Grabbing my shoulder, he roughly marched me

down the now-deserted block, stopping right in front of a bakery. The cakes in the display window made my stomach rumble. One had yellow frosted roses that I wanted to swallow whole.

"Sit on the sidewalk," Bodie commanded.

I obeyed, sitting down next to another old fire hydrant that he obviously still wanted to strap me to. I was betting I could slide the chains around and over the top to get free. Then I'd have to run with twenty feet of chain and try not to trip.

I chewed my lip, trying to think as he wrapped the hellish chain around my legs and then around the hydrant.

"Why aren't the damn Mage Police here yet?" I growled as a tiny bit of ash landed on my eyelashes and I shimmied to try and knock it away. The iron slipped to my bare ankles and dug into my skin like sizzling barbed wire, making me grimace.

"They never show down here," Bodie responded quietly.

What? My office hardly got any calls from down here—shifters didn't trust the MP, but... I suddenly became aware of human firetrucks wailing in the distance.

"You don't have much time," I told him.

He shook his head, eyes narrowing into slits. "The fire trucks won't be able to do anything. Regular water doesn't stop mage fires."

This wasn't a mage fire. They didn't do that shit.

They didn't have time to waste on bullshit things like setting fires, when they were too busy putting out metaphorical fires thanks to careless shifters all over L.A. who revealed our presence to humans right and left. All while running the whole fucking supernatural community.

I opened my mouth to spout off something sarcastic, but behind us, a building collapsed.

It sounded like an avalanche. Like television static amplified to the level of a sonic boom. Dust billowed out and I had to cover my face with my hands as the cloud of dirt rolled toward us.

"Fuck!" Bodie was off and running toward the collapsed building before he even finished locking my chains.

The desperation he felt was evident in his jerky movements as he ran through the cloud of debris, the trail of hair that erupted down his spine, and the wolf tail that protruded from the back of his jeans. He gave a howl as he started digging through the rubble, half human, half shifter.

Fucking hell. Had Drake really still been inside that building when it fell?

No! A strange mix of horror and elation rumbled through me as my eyes searched the skies frantically for any sign of him. I sat up and my jeans slid down my hips, revealing the top half of my ass covered by the stretchy black cheer shorts. Underwear, really.

This was my chance. I was outside. It was open air. I

just had to get these damn chains off and I'd be free. I let my feet slide out toward the street, clad in whatever hand-me-down off-brand tennis shoes the guys had found weeks ago. I could feel the heavy metal circles pressing against the thin black t-shirt and jeans they'd given me to wear.

If I could just slither out…

Suddenly, my throat burned with emotion. It was like my heart had tried to punch my brain, but it couldn't make it past my windpipe. It felt like a fist had gotten lodged in there. The thought of leaving Bodie behind didn't sit well with half of me, but that was the side that was fooled by stupid magic. It wasn't logical. It wasn't real.

I'd go home and get this shit spell of Larry's reversed.

Yup. That's what I'll do.

And when I saw my treacherous, lie-through-their-fucking-teeth-I'd-like-to-knock-out parents… Well, I didn't need to think that far ahead. I just needed to escape.

I pushed my hands out behind me and lifted into a bridge position. I slowly lifted my torso but kept my feet on the street instead of the curb. The chains slid down another couple inches but lodged on my hips.

Son of a bitch!

What the hell could I do to get this chain off? If I touched it, my fingers would sizzle like strips of bacon.

I glanced down. *Who needs pants?* I thought.

It was convenient that I hadn't gotten them buttoned earlier. I shucked them slowly, ensuring I could wrap the material around the chains and push them down. The chains slid off with relative ease until the links piled up around my ankles. I tried to slide my feet out while keeping the pants so I could pull them back on once I was free, but parts of the chain kept tumbling over the material, burning small patches on my legs.

Fuck it. I yanked the pants all the way off and tumbled backward at the same moment, trying to avoid the collapsed pile of chains that had just been at my feet.

Holy shit, it worked!

I didn't even have a chance to celebrate my victory, because the fire chose that moment to hop to yet another building.

Were the guys okay?

Drake was... who knew where. Bodie was still digging through the rubble—if his howls of frustration were anything to go by. And Easton had gone into the second building a long time ago and never came out. One or two other shifters had, though, I *assumed* at his urging. They'd scrambled past in their animal forms, not giving me a second look.

The third building should have already been clear, as people would have already evacuated.

I turned, ready to run, ready to put these crappy tennis shoes to the test. I ran a finger under the seam of my panties. Er, cheer shorts. The ones that only covered half my ass cheeks.

But people in L.A. wore less everyday. *Running through the city until Larry's magic wears off and I can glamour again will be easy, right? Right.*

I coughed again, using the inside of my shirt to suck in a semi-smoke-free breath before setting my sights on freedom. I'd taken one step. One single, solitary step... when I heard a heart-wrenching scream.

I turned back and looked up to see a little girl, no older than five, crawling out of a smoking window on the fourth floor of the newly burning complex. She balanced precariously on the ledge, holding a stuffed lamb doll, before her instincts took over and she shifted into a tiny white wolf pup.

A bullet to the heart would have hurt less than watching the scene before me.

The little creature howled in fear and terror, her voice calling up to the moon, praying for someone to save her from the smoke and flames.

Fuck me.

My feet pivoted.

She was a shifter. She might even become a damned criminal one day, but she wasn't one *yet*. And regardless of the fact that my boneless, insect-like parents had demoted me, regardless of whatever title I did or didn't have... I was a police officer. The need to help people was in my blood. It was the force that drove me. Always.

I ran toward the burning structure instead of away. I thought about going inside, but trying to find her exact apartment in that maze of a building would waste precious time. Instead I mentally kicked her parents for leaving her as I climbed up a fire escape on the side of the brick wall.

"Stupid, hairball-choking, flea infested fucks. Who leaves a kid that young home alone? Or leaves them *behind*?"

My shoes squeaked against the metal rails of the old, rickety ladders that composed the different levels of the escape. When I reached the fourth floor, I saw that I was still five windows away from the little white pup. She was standing closer to the middle of the building and the fire escape was along the side.

Damn it!

The heat was utterly intense, billowing across my skin like a giant hair dryer from hell. Smoke filled my nostrils like a repulsive cologne: hints of mayhem, death, and the choking scent of ash coming together to make up the unpleasant smell. I couldn't ignore the heat or the smell, but I could at least force my attention back onto the girl.

How the fuck could I get to her?

Instead of trying to kick in the nearest window, I tested my wings. They lifted me slightly, enough to hover, but not to truly fly. Larry's magic had worn off slightly but not completely. It would have to be enough. Because it was all I had.

I grabbed onto the side of the building and stepped off onto the nearest window ledge. I flapped my wings frantically, pushing my body into the bricks—bricks that were heating up like a pizza oven.

I shuffled sideways across the ledge to where it stopped, then stretched my foot as far as it could reach to touch the edge of the next window. I couldn't get a full foot on it. I was going to have to jump.

My heart squeezed tight, like a little kid clutching the sheets as they stared at the closet... knowing there's a monster inside... just waiting for it to come.

There's a fight at the end of this. I tried to lie to myself, to get the adrenaline rush to turn from stomach twisting fear into excitement. But the lie fell flat. There was nothing I could do... but jump.

I took a deep breath and then leapt.

My wings fluttered furiously, but they couldn't hold my weight. I sank, my fingers clawing at the bricks, scraping until they bled. Finally, they latched onto the next window ledge. My wings flitted furiously, shoving me forward so that my face rested against the glass window pane. I glanced inside the apartment as I fought to catch my breath. Smoke drifted under the door across the room. Going inside wasn't an option.

I turned and yelled toward the little wolf pup. "I'm coming!"

Her golden eyes turned my way and one of her ears cocked to the side.

I edged along the second window, nerves already

tense as I anticipated my next leap. But just as I got ready to make it, a huge claw closed around my waist, snatching me from the side of the building.

I looked up to see a giant black dragon, covered in dust and debris. He swooped forward and grabbed the wolf pup in his other claw and with one powerful beat of his wings, he pushed off away from the burning building and flew us down the street.

He dropped me suddenly and I fell, accidentally letting out a scream that would make me hate him forever. How dare he fucking damsel-in-distress me? I was the hero, damn it. I was in the middle of saving that little girl.

Arms caught me and I looked up to see a very angry pair of light green eyes. "You've been a naughty little butterfly."

AUBRY

BODIE DIDN'T STOP TO CHECK IN WITH EASTON OR Drake. He didn't even check on the little girl shifter who was crying in Easton's arms. Apparently, Goldilocks had caught her and then The Shadow had shifted back to human form. But I could only glance back at them for a moment, peering over Bodie's shoulder, just long enough to ensure they were okay, as he carried me down the street like a caveman.

Or... a groom.

Panic made me stiffen when the image of Bodie stripping off a bow tie and tossing it aside before he assaulted me. Fuck, that would be so hot.

How could I even have those thoughts right now? I was sore, aching, I'd just had some man swoop in and steal my save-the-day moment and all I could do was stare at Bodie's cracked lips, imagining us in the shower together with water running down his face, washing away all the soot, so that he wasn't dirty *that* way anymore. Instead, he got to be dirty my way. With me.

"You're wearing those booty shorts in the fucking street?" Bodie growled, his eyes half green, half golden. Ugh. I bet that was what his eyes looked like when he came.

Shock or something was sending me into a tailspin of horniness. *Shit.* Sometimes that happened after a big op. I needed release. And I'd never gotten any after El Fuego. I definitely needed something after tonight's antics. With hooded eyes, I stared up at Bodie, who dug his fingers into the outside edges of my thighs and put his lips to my ear.

"I'm gonna clean you up, Buttercup. I'm gonna touch every inch of this delicious body. Then I'm gonna eat you out until you scream. And once your legs can't hold you up, I'm gonna make you fucking hover in midair as I pound the shit out of *my* pussy."

Oh god. I am so screwed.

That fucking claiming tone he took, that sense of possession... I didn't want to melt. I didn't want this mate bond to be real. Maybe it wasn't. Maybe it was still some spell. But I was more turned on than I'd ever been at the start of a play session with any of my doms.

"Hurry up, then," I told him, running my hand down his chest. He was covered in grime and sweat, but that just added to the primal vibe he was giving off. That, or

I'd jilled off to one too many firefighter calendars growing up.

Bodie shoved open the door of a nondescript apartment building two blocks away from the fire, about two more blocks away from the building where I'd been held. He marched up the stairs with me, my anticipation rising with each step he took. I barely noticed the peeling paint or the discolored, 1980's red industrial carpet. I was too focused on the fact that Bodie wasn't even winded while he was carrying me.

Holy shit. He must have amazing fucking stamina in bed.

"Where are we?" I tried to sound sultry but ended up coughing. Goddamn smoke inhalation. Summer fae weren't completely immune to smoke. That's why we made our fire magic burn so hot, that way it emitted less of the stupid stuff.

Bodie ran a comforting hand up and down my spine. "We're at my place," his voice was soft, almost vulnerable. "I've been getting it ready for you."

I glanced up sharply. The look in his eyes was cautious. Almost like he didn't know how I'd respond. Normally, that kind of commitment talk would make me smack him across the face, jump out of his arms, and bolt like lightning. I'd leave his shocked ass behind and be outta there. But the stupid, fake mate bond had me leaning closer, pressing my chest into his, counting his heartbeats.

When he reached the third floor, Bodie pulled a

key out of his pocket while still managing to hold me. He unlocked the door of 3B and pushed it open. The inside of the apartment didn't resemble the exterior at all. Bodie had clearly had a ton of work done in there.

The interior had black slate floors and an accent wall with narrow, natural stone tiles in a variety of browns and greys. The rooms were small, like you'd expect from that kind of apartment, but the materials transformed the space and gave it a rich, cave-like feel. His couch was leather—typical male—but the rug in front of it was a delicious wine red. It was a sex rug, that was for sure. Or it would be, as soon as Bodie and I were clean. I pictured him pounding me from behind as I knelt on that rug and my knees went weak at the thought.

Something in my expression must have given me away, because Bodie slammed and locked the door behind us, hurrying into the bathroom. He set me on the grey concrete countertop and then turned around to flick on the shower. It was a small walk in shower, definitely not meant for two people. We'd be crammed in like sardines, our bodies wet and pressed against each other the entire time.

This was gonna be the best shower of my life.

"It'll take a minute to get warm," Bodie said when he turned back. "Or, you could just huddle close to me, because I'm already hot."

I laughed, teasing insults flying to the tip of my

tongue, but I swallowed them down when Bodie reached behind his head and yanked off his shirt.

Even the doms at my club didn't have six packs that chiseled. I pressed my lips together and pulled off my own shirt, determined to match him move for move. I didn't have a bra—the assholes had never given me one. I think Bodie had taken a sick pleasure out of watching my nipples harden everytime he whispered my name.

"Oh, Aubry." He did it just then, proving me right. His eyes traveled down my neck to stare at the pebbled peaks of my breasts before they burned a trail down my torso, settling in between my legs. I watched him clench his fists, watched how much he wanted to just grab me and take me.

But he resisted. Just like a good dom would.

Damn. That thought made the heat between my legs turn into molten liquid. We needed to shower, and fast. That red rug was screaming my name, or it was at least waiting for me to scream all kinds of names into it as Bodie rode me hard.

My hands reached down to slide off the booty shorts, but Bodie leaned forward and stopped me. "Wait."

He shucked his jeans and boxers so that he was completely naked first, then stood there taking me in. He was already half hard and he grew even harder as he stared at me. He reached down and stroked his length and I couldn't help but notice how his own hand could hardly fit around it. I imagined how much he'd fill up my mouth and I bit my bottom lip.

I rinsed my hands real quick and wiped them on a towel that lay on the countertop. Then I let my fingers travel up to my nipples and start to tweak them, which always made me wetter.

Bodie groaned. "Turn around and slide those shorts down so I can see some of that fine ass."

I slid off the counter and turned around, tucking my wings as I watched my breasts fall forward in the mirror. With my right hand, I reached back and slowly slid the shorts down.

"Fuck," Bodie released his dick and strode forward, kneeling and wrenching the shorts the rest of the way down. His teeth bit into the soft flesh of my ass, and I gasped as I kicked the stretchy material away. The pain sent a red-hot spike of pleasure through me.

Yes, man-handle me, wolf boy.

Bodie rose and grabbed my hand, leading me into the shower. I had to keep my wings tucked down so that we could both fit, but it was a sacrifice I was willing to make. He angled the sprayer so that it hit my chest and he aligned himself behind me, his hardness pressing against my asscrack and wings, sending a shiver of anticipation through me. He reached around me to the shelf and grabbed the soap, which he lathered up between his hands before setting it back down.

"I've been dying to touch you, baby," Bodie whispered in my ear as his hands stroked down my neck and shoulders, cleaning me. He rubbed in gentle circles, using his thumbs to dig down on pressure points that helped relieve tension in my neck and made me sag back against him.

Why did I resist this, again? I had no idea.

All thought fled from my head when Bodie lathered up again and caressed my breasts, cupping and squeezing. He cleaned my stomach, then knelt behind me and cleaned my legs while his hot breath warmed the back of my thighs. Then he did my hair and face. My skin buzzed like a live wire, sizzling with energy, ready to spark.

"I don't know how to wash your wings, Butterfly," Bodie admitted, when he was done gently feeling every other inch of me—except for that sweet spot between my thighs.

I turned, but the space was so tight in the shower that I ended up plastered with my face in his chest. The crevice between his pecs was the most delicious, lickable thing I'd ever seen in my life. I glanced up at Bodie, at his gorgeous yellow-green eyes. Then I slowly opened my wings, lifting them behind me.

"You can touch them," I whispered. "Just be gentle."

He reached out, gently stroking them as if they, and I, were precious to him. His hands roaming over my wings sent an explosion of sensation through me. Fae didn't normally allow anyone but a mate to touch their wings, because they were so delicate. But also because they were so sensitive. Bodie reached a spot in the middle of my wings that made my knees give out.

I arched forward and fell into him, rasping, "More. Please. Right there."

He stroked again and again, finding a pace that left me clinging to him, whimpering.

"Yes," I panted as colors streaked behind my eyelids and an amazing orgasm ripped through my body.

Bodie stroked me gently as I came down, then he quickly swapped our positions and cleaned himself up while I sagged with my back against the shower wall, mind still hazy from the delicious aftershocks of a 9.5 level orgasm. Maybe higher. The Richter scale didn't have enough numbers for the amazingness that was Bodie. My mate. *And just from touching my wings, too. I mean, holy fucking shit...*

I stared at him curiously as he scrubbed shampoo out of his hair. *Mate.* Was he actually my mate? Was I actually acknowledging that?

I'd had all kinds of kinky orgasms before. But they usually had to be given with a healthy dose of pain in order for me to rate them in the top ten. Bodie's fingers, not even his dick, had just given me this ridiculous, giddy, high-as-a-kite, happy orgasm.

He shut off the shower with a dirty smile. "I hope you're ready for round two." Then he swept me up into his arms. He didn't bother to dry either of us off, just stomped down the hall, toward what I assumed was his bedroom.

I stopped him, saying, "I want the red rug."

He paused for a moment, imagining the delicious-ness of my request, before he switched directions and headed back for the living room. He didn't even bother to look where he was going, just sucked on my neck and nipped at my pulse as he went.

He dumped me on the rug and towered over me. I'd never admit it to him, but I loved that rough treatment. How could he have known? How could he be so gentle with me one minute and so rough the next but do both exactly right?

I watched as he licked his lips at the sight of me. "Spread your wings and your legs. I wanna see all of you," he ordered.

I did, feeling promiscuous and wanton.

Then Bodie knelt in front of me and shoved my thighs down on either side so that my knees touched the floor. He brought his face close and let his teeth skim over my skin. He teased me, nipping around my core, at my stomach, my thighs, my pelvis. Nips turned to licking. His tongue stroked me in circles, promising me naughty pleasure.

My hands went to my breasts, but he stopped me, leaning up and over me. "One nipple. And the other I want free so I can stare at it. Stroke your wing instead." He grabbed my hand and moved it to my wing, to the spot he'd stroked earlier. "*There*."

Then he returned down south and blew his warm breath across my sex. My toes curled in anticipation. I tweaked my left nipple and simultaneously rubbed my hand across that sensitive spot on my wing.

Ohhh. Yes.

My head started to roll back.

His mouth latched onto my clit and sucked. And I entered bliss. I left earth and floated around the moon, waving at the asteroid belt. He sucked again and it was like I blasted off past Saturn and all its pretty rings. I left all solid thoughts behind. I was just a mass of pleasure, spinning around the sun. He was my sun.

"*Bodie.*" I panted his name breathlessly, somehow remembering to pinch my nipple and stroke my wing as he sucked. We found a rhythm that had me riding the very edge of pleasure. "Spank me," I cried as my hips arched and I pinched my nipple to the point of pain.

Bodie's hand came down hard on the side of my ass and I tumbled into ecstasy.

I thought the orgasm in the shower was amazing? Well, I was wrong. This one was so much better.

And Bodie wouldn't stop. He wouldn't let me flop down on the rug in numb submission, allowing him to fuck me raw. His mouth still gently circled my clit as he pushed three fingers into me at once.

He wasn't gentle. He didn't start with one or two. He used three. Like he knew I'd need a rougher orgasm after the one I'd just had. He was a psychic fucking sex god.

He roughly fucked me with his hand as his fingertips searched inside for my g-spot. I pushed up onto my heels, raising my hips, trying to help him find it. He finger fucked me so hard that my breasts shook with each thrust and when he had me right on the edge, he stopped.

He pulled his hand roughly away from me and his mouth left my clit.

"Suck my dick," he said gruffly, kneeling on the rug.

I was bereft. But at the same time, so completely and utterly in lust with him. I crawled on shaking hands and knees toward him and took his length in my mouth. *Even fuller than I'd imagined.* I used my tongue to flick the underside as I tried to choke myself with his cock.

His hands naturally went to my head and I expected him to fuck my face. But he didn't. He waited. He wanted me to impale myself.

Fine. I'd do it. And fucking love it.

I bobbed up and down, using my teeth to barely scrape the base of his dick when I bottomed out. Then I sheathed them with my lips as I slid up, using my tongue to stimulate him more. I added a hand at his balls, working them while my mouth fucked his shaft. He moaned softly.

The taste of his precum made me wild. It was different from salty human precum, different from fae precum, which was sweet. There was almost a rosemary undertone to it. I wondered what his cum itself would taste like. I sucked harder, determined to find out.

That's when Bodie yanked on my head, pulling me roughly off his dick and leaving my throat with a sore, raw feeling that I loved because I always associated it with a good, hard fuck.

"Protection," he gasped. "I gotta go grab some."

I shook my head and reached for his dick again. "No, you don't. Fae royals are injected with magical protection at birth. To prevent bastards." I rolled my eyes. "It isn't removed until marriage." I swallowed, thinking about how mine had been removed but then replaced. But I shoved the memories aside. They had nothing to do with today.

Bodie's brow furrowed but he didn't comment. Instead, he pushed my shoulder so that I would lay back down and straddled me as I sank back to the floor. His hips ground into mine and the heat of his dick made me writhe in anticipation.

"I like it rough," I said.

He leaned over me with a smile. "Too bad. I don't." And he leaned down and gave me the world's sweetest, softest, most frustrating kiss.

"No," I groaned, when he pulled away for a breath.

He didn't listen. He just peppered me with kisses. On my brow, on the tip of my nose. He nipped my lips and moved to my neck as he started to palm my breasts. I tried to reach between our bodies to grab his dick, but he shoved his hips down and simply ground his massive rod into my abdomen. "No, little Butterfly."

I stilled. I could fight him. I knew how to slide my leg up and flip him. But I was such a good little submissive. And I really really wanted his dick inside me. I decided to torture myself, and do as he wanted. He played with my nipples, gently plucking at them.

And just when I had resigned myself to a night of vanilla sex, he roughly flipped me over. Then he yanked on my waist, pulling me up onto my knees. He slammed into me, dick bottoming out roughly against my cervix. The pain was so fucking good I just about shattered.

But then his fingers stroked that little spot on my wing.

And I did fall apart. Every part of my body spasmed as he rode me and rubbed my silky wing with his fingers. My head tumbled to the floor, my cheek pillowed by the rug, my nipples roughly moving against the thick fibers with each thrust, getting a delicious rug burn as he punished my body and sought his pleasure. He yanked my hips up with his free hand and held me in place as he somehow managed to thrust even harder.

Black specks danced along the edges of my vision. Pain and pleasure blended into a song, like a baritone and a soprano harmonizing. *Yessss.*

"Come on, Butterfly," Bodie commanded with one

final swipe across my wing. "I want to see you come again."

For some reason, in my altered state, my mind pulled up an image of Easton. I imagined him watching us, stroking himself, saying, "I'm next."

The thought of the two of them sharing me, using me for their pleasure, drove me over the edge. I exploded with an orgasm that melted my fucking bones. Bodie had to hold me up with both hands as he thrust several more times before shuddering and spilling his seed inside me. When he was spent, he gently withdrew and lowered me to the rug. Then he turned me to the side, gently moving my wing back and creating a space for himself.

Instead of leaving like a dom would, intent on cleaning me up and getting the fuck out, he snuggled. Bodie, who by all the accounts I'd heard was a hitman, snuggled. With *me*.

For some unknown, ungodly reason, that brought a smile to my face. It grew even wider when he grabbed my hand and raised it to his lips, giving a soft kiss to the back of my sore knuckles before pulling me in even closer.

As the high from the orgasm wore off, this feeling of tenderness bloomed in my chest. And that made me scared. Made me second guess my instincts. I wondered... had I just royally fucked myself over? Could it be possible that I was—*somehow*—falling in love with my captor?

EASTON

WHERE THE HELL WAS BODIE?

The flames still chomped at the buildings behind us, but now they were surrounded by human firefighters who had a zero percent chance of containing this shit. Of course, the Mage Police had yet to respond. As always.

Mages were the only ones who could create these magical fires, and the only ones with the power to put them out. They always took their sweet ass time in doing so, too, making sure the buildings were nothing more than blackened bricks before swooping in and cleaning up the mess. Fuckers. There'd been a lot more fires lately too.

Next to me, Drake was spouting orders to a couple of shifter betas, making sure they would herd everyone else out of the area and take them to one of the apartment complexes we'd bought with our illegal weapons sales.

I shook my head, disgust and fury at the unfairness of it all causing my lip to curl. Thank god Drake had been prepared, that he'd had the foresight to shore us up for shit like this. Far too many shifters were already out on the streets, and now there'd be more.

My eyes scanned the heads and faces of every person we passed, looking for Bodie or Aubry. Last I'd seen, he'd had her. But neither of them seemed to be around anymore. Their absence created a roiling sense of uneasiness in my gut. It wasn't quite fear, but more like apprehension. Like a bomb was about to drop, and I was somehow going to get hit the hardest.

Drake pulled a shitty little cellphone out of his pocket—honestly, the man should have bought stock in burner phones—and quickly dialed a number. His clothes had remained unharmed since he'd shifted and fought fires in pure dragon form. I couldn't say the same for myself. My shirt was covered in soot and had a few holes in the front.

I ran a hand through my hair and ash rained down on me. My throat felt like I'd swallowed an entire sandbox. My lungs, like they'd been clawed from the inside out.

Someone handed me a water bottle. Some human paramedic or something.

"Can I check your pulse?" he asked.

I waved the well-meaning guy off, but opened the water and took a sip.

Oh, sweet life.

Next to me, Drake lowered his phone with a frown. "Bodie's not answering."

I handed him the water bottle and he tipped it up to his lips, letting it pour like a waterfall until he finished the whole thing off.

"Do you think they're back at her cell?" I asked, hoping I was right. "Reception that far underground sucks."

"Or she's giving him trouble," Drake's eyes narrowed.

Clearly, his thoughts were darker than mine. I got the sudden image of them in her cell, and her *giving him* something else entirely... My muscles tensed and my jaw ticked as I forced that image away.

I might have been crazy, but *somehow*, my gut didn't agree with Drake's worries. I didn't argue with him though. Nobody argued with Drake. Except Bodie. And when they did go head to head, it felt like two planets colliding, sending shockwaves into the entire universe.

I wasn't sure I could handle watching that right then.

"You wanna check the cell, and I'll check his place?" I offered, trying to avoid what I was certain was gonna be an intergalactic meltdown. I dug my hands into my pants' pocket and pulled up my key ring. I had a set of keys to both Drake and Bodie's places, just as they had a set to mine.

Drake's lips scrunched, the corners almost tugging into a feral grin. He wasn't happy, but he nodded anyway. If I wasn't there to run interference between the two of them, he'd get to go volcanic for a couple minutes. And I think, after all this tension, he wanted that.

He marched on ahead, while I peeled off to the left.

I'd duck into Bodie's place, rinse off, borrow some fresh clothes, and then go break up the fight of the century. I could only hope they wouldn't draw too much blood before I got there.

Part of me chided myself for not going with Drake right away. But I was fucking exhausted. My muscles ached. My *heart* ached. I'd seen at least fourteen lifeless bodies this afternoon. And then, I'd been forced to watch Aubry clinging to the side of a building, damn near falling to her death as she tried to save a child.

Fuck me.

I didn't know what was worse: fearing for her life, or watching the kindness pour out of her as she self-lessly risked it all for a whimpering pup. That kind of compassion and devotion was downright sexy.

I rubbed at my chest, as that sensation of a bomb dropping assaulted me again. My heart couldn't take much more of this shit. But it felt like there was always more coming. Always something bad around the corner.

Speaking of corners, I rounded the next one and yanked open the door to Bodie's apartment building. Sooty footprints covered the filthy old rug. *Good.* Hopefully that meant more people had fled and escaped the fire.

Tragedy is the terrible seed that allows kindness to bloom. That was what my mother used to say. It wasn't always true. Kindness certainly hadn't resulted from the torture and devastation I'd experienced within my own family. But around here... shifters of all stripes and colors had been forced to band together. It was kind of beautiful when I thought about it.

And even for me, I'd at least found some sense of happiness now that I'd left my past behind. But still, I wished the world was different. I wished life was easier and fairer. I wished I could plant a seed of kindness and watch the blooms spread like wildflowers, skipping the seeds of tragedy altogether.

But it never seemed to work like that.

I stymied my philosophical thoughts as my sore hands fumbled with the key to Bodie's apartment. The prospect of a cold shower was calling to me, and already, I felt guilty about the potential fight going down at Aubry's cell. I needed to get back there as quickly as possible. I shoved open the door... and I froze.

My eyes widened. My mouth fell open. My heart plummeted straight to my toes like a cinder block, leaving my chest hollow and empty.

There, on the living room floor, were Bodie and Aubry. Both of them were completely naked, and clearly, riding the high in the wake of a good fucking. Her white hair fanned out over the red rug like fresh snow over an open wound. He was gently caressing her delicate skin, and she was gazing up at him, smiling softly.

Aubry was… smiling. She was… happy…

My eyes didn't even rove down her perfect body because that smile was like a grenade exploding in my chest. It was a bomb. The very bomb I'd been dreading this entire time.

Fuck. No… This can't be happening.

Aubry was the first to spot me, immediately curling up into a ball and using her wings to hide her nudity. From *me*. She was hiding from *me*. Pain ripped through my chest like a serrated knife hacking into my very bones.

Bodie turned around and sat up. "What the fuck, man? You don't even knock?"

I dropped the keys. My fingers were too numb. They fell to the floor with a *ping* that was the only sound in the airless room. This was worse than the fire. I couldn't breathe.

I can't breathe…

I turned, unable to speak, and stumbled back through the doorway. My broad shoulder crashed into the frame, knocking me sideways before I pushed off and ran down the stairs. Two steps per flight, two flights per floor, three floors… a dozen steps later, and I was barreling out the front door.

I had to get away.

My feet pulled me down the sidewalk with no comprehension or interference from my brain. I had no idea where I was going, where I was even at anymore, and I didn't really care. As long as I was separating myself from them.

How could I let this happen? How had I managed to get so attached?

There was a connection and a pull right from the very beginning in the pub, I knew that. I was aware of it, even though I'd tried to ignore it. And then Bodie felt the mate bond with her, and it was like a slap in the face. That connection we'd had? It suddenly meant nothing.

I tried to let it go—let *her* go—again, but then her stupid fucking parents ripped a hole right through her chest. Better men than I would have walked away, but I couldn't stand to see her hurting. I'd comforted her, and we'd talked, and I'd fallen a little further into that forbidden black hole of desire.

I'd walked her to her cell, and *again*, tried to leave… but she'd asked me to stay. And I'd listened.

My heart squeezed at the memory as I stared blankly ahead.

No matter how attracted I was, no matter how much I wanted her… I shouldn't have stayed. I shouldn't have opened my heart to her. I shouldn't have damn near kissed her... And now that she was with Bodie—her true mate—I definitely shouldn't be feeling heartache and jealousy.

I bit my lip hard enough to break through the skin as I willed the aching, unfamiliar feelings to take a hike. Of course, the bastards didn't. They hung around, clinging to me like anchors, pulling down to the bottom of a hopeless sea of longing and regret.

Fuck, this was bad.

I walked and stared and tried not to think, strolling through the darkness of night completely aimless for a while, until I spotted Larry's frazzled hair in the distance. Distraction. I needed a distraction. I couldn't think about what had happened. Not now. Not ever.

I hurried over to him. "Hey, Larry. Whatcha doing? Can I help?"

The old mage glanced up at me in surprise. "I thought you'd be with Drake."

"No, we, uh... split up to help." *Not a total lie*, I told myself.

Larry scratched his grizzled head. "Well, I think evacuation's taken care of. And the humans won't be able to stop the flames, but they can at least contain the spread for us... so... I'm off to the Los Angeles County Crematory Cemetery. You're welcome to come along, I suppose."

I nodded. "Sounds good."

"I need to pick up a few things at my apartment... a bone saw for one."

My eyebrows rose. But after working with Bodie and Drake, I was a little hesitant to ask why he needed that. "Um... mind if I clean up at your place while you grab what you need? I kind of lost my keys."

Larry checked his watch. He was one of the only guys I knew who still wore the outdated things. Then he sighed, the sound almost sympathetic. Like he somehow knew how much I needed this physical and emotional cleansing. "Sure."

Five minutes later, I was inside his cramped apartment, picking through meandering stacks of books. Ten minutes after that, I was showered and wearing some grey sweatpants that ended mid calf and a black t-shirt that said "Officially the World's Best Daddy." The t-shirt was about two sizes too small so it clung to me, emphasizing every dip and rise of my muscles, but I didn't give a shit. I slid back into my dirty tennis shoes sans socks.

"Ready," I announced.

Then we set out.

I didn't know if Larry's beat up Honda could make it. Luckily, it was so late at night the streets were nearly deserted so we made it to the cemetery in under ten minutes even with his car stalling out once.

Drake called me just as we parked, but I didn't answer. I already knew what he would say, and honestly, I didn't want to crack open that can of worms ever again. Eventually, after three missed calls, I texted: *Helping Larry. Bodie and Aubry are fine at his apartment.*

Even writing that much made my throat burn with…
something.

We got to the white, mission-style building without
incident. But when we arrived at the gate, Larry
cleared his throat and stopped walking. He didn't make
eye contact with me as he shuffled his feet. I got the
distinct feeling that he was embarrassed about
something.

"I don't like what we're about to do, but it's necessary," he admitted.

I raised a brow, finally wondering what the hell he
was up to. "What is it we're about to do?"

"Steal some murdered person's bones."

My brows furrowed and my lips thinned just before
they curled in sarcastic amusement.

Hmm, maybe I should have stayed and faced Bodie,
instead. I stared up at the barbed wire that topped the
dark chain link fence. *Nope. I still feel better about*
burglarizing some bones.

"The county cemetery is where they send all the
unclaimed bodies. Gang member victims. Unidentifiable murders. Stillborn children. Loved ones who
couldn't be afforded a proper burial. This place is a
veritable clearing house for forgotten souls."

Well, that sounded promising. Tons of bodies, all of
which with dangerous or depressing backstories. Shit,
maybe the place was haunted?

"How are you gonna know which ones are…?" I
began hesitantly.

"Typically, you go for someone without a face." Larry made a disgusted grimace. "That's usually a murder."

My stomach churned. Tonight was just going from one god awful depth of hell down to a new layer I didn't even know existed.

"So, we're not digging up bones?" I clarified hesitantly. "We're cutting them out of unclaimed corpses?"

"Right," Larry agreed, his face paling in the moonlight. "This is a crematorium, after all. All that's buried under those headstones is ash."

Jesus fucking hell... I scrubbed a hand across my face, contemplating getting the hell out of there and just leaving old Larry to figure this shit out on his own. But Larry had already headed over to a length of fence near the building.

"Just, follow my lead," he whispered.

I had to force my feet to shuffle along. It was after midnight. The cemetery was closed to the public. And by the smell in the air, the fires were still raging—and I hoped to god those were the fires from back in Skid Row that I was smelling and not some roasted, faceless gangster.

We needed to steal these fucking bones and get the hell out of there fast.

My eyes tracked a lone flashlight beam in the distance. The sounds of keys jingling and an off-tune whistle accompanied the light.

"Security guard." I pointed him out to Larry.

"Yeah. He's not the one to worry about," Larry assured me. "Help me climb the gate."

Cryptic much, Lar?

I shook my head and interlocked my fingers to make a step, then I boosted him up. He scaled the diamond-shaped links with more piss and vinegar than I expected from the old man, and when he reached the top, he poured a little powder over the barbed wire and they completely disappeared.

He straddled the fence and peered down at me. "Hurry! This spell only lasts about forty-five seconds."

"Fuck!" I cursed, scrambling to get my huge-ass feet to fit into the little diamond squares. Eventually, I just said fuck it, and hefted myself up with my armstrength alone, allowing my legs to kinda dangle uselessly beneath me.

"Why didn't you tell me that *before*?" I scolded him as I straddled the spiraling wire while he began lowering himself on the other side.

"Forgot," Larry shrugged. "Oh shit."

I didn't look down. I didn't want to see what I could already feel poking the insides of my thighs. Against the most precious part of me. "Damn it, Larry. Gimme some more of that shit. Now."

"But then we won't have enough to get out."

"I don't give a fuck. We'll worry about that when it's time to leave," I growled, my bear coming to the surface. My fingernails elongated into claws and thick golden fur sprouted along my forearms.

I took a deep breath and tried to calm my animal, reining him in so I could shift my hand back to human form and grab the pouch that Larry had handed me. I sprinkled the rest of that anti-barb shit all over, using every last speck.

A second later, the sharp scrape of metal against my scrotum eased and I breathed a sigh of relief before I cowboyed over the top of the fence and jumped all the way down.

When Larry finally shimmied his scrawny ass onto the ground, I shoved a finger directly in his face. "Next time you want me to put my balls on the line for you, I expect a warning."

I heard a gun cock behind me.

Larry's eyes widened and his hands slid up slowly in surrender. "Um... Easton? I think your balls might be on the line."

I froze and used my shifter senses to tell me about the threat behind us. I heard two staggered heartbeats, one toe scrape, and one inhale. I estimated we had two attackers. But who were they? What powers did they have?

I gave a subtle sniff. Not shifters. They smelled human. But I could also smell gunpowder and ashes. I couldn't tell if that was from them, or just the particles in the air.

A rough male voice spoke. "We told you not to come back here, Larry Faerie."

I watched Larry's face go through a multitude of

expressions. He knew our attackers. Hated them. Had a history with them. And they'd just insulted him in a way that only mages could. Fae were born with power. But mages took pride in earning it.

Which meant these fucks were probably mages themselves.

God fucking damn it.

I couldn't catch a break tonight.

Had Larry known these guys would be here? Was that why he wasn't overly concerned about the guard? He was kind of a pacifist, which was probably why he'd deflected my comment, but fucking hell, he hadn't even told me to watch my back.

I was a little pissed at him. More than a little pissed. All the damned emotion I'd been holding back and bottling up over Aubry suddenly uncorked. Coupled with my rage over Larry, I'd finally hit my limit.

Fuck it. I was ready to tear something completely apart. It made me rash, careless, cynical. The shifters needed Larry, but they didn't need *me*.

"Go," I ordered him, my voice coming out as a growl.

I whipped around, keeping myself between Larry's retreating form and the others, using my body like a shield as I shifted my right arm. A grizzly's reach was nearly five feet, so when I swiped my claws over the mage holding the gun, I knocked the weapon right out of his hand.

But not before he got a shot off.

My foot exploded with pain.

Son of a bitch!

I roared, backhanding that motherfucker, and then swinging forward again toward the other mage. This man had dreadlocks—he was younger, maybe college age—and he was chanting something, trying to do a spell. But I knew from experience—mages might be more powerful than me, but their magic took time. Mine didn't.

My claws raked into his side, and he went down screaming.

His buddy, an older gentleman wearing a Mag-Sorgin University sweatshirt didn't give me a chance to pick him up and shake him like a chew toy. He kept his gun carefully trained on me as he stooped to check on his friend. He held the weapon in his left hand because I was pretty sure I'd broken his right.

"You're gonna want to get him to the hospital," I said as I watched the red stain on dreadlock boy's blue shirt grow darker and spread farther. His screams slowly faded into gasps as his whole body shivered.

I pressed my lips together. *Shit. That was stupid. I shouldn't have said something so obvious.*

But the mage with the gun, the only mage still standing, just shook his head. "No need. Stay the fuck back."

He pulled a metallic white sleep grenade from his pocket and waved it at us threateningly as he holstered his gun and bent down to heft his friend over his shoulder. The dude I'd mangled grunted in pain, but was too weak to do anything else.

Larry, who had apparently emerged from a hiding spot instead of running away like I'd told him, grabbed my arm and guided me backward a few steps.

The remaining mage gave us a wry look, his eyes traveling up and down Larry's hunched over form, judging and dismissing him. "If I ever see you again, Larry... I'll be using *your* bones."

He whistled and two fae swooped down out of the sky and plucked the mages up, flying them off before I could blink. Watching their gossamer wings flutter on the dusky breeze reminded me of Aubry and all that I'd lost before I ever even had it.

My heart sank once more.

I exhaled hard. "Well... that could be worse." Or better, depending on how morbid I was feeling. "I hope that dude's okay."

Larry stared up at me. "He won't be. Murder bones are too valuable to waste."

I had to physically stop myself from breaking anything within reach, which would have been poor Larry.

That mage was gonna let his friend die? So he could cut out his bones and use them in a spell? That was vile. That was abhorrent. That was the very fucking reason we couldn't lose this war to the mages. They cared about nothing but power. They always had.

I shook my head and a thought came to me. *We*

were about to break into the crematorium and steal the very same thing: murder bones. Suddenly, our endeavor took on a whole new light.

"Is there any other way for you to stop that fire?" I asked.

Larry gave me a sad smile. "If there was, I promise you I wouldn't be here."

I stared at Larry, finally realizing how much this took from him, from his ethics, how he bent his moral compass to try and do what was right for *shifters*. For *us*. For the *group*. Even if it left an awful taste in his mouth.

Fuck.

Aubry's beautiful face drifted through my mind once more. Her pale skin, her plump lips, her silken wings, and her selfless heart. And I realized... I, too, had to do what was right for the *group*.

That thought sent a mudslide of grief through my veins. Like the top of my heart had been sheared off and sent tumbling through my body down to my feet, liquefying and destroying everything in its path. It was heartbreak on a level I'd never felt before.

All because of a fae.

Because of a woman I hadn't even kissed.

A woman I never should have fallen for.

I followed Larry like a zombie after he healed my foot, after he did a Compulsion Spell to send the human guard to stare at a tree, after we broke into the sanctuary and he took a couple femurs. While he worked, I stood off to the side, staring at nothing. I leaned against a table, my hands skimming over something rough. I looked down and saw a small grave marker, the size of my hand. It only had a year inscribed on it.

Larry came back over just then, carrying a bag over his shoulder. "Time to go."

"What's this?" I asked, softly.

He looked down and sighed, the ghost of a forlorn smile touching his lips. "It's the marker for the pauper graves. If bodies go unclaimed for three years here, they are cremated and put into a mass grave. The year of cremation marks the spot."

I stared down at the little stone. I'd thought mass graves were a thing of the past. Apparently, I was wrong. I wondered how many shifters were included in these mass graves. Most shifters lived paw to mouth, day by day, barely scraping by under strict mage scrutiny.

Larry put a hand on my shoulder. "Time to go." He held up a pair of giant hedge shears. "Let's hope these work on chain links."

I took the tool from him and followed him outside. Cutting a quick flap in the metal, we left without incident and made the long walk back in silence. Too many emotions filled me to even begin processing them. I just let them swim around unguarded as I sank deeper into despair.

Back at his apartment, Larry gave me careful

instructions, and I mixed potions for his spells with robotic arms, my mind shut down. I followed him wordlessly as he walked toward the fire, chanting and waving his arms and splattering an orange potion that looked like orange juice on buildings like he was anointing them.

The entire time, I repeated the same phrases over and over. *She's Bodie's. She doesn't belong to you. He only gets one mate. Ever. He's an important part of your three-man pack. You can't mess with that. You can't fuck it up.*

But pack or not, I knew one thing with startling clarity: *I was hers.*

My beast roared each time these painful thoughts flooded my mind. It made no sense. Bears could get a new mate if their old mate passed, but we only ever had one at a time. There was no way Aubry was mine, too. No way. It was one hundred percent impossible.

She might not have been my mate, but the things I felt for her...

It was the worst fate imaginable. Because even though I longed for her, I would never lift a finger, never take a step, never make a move. I could never hurt my friend like that. Even if it meant living the rest of my life in unrequited longing.

16

AUBRY

OH FUCKING HELL, I THOUGHT, AS MY HEART THUMPED wildly at the sight of Bodie smiling above me.

I was definitely falling for him.

Them? I couldn't forget, Easton's face had popped up in that little fantasy before I came the last time. Was it possible I had feelings for him, too?

Suddenly, as if the very thought of him had somehow conjured him up in bodily form, I saw Easton standing in Bodie's doorway. Blue eyes wide, mouth ajar, he looked stunned out of his mind. But the way his shoulders slumped and his golden brows furrowed, I knew he was also hurting. Because of *me*. Because I was lying there naked with Bodie.

I quickly covered myself with my wings, hoping it'd make this less awkward for all of us, and somehow make his hurt go away, or at least fade some.

But it didn't. It only seemed to hurt him worse. His expression fell even further.

Bodie noticed the strange look in my eyes as I focused on Easton over his shoulder. He jerked around and sat up quickly. "What the fuck, man? You don't even knock?"

Easton dropped his keys and scrambled for the door, smashing into the doorframe before sprinting away down the stairs.

"Easton, wait!" I shouted, hopping to my feet and running over to the doorway. But he was already gone. He had to have hopped entire flights of stairs at a time to get away that fast. My back slumped against the frame and my head fell back into the wood.

Fuck. How the hell am I going to fix this?

Bodie remained eerily silent as I sat there and wallowed, trying to process what had happened and figure out a way to make it right, so I turned my head and shot him a forlorn glance. He was sitting on the rug, arms draped across his knees, staring at me like he couldn't quite figure me out.

Well, good luck, buddy. I can't even figure me out nowadays. You assholes swapped my brain with a bag of beans.

"Why'd you run after him?" Bodie asked me quietly. "Why'd you call his name?"

I swallowed hard and turned my head so I could stare up at the ceiling above me. "I don't know."

And truthfully, I didn't. My feelings for both Easton and Bodie were a fucking ball of jumbled up knots that I did *not* have the time or energy to untangle.

"Do you..." Bodie trailed off, his light green eyes dropping to the floor.

But he didn't have to finish that sentence. I *knew* he wanted to know if I liked Easton, if I had feelings for the bear shifter. How the hell was I supposed to answer a question like that when I didn't even know what I was feeling myself?

"Can we just not talk about this?" I asked, exhaustion masking the little bit of irritation in my tone.

Bodie stood and disappeared down the hallway, returning in a pair of low-hanging sweats and carrying a handful of clothes. He tossed me a clean up towel, a pair of black yoga pants, and a heather gray camisole. *Women's clothing.* Where the hell had he gotten those? Were they remnants of a night he spent with another woman, here in this very apartment? A night like he'd just spent with me?

My lips pursed as I wiped away the remnants of the best orgasm of my life. When I was finished, I grabbed the stretchy pants and shimmied into them. Bodie watched me in amusement as I slid the tank over my head and adjusted my breasts before smoothing it down my waist. I realized he'd slit the back so my wings could fit. So, at least he'd modified this hussy's shirt for me.

"You look jealous, Buttercup," he said in a mildly taunting tone. "Maybe now you know how I feel?"

I stared at him as he moseyed out of the living room and into his tiny kitchen. Marching after him, I flopped into a dining room chair and crossed my arms, glaring as he moved around collecting items for a cup of coffee.

"There's a big difference, actually," I argued as he popped a k-cup into his coffee maker.

"Oh? And what's that?"

His nonchalance was driving me insane. "*You're* jealous over nothing, a man who's your friend, a man I've never even kissed. *I'm* jealous over a woman who clearly left clothes behind in your apartment, a woman you slept with."

Bodie started the brewer and turned around, bending over to grab the edges of the table on either side of me. "Ah, but that's where you're wrong, Princess. I told you I was getting this place ready for you. That outfit you're wearing? I bought it specifically for you. No other woman has worn it. In fact, no other woman has ever even seen the inside of this apartment."

I raised a disbelieving brow.

He chuckled. "I'm not saying I haven't fucked other women. I'm just saying I never cared enough about them to bring them here." His face darkened. "I never trusted them enough. Any one of them could have betrayed me in a hot second to the stick swingers."

His look was hot. So hot my pussy flared back to life. But my mind was still stuck on the fact that he'd said he'd fucked other women. It was illogical. But it made me furious. It made me want to bite and mark and spank his tight ass.

He leaned in even closer, his nose caressing the side of my neck, causing my eyes to flutter shut. "You're hot when you're jealous, you know that? I like that my mate is territorial."

My eyes popped open. Is that what I was being? Territorial? Like some freaking animal? I needed to get my shit together. I reached out and touched his chest, almost allowing myself to get sidetracked by the heat of his hard pecs, before pushing him away from me.

"I'm not your mate," I denied softly. "And I wasn't being territorial."

He chuckled once more. "Yes, you are. I know you feel what I feel. And after sex like that?" He shook his head and bit his bottom lip before turning around and grabbing the finished cup of coffee and setting it before me. "Fuck, that was incredible. I've never come so hard in my life. It's like I poured a piece of my soul into you when I got off."

I took the cup, which I now realized he'd made for me, and stared down into the steamy black liquid, trying to ignore his words and the images they brought back to life in my mind.

"And based off the sexy fucking looks that crossed your face—utter shock and disbelief coupled with ecstasy—I'd say you've never had an orgasm like that either."

233

To my relief, he turned around and busied himself making a second cup of coffee. Thank god. I did *not* want to admit to the arrogant claims he'd just made... even though they were true. I mean, getting off on someone stroking my wings alone? That had *never* happened before.

It made my pussy clench just thinking about it and, suddenly, I was daydreaming about him bending me over the kitchen table while he spanked me with a spatula.

"You don't have to answer," he continued, pressing the start button on the brewer. Then he turned back towards me and leaned on the counter, crossing his deliciously ripped arms. "But what we felt? That inexplicable carnal bliss while I pounded you over and over again? That was because of our mate bond. So, you can deny it until you're blue in the face, but I already know the truth."

I rolled my eyes, wondering how either of us had actually fit in the room alongside his massive fucking ego. "Just because you're good at sex, doesn't mean you're some fated gift to my cunt and my soul. Don't be an asstrich."

"What?"

"A jerk who is so pompous and ignorant at the same time that his own head is up his ass like a damned ostrich." I smirked like I was feeling superior. But inside, I wasn't sure I believed my own words. Because my eyes couldn't stop tracking him. My heart couldn't stop pounding. I swallowed hard.

Bodie heard it. The fucker could probably hear my traitor heartbeat too. His lips tugged at the corners and he spun around, carefully taking a sip of his finished cup of joe. My gaze raked up and down his muscular back, following the rigid muscles along his spine out to his broad, stacked shoulders.

Fuck, he was hot.

I took a gulp of blazing hot coffee and barely even noticed the burn compared to him.

Bam, bam, bam! Three pounding knocks rattled the thin door of Bodie's apartment.

He turned around and waggled his brows at me. "*Ah*, that'll be Drake. Probably freaking the fuck out." Holding his cup, he shuffled into the living room and over to the door.

How was he so sure it wasn't Easton? Coming back to deck him right in his smug face?

Oh god, Easton… How could I have hurt him like that? Even if Bodie really was my mate, how was I supposed to be with the wolf shifter knowing full well it was killing his friend, his packmate? Easton and I had had a connection. Whatever it was… I knew it was mutual. And I knew if the situation was reversed...

"What the fuck were you thinking?" Drake's booming voice filled the small space.

Good guess. One point for Bodie, I thought as I brought the cup of coffee back up to my lips.

"Morning, Drake. I see you're bright eyed and spiky-tailed as usual," Bodie replied, unfazed.

"I grabbed the girl and the pup," Drake said darkly, continuing his rampage. "And handed them off to you and Easton. Next thing I know, you and the faerie are fucking gone."

"Got the *fucking* part right," Bodie mumbled as he reentered the kitchen, grinning over the rim of his mug at me.

I got the sudden urge to swat the damn thing right out of his hands, but I resisted. Barely.

"Did you seriously just...?" Drake was fuming. Literally. Smoke drifted from his nostrils as he strode into the kitchen and stared at us.

I did my best to concentrate on my coffee instead of the pissed off dragon shifter growling in the very tiny room. The temperature rose a couple degrees. And not just from discomfort. It literally rose.

"No, you know what?" Drake said to no one in particular, his lips curving sharply as he put his hands on his hips. "I don't even give a fuck. My packmate's alive, my hostage is alive, and I just saved as many shifters as I could from that fire. Easton's off helping Larry now, so they can make a potion or something and end that damn fire. It's been a long fucking night, and quite frankly, I'm exhausted."

He marched over and snatched both mugs right out of our hands and poured the coffee down the drain.

"Now's not the time for caffeination," he informed

us mockingly, setting the empty cups in the sink. "It's time for *sleep*. And that's not a suggestion, it's a fucking order: get some goddamned sleep. Because you and I," he said, glaring at Bodie, "have some shit to discuss when we wake up."

Bodie sighed but nodded. "I'm only agreeing because I'm gonna sleep with Aubry."

"*Actually* sleep. I don't wanna hear anything," Drake growled before he stormed into Bodie's living room, grabbed a furry gray blanket from behind a chair, and sprawled out on the leather couch. He took a deep breath and his head jerked down toward the red rug. He must have been able to smell the sex we'd had there. He let out a low growl before sighing and closing his eyes.

Without saying a word, Bodie stood and quietly took my hand, leading me into his bedroom. The smell in his room was so fresh, yet so distinctly male, I couldn't help but take a deep breath, smiling in contentment as it swirled around in my lungs.

He tucked me into the charcoal gray sheets, and curled up behind me, being careful not to smash my wings, before kissing my shoulder. Then he slid his hand down my arm and rested it protectively on my hip. Exhaustion hit as soon as I snuggled back into him, despite the bit of coffee I'd managed to drink.

And soon, I drifted to sleep... with thoughts of Easton's devastated face haunting my dreams.

It was dark when I opened my eyes to a cold, empty bed.

I felt around for Bodie, but he was gone. My eyes blinked and squinted, trying to adjust to the minimal light, but the room was empty. I trained my ears, listening closely, and the faint sound of voices drifted in through the cracked bedroom door. Climbing out of bed, I tiptoed over, peering through the slit.

Drake, Bodie, and Easton were in the living room.

Drake paced around throwing his arms as he talked, Bodie sat on the couch rubbing his temples as he listened, and Easton sat on the other side of the couch staring blankly ahead. I couldn't make out any words or phrases at first, but I had a feeling they were talking about me. Or at least, shit involved with my kidnapping and their future plans. Whatever the hell they were.

I watched and listened harder, my brain working overtime to add up whispers, body language, and the moving of their lips into something decipherable, and finally I started making things out.

"I don't give a shit what Larry says," Drake hissed. "The mate bond can't be real. If it was just Bodie? Maybe. But Easton, too?" He shook his head and ran a hand through his ebony hair. "Bears and wolves don't share fucking mates!"

"But dragons do!" Bodie said. "So, it's not unheard of for shifters—"

"You aren't fucking dragons!" Drake shouted.

The other two immediately shushed him as he paced frantically.

My heart pounded like the soundtrack of an action movie. Hope and elation filled me, and I had to mentally slap myself in order to beat those emotions back down. I shouldn't be happy that *one* of them was smitten with me, let alone *two*. That was just plain stupid of me. I should have turned around and tried to sneak out a window. But I was desperate to hear what the hell was going on. What the connection between Easton and Bodie and I might be if it wasn't a damn mate bond.

"It's not real," Drake repeated softly.

Easton paused at Drake's words, sitting up to stare at Bodie with a nervous expression. Bodie glanced right back, his face still, blank, and questioning. His green eyes looked uncertain.

And just like that, the elation that filled me like a misguided hot air balloon, popped and leaked out in waves of what almost felt like... *hurt.*

Fucking Bodie, I thought shaking my head snidely. *He almost had me convinced. But even* he *wasn't sure, apparently.*

I turned away from the door and took a deep breath, letting it out slowly. That's when I heard a gentle tapping on my window. It was so soft, it could have been the pitter patter of raindrops, but there weren't any clouds in sight, no wispy edges shimmering in the light of the moon.

I took one last glance over my shoulder and out through the cracked door—gazing out at the two men I'd almost thought I *liked*—before moving toward the glass pane. *Oh shit!* Someone was out there, crouched on the ledge. A person in a black trench coat, whose feet turned out toward the street as they edged along the exterior windowsill.

Adrenaline immediately punched me in the chest and I took up a fighting stance. I didn't yell for the guys. It might have been because I was furious with them or because Drake had stolen my heroic win and mate bond and I was more likely to kill him than any attacker. But it was also partially because I was curious. Who was coming after Bodie? My... whatever he was. My hackles rose at the thought of someone hurting him. Or Easton. Bodie had said he'd never brought anyone here. And he hadn't even been on the Mage Police radar. So, who knew about him?

The figure's thick hand moved along the top of the window. A man. He slowly pivoted. Wind tugged at his jacket, reminding me that he was three stories up and balancing on a damned ledge. One wrong move and this hair-brained idiot would find himself lying in the Southern California Hospital in a full body cast. Or worse. If the shifters in the other room got to him, I was sure it would be worse. I waited curiously as the stranger crouched cautiously in order to pull up the window.

I was stunned by who I saw.

I ran forward and pushed the glass the rest of the way up myself. "*Triton!*"

His jaw dropped like he was surprised to see me. But then he grinned. The wind picked up and his normally perfect hair whipped in the breeze. "Aubs."

He looked like he was halfway to the madhouse as the cold moonlight reflected in his wide blue eyes. His carefully trimmed beard had grown out some and the stale scent of smoke clung to his partially unbuttoned shirt. He had bags under his eyes, like he hadn't slept.

The relief in his tone was welcoming. "I found you! I can't believe it."

"You've been looking for me?" I asked, emotion clogging my throat and eyes. I couldn't help but feel uplifted. More than uplifted. Buoyed. Floating. After feeling so alone, abandoned by my parents, tossed aside by the Mage Council, it was such a momentous thing to realize that not everyone had given up on me. *Someone* had been looking for me all this time. *Someone*, at least, cared. My best friend hadn't given up.

"Is anyone else in here?" Trite said. "Where are those assholes who took you?"

"Shh," I warned, leaning closer to him. "They're in the living room. If we want to get away, now is the only chance."

Trite's eyes dilated as he peered toward the

bedroom door, as if he could see through walls and determine who my kidnappers were, as if he could attack them with his mind alone.

"Who is it?"

I shook my head, recognizing the brutal look on his face. Triton wanted to fight. But he was too exhausted. He'd obviously been up all night. "There are three of them. And I don't have any of my powers."

His gaze flicked over to me and his eyes widened. He shook his head. "Shifter scum. Always out to steal other people's magic. Okay, let's get you out of here." Trite waved his hand in a circular motion that told me to hurry the fuck up. "We have to leave before they realize what's going on."

For some fucked up reason, I hesitated. Biting my lip, I glanced back at the door *yet again*.

My ma—No, *Bodie* was waiting beyond that thin strip of door. He'd feel it if I left—thanks to that fake-assed mate bond—and he'd be after us in an instant. My chances of escape were slim to none, if escape was even possible at all.

Beyond the probability and statistics… there was a muted pain in my chest at the very thought of leaving him and Easton behind—Drake could go fuck himself. My heart didn't want to go. But my parents had long ago taught me to mute my heart. My mind was stronger.

Go, Aubry, I pep talked myself. *These men aren't your mates, they're your captors. You're not falling in love with one or the other, you're just drunk on a delusional cocktail made of Stockholm Syndrome and mage magic. Drake's right. This connection isn't real. And if it is, they still fucking kidnapped you! Now, take the fucking blinders off, and be the badass bitch you know you are.*

I took the deepest breath I could manage, fingers twitching as my body still fought against my mental argument to leave. But finally, I threw a leg out over the sill.

"We have to hurry," I told Trite in a harried whisper. "They'll know the moment I'm gone, and I don't have the use of my wings, glamour, or fire right now."

His eyes went wide, and his brows furrowed. "Jesus, what'd they do to you?"

"Nothing. I'll tell you later. Just get the fuck moving."

Before I change my mind.

We scooted along the ledge, our backs and palms pressed firmly into the siding of the apartment building, until we came across a fire escape ladder. Triton climbed on, then helped me over, and the two of us shuffled down the stairs as quickly and quietly as we could. My freaking heart was beating louder than the gentle *ting* of the metal steps against Trite's feet. My own were still bare, and I felt every tiny rough edge that fire escape had.

Trite glanced back to check on me when he reached the bottom. "My car's parked a block down the street, as soon as we get there, we'll be golden."

He didn't offer to use portal magic, which surprised me. The Mage Council was able to monitor the whole world by travelling instantly with Portal Potions, which allowed the user to go anywhere they'd previously been. But... maybe he wasn't authorized to use one. Maybe I didn't rate that kind of magic. I probably didn't, considering my parents had publicly fired me, probably at the Mage Council's request. They were little mage puppets. Always had been.

I studied Trite's face again. Was he supposed to find me? Was everything on TV a front? Was that all just to strip Drake of negotiating power so that Trite could perform a behind the scenes rescue? Was he taking me back to my parents? A million questions flew through my head as I followed my best friend toward his fancy-ass car.

The government made sure that MP cars were bullet-proof, magic-proof, and shifter-proof. If we made it inside, Bodie would be helpless to stop me from peeling away, leaving nothing more than a tire burn on the road as well as his heart.

Again, my chest ached at the thought.

Please, Aubry, don't leave him, my feeble heart begged. My pussy joined in on the pathetic pleading, and somewhere deep inside, my soul even nodded her agreement.

You shut your whore-mouths, my brain snapped back. *Leaving that wolf behind is nothing our dino dildo can't fix.*

244

My other body parts were *not* amused, *nor* convinced.

Neither was my brain, if I was being honest.

I'd taken less than five running strides toward Triton's car when a familiar voice cut through the night like a hot knife through butter, instantly halting me in my tracks.

"Going somewhere, little Butterfly?"

My heart trilled at the top of her lungs like a fucking opera singer as Bodie's voice filled the air around me and infiltrated my system.

Triton spun around, prepared to fight Bodie, and immediately came face-first with a hard-knuckled fist. Trite dropped like a sandbag, all the air whooshing out of his lungs as he gasped on the ground.

I sighed and rolled my eyes.

He's a council member, Aubs, I reminded myself. *He can only spar with you because you've done it since Mag-Sorgin days. In a real fight Trite's actually a bit of a pussy. Also in the fine print.*

My lips parted, but I didn't know what to say. What the hell *could* I say?

"Bodie, I—"

"*Don't.*" The word was harsh and raw, spoken through gritted teeth and a thick veil of emotion. If I didn't know any better, I might worry he was on the verge of tears.

"Aubry," Triton gasped, once he was finally able to breathe. He held up a small glass ball full of pink and purple swirling magic. A Portal Potion. So he *did* fucking have one. "I'll come back for you."

"The fuck you will," Bodie growled, launching at my old friend just as the mage slammed the potion to the ground. The glass shattered and Trite disappeared in a puff of sweet-smelling purple smoke.

While the smoke still lingered, I got the urge to run. But, the next thing I knew, rough hands had clamped around my shoulders, fingers digging painfully into my flesh as I was yanked down the street. Adrenaline spiked for just a moment, followed by arousal, and a quick mental slap to the face.

This is not *sexy time!* my brain screamed at my vagina in frustration.

Drake's menacing voice echoed through my skull as his harsh breath skimmed my ear.

"You just made a big mistake, little fly."

17

AUBRY

ANGER LIKE I'D NEVER FELT BOILED THROUGH MY VEINS
as Drake dragged me out of there.

I was two seconds away from freedom. Two
seconds, and this fucking firebreathing tadpole had
torn it away. The anger was quickly followed by
despair as Drake shifted. There was no way I was
escaping now.

The hands gripping my shoulders turned into black
claws. He pulled me tighter to his chest and leapt into
the sky, jerking my body up like a yo-yo handled by a
toddler. He obviously didn't carry people often. He
flew away from Bodie without a word, just up, and
then right through the smoke of the diminishing fires
in order to hide us from view. Larry's spell, whatever it
was that Drake had mentioned, was working to stop
the flames, thank fuck.

Before my entire view was eclipsed by grey smoke, I

looked down over the streets of Skid Row and thought I saw a blond head. My heart clenched. But I honestly didn't think it was Easton; he hadn't followed the other two outside as far as I knew. It was just ridiculous, wishful thinking on my part.

But then I questioned myself. Why was I even wishing I saw him? What the fuck? I had been *this close* to freedom, *this close* to never seeing them again...

My heart punched me painfully. Not a knockout blow, but the kind that made me see red around the edges of my vision.

Or maybe that was just a lack of oxygen due to our height?

If Bodie and I actually had a mate bond... Did I believe in that now? That the wolf man and I were mates? Drake said no. But what other explanation was there for why I hadn't wanted to escape? For why it had been so hard?

Based on Larry's constant need to redo spells, I had to assume he was some kind of shit mage—Trite never had to redo spells that often. I hadn't heard or seen anything from 'Larry the Ethical' that would lead me to believe his spells were consistently renewing some ridiculous love spell.

I doubted he'd even have the power to pull something that big off. Trite had told me once that he'd tried a Love Spell—just for shits and giggles—but it hadn't worked... and Trite was on the fucking Mage Council. So, if *he* couldn't get a Love Spell to work, the chances of *Larry* being successful were… none. Just none. There was no fucking way that Larry had done this to me.

I'd done it to myself.

With both Easton and Bodie. Why the hell had I become addicted to assholes over the years? Why was I so attracted to them? Why was I attracted to Easton even when I thought that my connection with Bodie might be a real mate bond?

Those were questions I didn't understand or have any answers to…

Fae rarely got mate bonds. Our loyalties were too fickle. Our natures were so fierce that it was hard to find someone we could trust.

Shifters, on the other hand, were loyal first and fierce second… and maybe I admired that a little. Their sense of pack. Maybe I wanted that. Maybe that desire had sparked this wannabe mate bond or whatever it was *and* this attraction to Easton. Maybe that's what had drawn me to them, and now left me confused, heartbroken, and angry even.

I'd wanted to leave with Trite. A huge part of me longed to escape and go back to the known and the safety of order and predictability. But another part of me had wept. Because I'd tried to leave and Bodie knew it.

He knew I'd betrayed him.

His face, that hurt expression, the tears filling those light green eyes—they didn't fall but they were there nonetheless… I couldn't handle it. I shut down my mind the best that I could.

Drake flew us higher and higher and I drifted through the night sky in his claws, my feet floating, skimming clouds. Eventually, he got us so high above the smog that I could actually see the stars. I rarely flew this high. My own wings were sensitive to changes in temperature and stronger wind currents.

Come on, Aubs, I urged myself, mentally hopping around like a boxer trying to get energized for a fight. I tried to reason away the ache in my heart, that grew with each mile we got further away from Bodie. *Feelings are bullshit, and you don't need them. Those shifters? You don't need them. You only need yourself; you only* have *yourself.*

I shoved my asshole feelings aside, the ones that wanted to rend me limb from limb for trying to leave. The ones that wanted to rip me apart but not quite kill me, leaving me gutted and suffering in agony.

Fuck them.

Drake had dragged me out of there so furiously, I wouldn't be surprised if he planned to drop me. I'd caused them too much trouble. I'd probably deserve it if he did let me go. My wings still wouldn't hold my weight so I'd plummet to my death. There were worse ways to go.

But when Drake dove down like a hawk, gaining speed, I suddenly didn't want to die. My heart shivered in my chest and I closed my eyes tight, not wanting to see the ground when he threw me hard from thirty feet so that I'd break my neck.

CRUNCH.

I peeled open my eyes, confused and disoriented. Drake had landed on a gravel road, his claws sliding across the small pebbles as he dug in to latch onto the dirt beneath. My eyes flickered from side to side. We were in the middle of the mountains. In the middle of a forest. There was a cabin in front of us that looked like it hadn't been used since *The Strangers* had come out here to film their horror flick.

It was my personal nightmare. Nature? No takeout? What the fuck? I might have been a summer fae, but I was a city girl.

Drake dragged me forward and it abruptly registered that I was going to be stuck out here with him. Alone. That made the bile in my throat rise about five inches higher. Suddenly I wished he had dropped me. The only reason he hadn't tortured me before was because Bodie and Easton had run interference. Now, they weren't here to save me.

I fought a shiver.

I didn't want him to see how easily he could cow me. I didn't want him to know that my stomach was tying itself in Celtic knots and I was pretty certain that whatever slasher film had used this cabin as their set was gonna look like a picnic compared to Drake's plans for me.

Fuck my life. If body-swapping was actually a thing

and not some human fantasy, I would have swapped places with the ugliest, poorest, loneliest shifter in existence. I would have swapped with a worm shifter shriveling in the sun. Anything would have been better than this.

Drake pulled out a key ring and unlocked the cabin door.

I glanced around wildly, thinking that this view was going to be the last I ever saw. I fully expected a Dexter-style table and plastic sheeting to be the only things inside.

Instead, when the door swung open, I saw a couch with a red and gold fish scale pattern from the 80s. There was a box TV with a DVD player attached to it. And a kitchen that was all wood. Even the countertops. It was rustic times a million. *The Beverly Hillbillies* on crack.

Drake shoved me inside and followed me in, shutting and locking the door behind us. He then pulled out one of those spelled pouches, the ones that were somehow infinitely deep. "Sit on the damn couch. And if you so much as move a muscle, I swear…"

He didn't finish the threat, just reached into the pouch and brought out a length of iron chain. He came forward and secured one end around a couch leg. Then he grabbed my ankle and wrapped the other end around it outside my pants. I heard a lock click into place. I was surprised he didn't lift my pants to make it burn. But he probably wanted my fear to build first.

That done, Drake walked around the room closing all the dusty-ass curtains, making us both cough. Then he threw thin metal nets over them, which I assumed were made of iron.

The front door was unlucky enough to get the treatment of his crap carpentry skills. He hammered a support into each side of the doorframe, and pulled out an iron bar, battening the entryway so if I wanted to get through, I'd have no choice but to touch the fucking thing.

I analyzed all his 'containment' measures, which weren't actually that different from what he'd done with my cell, with a crude eye. Was he trying to lull me into a false sense of calm before he started the torture? If death was coming, I wanted to rip the fucking Band Aid off and get it over with. I couldn't stand these adrenaline spikes and falls. I was gonna die of a fucking heart attack.

That'd piss both of us the hell off.

"Thorough aren't you, Drogon?" I goaded him.

Drake raised a brow then got back to ignoring me.

I leaned back on the couch in shock. "Don't tell me you don't get a *Game of Thrones* reference. Everyone fucking watched that show."

Drake just blinked. "Oh I got it. I just didn't think it was a very good burn, Dollface."

What the fuck? That was the most demeaning, stereotypical goddamned nickname ever. He could see how furious it made me and I swore I saw his lips twitch.

I clenched my fists. "I'm happy to try harder. Your beast? Not so scary."

"No?" Drake was about to dismiss me but for some reason that comment made him stop short, I could tell.

"Yeah." I scrunched my nose. "You look more like the Geico Gecko."

"Well, you're nothing but a parasitic wasp."

I scoffed. "You said *my* insults were bad but that was just—"

Drake cut me off, his blue eyes flashing gold. "A parasitic wasp uses her stinger to inject her eggs in another species and when her children hatch, they tear their host apart."

Oh. *Okay…* "Fine," I admitted. "That was a semi-decent, albeit crazy-nerdy, burn."

Drake walked off. I turned on the couch, watching him open a door and climb a set of stairs I hadn't noticed previously.

Who puts a door in front of their stairwell? This was definitely a serial killer's house.

"Where are you going?" I shouted after Drake. Suddenly, I wondered if all the evil torture devices were upstairs like Frankenstein's lab with panoramic windows and lightning in the background and everything.

Drake didn't answer. I turned around and crossed

my arms. I hadn't really expected him to respond, but sitting on the stupid couch was anticlimactic.

I'd just tried to fucking escape! He hated me! I was pretty certain I'd heard Drake arguing to 'get rid of me' with the guys tonight. And I knew what The Shadow did to get rid of people.

So, where was the punishment? There was no way in hell I'd believe that there wasn't one. Unless he was using reverse psychology to make me punish myself by not telling me anything and leaving me in this god-awful state of anticipation.

Calm down, Aubry, I told myself. *Remember your MP training.*

I sat there for an hour, maybe two, listening to mysterious noises drift down the stairs. A thump. A pounding sound. Jumping. A series of thwacks.

He was practicing with whips. Discarding the last body he had tortured to make room for me. Maybe he had a stretcher up there, some crazy homemade medieval torture device. My mind swirled in ridiculous circles getting more and more absurd.

Finally, I couldn't stand myself. I stood up and walked over to the TV. I turned it on, finding nothing but static. *Great.* I bent over to the DVD player. There was a single DVD in the machine, and no others anywhere else. It was Disney's *Beauty and the Beast*.

Fuck me.

I'd been kidnapped by a kindergartner.

But it was either: a) watch the stupid fucking movie,

b) try to figure out what terrifying things Drake was up to, or c) wallow in the horrid feelings that had taken over my stomach like a pit of acid—the ones that said I was a truly awful mate and that I'd destroyed Bodie's beautiful heart forever. That didn't even include the guilt about Easton and that fucked up scenario.

I hit play.

Annoying, happy songs blared out of the TV. A line of static raced across the bottom third of the screen and at least one of the speakers sounded like it was about to blow.

Drake stomped downstairs. "What the fuck is that shit?" he asked, marching toward the couch.

I turned, ready to insult the interfering dickhead by calling him LeFou, but I stopped short.

Drake wasn't wearing a shirt. And he was dripping in sweat. Beads of it trickled down his pecs like rain trickles down a windowpane. A bright white scar cut across his chest. But I hardly noticed that. Instead, I noticed that he'd taped his knuckles. Like he was punching something.

My spine shot up straight. "Are you fucking exercising up there? You have a fucking workout room and a punching bag and you're leaving me stuck down here with a *children's movie!*"

Drake's eyes flicked up and down my figure, taking in my fury. My balled up fists, my thinset lips, and my open wings which were aggressively tilted toward him.

The tiniest of smirks crossed his face. "Yup."

The bastard turned and walked back upstairs and the *thwacking* started up again.

Asshole.

I debated watching the movie, but "Be Our Guest" wasn't gonna cut it. Not when I knew that upstairs, Drake was doing what I longed to do, punch my stupid fucking emotions into oblivion. I stopped the television and dropped to the wooden floor, doing push ups until my arms shook too much for me to continue. Then I moved to sit ups. Then squats. At least if he came downstairs and killed me after all that, it would be quick. I wouldn't have any energy left to fight.

I couldn't keep track of time, but I pushed myself until I collapsed on the couch. I had no idea what the hour was, only that it was still dark outside. I'd just started to drift off when Drake came tromping down the stairs.

I sat up, turning to keep an eye on him as he went into the kitchen behind me and got himself a glass of water. I watched as he drank, gulping, the water spilling down his lips, over his chest, splashing onto his happy trail.

My eyes glared at the thin line of dark hair. There was nothing *happy* about that man. His wasn't a happy trail; it was a trail down to hell, where torture awaited. He didn't have a dick. He probably had a demon in his pants.

What was supposed to be a funny, ironic, snarky thought morphed as I thought about sinfully demonic levels of torture. He could burn off my clothes, spank me with a pitchfork, then flip me over and spread my thighs, bringing that pitchfork up to tease me dangerously—

Fuck.

I did *not* want to get hot thinking about Drake. Not now. Not ever.

I tore my eyes away from him and flipped around to sit back on the couch. One of the springs pressed into my ass and I scooted over.

To my surprise, Drake walked over with a glass of water for me and I took it carefully, ensuring I didn't touch any of his fingers. I gulped the water, realizing just how thirsty I was.

When I looked up, Drake was gone.

Twenty minutes later he showed back up looking fresh and showered. He reached into his magic pouch and pulled a can of chicken out of it. Then, he strode into the kitchen and grabbed a can opener and two bowls. My brows raised as I watched him open the can and divide the chicken before returning to hand me a sad, pathetic-looking bowl of plain chicken.

"I'm sorry. I don't eat cat food."

He shoved the bowl at me. "Take it or don't eat."

"Don't they have spices over there? Or do you have noodles in your pouch or something?" Chicken alfredo would be okay, or even just chicken spaghetti, but plain canned chicken sitting in a broth of salty chicken juice?

He had a better chance of me eating his dick. And that wasn't fucking happening.

Drake raised a challenging eyebrow at me. "You know how to cook?"

I was raised in a fucking fae mansion full of servants. Of course, I didn't know how to cook. But if he'd unchain me and I could bust through one of those iron covered windows and fly out of here...

"Yup." I tried not to eye the windows as I answered.

Instead of unchaining my ankle, Drake unchained the coil around the leg of the couch. "Well, come on little gnat, get to work." He yanked the chain and walked me toward the kitchen.

I grudgingly followed with my bowl of nasty chicken in hand, trying and failing to not feel like a pet sub on a dom's leash. My downstairs prickled with heat while my upstairs scolded me.

We looked through the cabinets, which contained some dry goods, like flour and rice, and a couple cans of beans. No sauce. *Awesome.*

I clomped over to the fridge, chain clanking along on the ground like I was some stupid actor in a bad community theatre remake of *A Christmas Carol*. When had life decided to make a Jacob Marley out of me?

There was mayo in the fridge. And some cheese that didn't look bad. Could that be made into a sauce? I grabbed it and swung the fridge door shut with a sigh as I said, "You could just take one of those kitchen knives and end both our suffering."

"You really think I'd stab myself to make your precious little life easier?" Drake rasped.

I turned back to look at him. "No."

A long, drawn out moment passed and a shadow crept over Drake's face as he stared down at me. "You think I brought you out here to kill you?"

"Deserted cabin in the woods. Pretty cliche, yeah, but you're not the brightest crayon in the box, so..." I trailed off.

"You kill more than I do, fly," Drake sneered, taking a step toward me.

"I only kill criminals."

"They aren't criminals if the laws are unjust."

"Who gets to decide just and unjust?"

"Not shifters. Is there a single damn shifter on the Mage Council?" Drake stepped again into my space, trying to intimidate me.

I straightened my spine and slammed the mayo down on the counter, flaring my wings. "You think fae have it that much better?" I took my own step forward, until we were toe to toe. "My family has to watch every single breath they take. A mage ended my grandfather's life because he met with the sirens alone, without one of them present." I glared up at Drake, breathing hard. And I realized I said something I shouldn't. Damn it all. He'd pissed me off so much that I was revealing family secrets. Shit my parents had put on lockdown, stuff I'd only been trusted with after I'd gotten the chief enforcer gig.

Drake's voice was soft when he asked, "Then why serve them?"

I gave a bitter laugh. "You don't know the answer to that? Then you're dumber than I thought, you skink."

Drake turned away. "Just make the food, mosquito."

"Who says I'm making any for you, iguana-face?"

He turned back to face me. "What's your relationship with the guy who tried to take you tonight?"

That was a one-eighty.

He followed it up with a stab to the heart. "I'm about to call Bodie and I'm pretty sure he's gonna want to know."

"Triton's my best friend," I blurted out before my brain could stop my heart. "Never been anything more."

"Triton who?" Drake's face grew ashen.

"Triton Vale. And he will kick your asses when he finds me again—which he will," I promised. "He'll bring a shit-ton of mage wrath down on you now that he knows it's you who has me. There won't be anywhere dark enough for you to hide, Shadow," I mocked.

Drake didn't answer, just stared at me stone-faced for a moment before walking off.

I turned toward the countertop, furious with myself for saying anything as I grabbed my mayo and reached for a pot. I had to go back for the cheese, because that asshole Drake had pissed me off and I'd forgotten it.

I shouldn't have said Triton's name. Of course, Drake knew who Trite was. My best friend was on the damned council, for god's sake. Everyone knew who he was. By name at least. But if Drake hadn't known his face… I'd just put a target on my best friend's back. The only person who'd tried to rescue me. *Fuck.*

I grabbed onto the countertop and dug in, wishing I had the strength to just crush it. I wish I had the strength to crush Drake. Or go back in time and just erase this whole mess. I breathed deep.

But maybe I was wrong. Maybe I was reading too much into this. And Trite wasn't a fae. He couldn't glamour. But he'd used a Portal Potion and could be halfway across the world in the blink of an eye. He could make another one. Maybe he could even make something to disguise his looks. Or at least dye his hair or something. He'd tried dying it dark once in college when I'd dared him. Maybe he'd think to do that again.

He wasn't without resources. And these shifters were busy. They had other priorities. I was a small fry. Not even worth a ransom from the mages.

Having logicked myself into a state of semi-calm, I let go of the countertop and got to work.

I started up the fire and tossed in some mayo and then cut some cubes of cheese. When I tossed them in, it didn't look quite right. It was lumpy. I watched for a few minutes, but nothing happened. How long did it take cheese to melt? Did I need to add some water? Did it need water to boil?

I got a cup of water from the sink and dumped it in. The water sat on top of the lumpy mess beneath. I hissed in frustration. I had trained for life and death situations all my life. But as an officer. Not some damned, stuck in some post-apocalyptic style cabin in the woods with an asshole.

When I got out of this, I was taking cooking lessons. I rooted around in the cabinets as I decided that. I found some takeout packets of pepper. Those might be good. They also made me wonder if we could get delivery out here. I ripped open the little paper pouches as I watched Drake standing near one of the far windows, talking quietly into his phone. I dumped the pepper in and moved back toward the edge of the kitchen.

What was he saying? What was Bodie saying? Curiosity clawed me like a cat. I tried to read his lips.

That's when the burning smell hit my nose. I turned.

Fuck!

I ran back to my pot to find a disgusting mess. The sides of the pot were ringed in brown.

"What the fuck's going on?" Drake roared, returning to the kitchen. He grabbed my pot off the stove and dumped it into the sink. He turned the faucet on. A hiss and a curl of steam erupted from the hot metal.

I turned the burner off and faced him defensively. "You distracted me."

"What?"

"Don't try and have a secret conversation about someone while they're cooking."

Drake balled his fists and raised them like he wanted to punch me.

"Go ahead, but if you do it, I'm not holding back."

He lowered his hands.

I struck anyway. I gave him a right hook so hard that I felt it all the way up to my shoulder. My bones rang with pain.

Drake looked startled. But only for a second. Then his black brows drew down and he was on top of me, pinning me to the floor as I kicked and tried to punch him.

"Stop it!" he growled, smoke escaping from his mouth in rings, like a fucking mobster smoking a cigar. He wrapped his hands around my wrists and his thick thighs pinned down my legs and the bottom half of my wings.

"What did you tell Bodie?" I snarled up at him, then coughed. Fucking smoke. I stretched my fingers and used my nails to rake bloody streaks across the back of his hand.

"You bitch!" Drake snapped. Then he lay full on top of me, his weight pressing down on me so that I couldn't breathe.

Fucker was huge. Not as big as Easton, but his chest was twice as wide as mine. His hands turned into claws in order to better escape my nails. I realized almost instantly that those claws had a very good chance of puncturing my wings if I kept fighting.

But I was past the point of caring.

I wiggled to get my hip out from under him, then wrapped my unchained leg around his waist, using my heel to kick inward and jab the back of his leg. He didn't even react. The motherfucker was made of steel or something. His pecs certainly felt like it. I tried to roll my hips and shift him off of me, but he was too heavy. I let out a frustrated cry.

Drake leaned down and got in my face. "All I fucking told Bodie was the name of the asshole who tried to take you. Triton Vale. He'll do the rest."

No. Fear slithered into me like a snake. I froze, staring up at Drake's blue eyes. I took in his serious expression and the set of his jaw. Trite was a mage... he was protected. But Bodie had lived off the radar for so long... I knew. In my heart of hearts I knew what the outcome would be.

"He's gonna kill Trite, isn't he?" I whimpered.

Drake didn't even crack a smile. "Would you expect anything less?"

BODIE

I STALKED AFTER MY TARGET LIKE A DEADLY PREDATOR.

His putrid aroma had disappeared when he had, so I didn't have a scent trail to follow, but I'd already committed his scent to memory. Hunting him down was now my top priority.

The fucker had tried to steal my mate away, and I was going to end him for it.

Prowling through the streets of Santa Monica, I carefully sifted through the air for any trace of him. I didn't know his name, but I knew he was a mage. I didn't know where he lived, but I knew he was a friend of Aubry's. Since Aubry lived in Santa Monica, I figured I'd start there.

Humans walked up and down the sidewalks, just as relentless as the traffic on Wilshire Boulevard. They bumped each other's shoulders and ignored manners as they went about their business, each acting as if they were the only people left on the planet. Like the world somehow revolved around them.

They never bumped into me, though. No matter how crowded the sidewalk was, my wolf emitted a predatory vibe so strong that the humans subconsciously shied away.

Good. I didn't need naive non-magicals getting caught in my crosshairs.

Hours passed as I strategically scanned the various Boulevards—Santa Monica, Olympic, Pico, Lincoln, Cloverfield—sniffing at the air like a bloodhound. I carefully compartmentalized where I'd been and what I'd smelled so I could continue narrowing down my search. The asshole didn't seem to live within five miles of Aubry's apartment, which was a good thing for him, even though I was still going to graffiti the walls with his brains when I found him.

I'd almost made it to Ocean Park Boulevard when I felt my current cell vibrate in the back pocket of my jeans. I swiped at a bead of sweat about to drip into my brow, and I quickly brought the phone to my ear.

"What's up?" I never bothered with formalities such as *saying hello.* I didn't have time for that shit, and quite frankly, it didn't really fit the assassin vibe I had going on.

"Triton Vale." Drake's voice filled my head like a broken record echoing in a cave.

I didn't say a word. I just hung up to book an Uber ride. Now that I had a name, I could do a much more thorough and much less time-consuming search for his whereabouts. But I couldn't do that in the middle of the street. I needed some privacy.

When I logged onto the app, I made sure to put "underground" as the password, which opened up a special supernatural login screen. I scanned my thumbprint and, seconds later, a whole new map appeared, showing the locations of various supe rides I could request. After all, I couldn't trust just anyone to pick me up and drop me off.

I found Drew, one of my old packmates nearby, driving a rundown baby blue El Camino. It wasn't going to be pretty, but it would have to do. I chose a pickup location up ahead, so that I could keep walking instead of standing around wasting time while I waited for him—Sweat City Fitness. I'd never been there, but I sure as hell wouldn't look out of place lounging by a gym. It was better than the girly clothing shops nearby. What a weird name though. I couldn't imagine a conversation where I'd want to say I was at Sweat City. I found the building and lounged up against the wall for just a second before I saw the car.

As soon as Drew rolled up, I climbed into the back-seat and got to work. Larry had encrypted my phone with magic to make it untraceable, allowing me to access the dark web without ever getting caught. He'd done the same to Drake and Easton's, but the dragon was too paranoid to trust the magic. No offense to Larry, Drake didn't really trust anyone that much. Not even himself. I saw the way he looked in the mirror after he'd shifted and flamed. There was a lot of guilt weighing down his shoulders. Me? Not so much. I had people to protect. I'd tossed aside guilt and spat in her face long ago.

"Where to, dude?" Drew asked, glancing in the rearview mirror.

I shook my head, barely paying any attention as I searched for Triton Vale on the dark database. "Any-where. Just drive."

Drew grinned. My pack had long ago gotten used to my brash demeanor. "Whatever you say, Bodie-man."

I tapped enter, and file after file appeared under Triton's name. Some of them were outdated and possibly even the wrong guy—that stupid mermaid movie had caused a rash of sirens to name their kids Triton in the nineties—but others triggered my instincts, and I knew in my bones that I was on the right track. I clicked the third file and opened it up.

Triton Vale. Blond hair, blue eyes. Five foot eleven inches tall. One hundred eighty pounds. Graduated from Mag-Sorgin University six years ago. Youngest member of the Mage Council.

The Mage Council? Jesus, how important was the scrawny little fuck?

I got back to reading, scanning the file for an address. The only one I found was from downtown, nearly six years ago—clearly from his college days. Nothing newer. *Shit.*

"Take me to the Venice Beach precinct," I told Drew, who immediately hung a hard right and made a U-turn.

"You got it, dude."

I narrowed my eyes and gazed out the window as I thought. If this bastard worked for the Mage Council, then his scent trail was bound to be found near the precinct where Aubry worked. A cluster of magical buildings were in that area and he could have visited any one of them. From there, I'd be able to trace him back to anywhere, but preferably his apartment where I could skin him alive before blowing a hole through his dumbass head.

You fucked with the wrong shifter, Triton.

He'd picked *my* mate to kidnap—rescue? Fuck it, it didn't matter. *Mine.* He'd pissed me off—*me*, the best assassin on the shifter's side of the war. And he wasn't going to live another day to regret that decision.

I pulled a handgun from my hip holster and busied myself with readying it, making sure I was full on ammo, that the silencer was screwed on tight, and that the sights were still perfectly aligned. It would be more satisfying to let my wolf kill him slowly. But, unlike other assassins, I didn't go for satisfaction. I cared about results. It was why I'd never been caught.

"You, *uh*, planning on knocking someone off?" Drew asked, as he stared at me in the rearview mirror.

I leaned forward and smacked the back of his head and then averted the mirror. "Just drive."

Twenty minutes later, thanks to the godawful fucking traffic, I had him drop me off on Washington Boulevard—far enough away to avoid anything conspicuous on either of our parts. I handed him a fifty and shut the creaky car door behind me, patting the roof to let him know he should leave. As he pulled back onto the street, I made my way toward the precinct.

Sniffing carefully, I scanned the air for any signs of Triton soon-to-be-dickless Vale floating on the breeze. But I found none. Odd. If he was on the Mage Council, his scent would be all over around this part of town. Maybe I just wasn't close enough yet.

At the next corner, I turned right onto Venice Boulevard, assessing my surroundings while with a bored, unassuming expression, like I was just some normal fuck on a grocery run. I tilted my head at a slight angle toward the ground, hunched my shoulders just enough to look casual but not enough to appear weak, and carefully stuffed my hands into my jacket pockets. It was way too fucking warm for a jacket tonight. But appearances had to be kept up. And I couldn't just walk around with my gun in the open. My finger stayed on the trigger just in case.

Murder was a fucking art. One I'd mastered long ago. My acting skills definitely aided my success. That, and the fact that I had incredible aim, could assemble and disassemble a firearm in the dark in under a minute, and had approximately zero emotional baggage surrounding the act itself.

Jesus, when I put it like that, no wonder Aubry tried to run away...

Glaring, I shoved that thought down and shot it through the chest. I didn't need any more reasons to be pissed at her *or* myself. Right now, I just needed to do what I did best—track and annihilate.

As I approached the precinct, I realized rather quickly that something was off. There was no scent trail that matched the man who'd disappeared outside of Drake's apartment. So, either *that man* and *Triton* were not the same man, or Triton hadn't been in and out of the precinct in days. As a council member, I didn't see how that could be possible for old Dickless to achieve; mages were in and out of there nonstop and even with their portal potions, they still left traces of their scent behind.

I took another deep breath and continued walking, never once glancing toward the building beside me or looking up at any of the people who filtered in and out. Still, I found nothing, not even the smallest hint of his scent on the breeze.

Growling quietly, I rounded the next corner and pulled out my cell. I dialed and, as soon as the phone stopped ringing, I spoke. I didn't even wait for him to answer. "Goldilocks, meet me at the cottage," I ordered, using our code words.

Easton arrived at my place just as the sun went down. He looked all pained and distressed, which irritated the ever-loving hell out of me. I didn't care what he thought he felt. Aubry was *my* mate, not *his*. *He* didn't get to feel like shit because of her, *I* did.

Normally I wouldn't argue on behalf of a woman who made me feel like shit, but clearly, I'd lost my damned mind. I couldn't get her out of my head no matter how much I tried. Her scent was constantly clogging up half of my nose. Even my shirt had a trace of her on it, which was like a stupid fucking balm since I was away from her. Fate was a fickle bitch, teasing me with a mate who didn't want me in return.

"So, what'd you need?" Easton asked, crossing his arms and leaning against the outside of my building.

I gazed out across the dusky parking lot and over to where the mage had damn near escaped with my mate. My lip curled and my teeth elongated slightly as my eyes flashed with warmth. "I need help tracking that bastard-ass mage."

Easton had the good sense to look surprised. "You're the best tracker we have."

"Yes, and I've hit a dead-end."

Goldilocks shook his head. "I wasn't out here when it happened. And by the time I arrived, the smoke from the Portal Potion had overridden any scent trails."

"I know," I ground out, feeling far more aggravated than I had before he'd shown up.

I had to remind myself that I'd called him, he hadn't just shown up uninvited. I needed his help, so I needed to play nice. Even if I did want to sucker punch him in

274

the mouth for feeling heartbroken over my mate trying to leave us. *Me*. Trying to leave *me*.

Easton shrugged. "So what, then?"

I sighed heavily, biting my bottom lip to keep from cussing him out. I mean, seriously, how many bears did it take to screw in a lightbulb? Yanking the stairwell door open, I gestured curtly for him to step inside. "We'll talk more in private."

After we hiked up to the third floor, and shut and locked my apartment door behind us, I got down to business. "Drake gave me a name: Triton Vale."

"Okay?" Easton said cluelessly, as he rummaged through my cupboards until he found a bag of chips. He opened the bag and immediately started munching.

Fucking bear shifters. They didn't actually hibernate like their animal counterparts, but they sure as fuck acted like they were constantly preparing for it.

I sighed and grabbed a handful of chips for myself. "Average height, weight, and build. Blond hair, blue eyes. Smelled kinda like a mothball with an underlying note of smoke and rotten eggs."

"A mothball?" Easton asked, his pale blue eyes lighting up with recognition. "That's what the guy from the pub smelled like. The one Aubry was with the night I met her. His description sounds the same, too. Is he the one who tried to rescue her?"

My nostrils flared, and the blood in every inch of my veins started boiling. "It appears that way. So, they were... *together*?"

So help me fucking god, if he'd stuck his lanky, limp dick in my mate's cunt, I was going to rip it off and shove it in his mouth like a gag before I killed him. *Slowly*. Fuck efficiency.

Easton glowered, telling me all I cared to know.

"I don't know," he admitted. "I don't think she had any kind of romantic feelings for him, but he definitely seemed interested in her."

"How? I need every ounce of information right now." While that might've been true, I'd never admit that this was more of a masochistic punishment than a necessary piece of information.

Goldilocks shook his pale blond head. "I don't know. It wasn't in anything he *did*; he played the part of overprotective bestie. It was more in what he *wasn't* saying or doing, coupled with the pheromones and testosterone in the air."

I clenched my jaw so tight that I was surprised my teeth didn't shatter. "Anything else you can tell me about this punk-ass bitch?"

"He ended up going off with some random chick," Easton sighed and shook his head.

Great. Then I was back to square one: sniffing up and down every mother fucking street from Santa Monica to Venice Beach. Son of a bitch. At least I had an extra nose this time.

I patted Easton's shoulder, and he immediately tensed, his eyes flashing gold like he was ready for a fight.

Yeah well, back at ya, Baby Bear. You just keep your spoon in your own porridge bowl and sleep in your own fucking bed, and we won't have any problems.

THREE DAYS.

Three hot as shit, frustrating as hell, never ending days... we searched for that shit-dick mage.

Three.

I'd never had so much trouble tracking down a target in my life, and the worst part was, I wasn't even sure if he was trying to hide. My fucking heart was more invested than my head in this situation, and that had never happened to me before. It fucked up my concentration, and ate away at my sanity like worms on a corpse.

Easton and I met back up in front of Tortoise General Store on Venice, and he looked just as pissed and empty handed as I was. We both pretended to look into the store window at this weird hanger art thing someone had stuck on the ceiling as he reported back to me. His hands fidgeted as he said, "Seriously, where the fuck has this mage disappeared to? The fucking Alps? The Sahara?"

Great. He'd come up as empty as I had. I growled in frustration. "Not even a hint of a scent?" I asked him.

"Nope. You?"

"No."

Easton ran the back of his hand across his brow and gazed across the bumper-to-bumper traffic. "So, what do we do? Just keep looking forever?"

Yes, my heart shouted, and the yell echoed through my chest and rattled my bones. Externally, I was able to keep a better handle on things. I didn't fidget like Easton. "He'll turn up eventually," I replied darkly. My brows lowered, my eyes narrowed and my lips grew taut. I didn't give a shit if I had to search for the rest of the week, I was going to find and execute this mage.

Easton wasn't used to the dogged determination of an assassin. But whatever, I didn't need him. "Leave, if you want," I said, and I strode off down the sidewalk. "I'll track him on my own."

"It could take you weeks on your own," Easton protested. By the sound of his voice, he was keeping up rather than giving up.

"It never takes me weeks," I told him, feeling the frustration of this goose chase crawl up my throat again as the scent of over-perfumed humans assaulted my nose and a cluster of giggling girls passed, eyeing me appreciatively. My dick didn't even twitch. Not interested.

"I'm not leaving."

The bear was being stubborn. Normally, I'd have appreciated his tenacity and his help, but right now? It made me suspicious. I slowed my walk, waiting at a light for him to catch up.

"Why are you so hellbent on helping me when two

seconds ago you whined about forever?" I asked, glancing over at him with a raised brow. "Couldn't have something to do with *my* mate, could it?"

I turned back around, but I both heard and felt his growl on the air.

"Yeah, that's what I thought."

I shook my head as a sneer captured my lips. How the hell had it come to this, our three-man pack crumbling over something as simple and beautiful as me acquiring a mate?

"Why the hell can't you just be happy for me?" I asked. "Why do you feel the need to butt in and stake a claim of your own? Huh?"

"I saw her first."

That made me stop on a dime and whip around to face him. "The fuck did you just say?"

His eyes were pure gold, his fists clenched and his shoulders lifted, like he was one insult away from going Hulk.

When he spoke again, his voice was little more than a growl. "I said, I saw her first. I met her at the pub that night because you two thugs couldn't trust yourselves not to kill her. I flirted with her. I worried about her. I second guessed our plan to kidnap her because she made me feel things I wasn't expecting. Me. Not you. ME!"

"Fuck you, Goldi—"

But he cut me off and got right up in my face. "And then you come down with fated-mate-fever and

279

suddenly my feelings for her don't matter anymore? You just waltzed in and snatched her away."

I shoved him hard in the chest but he only took a half-step backward. The crowd was too thick. It was midday. And we shouldn't be fucking doing this, drawing attention near the precinct. But my wolf howled.

"I tried to leave her alone," he snarled, and a couple thick veins bulged in his neck. "But she asked me to stay."

My brain short-circuited. Somewhere between an overload of emotion and a knee-jerk reaction, I found my fist connecting with Easton's face. Right in the middle of the street.

He took the hit like a champ and swung at my face in return. I ducked out of the way, but only barely, as his other fist flew up to meet me.

People scattered away from us as if a sinkhole had just formed beneath our feet. We were making a scene. *Shit.*

I clenched my fists and shook my head, signaling to Easton that we needed to knock it the fuck off.

Like always, Easton listened. He actually hated to fight, unlike Drake and me. Our eyes flashed gold and we bared our teeth at one another, circling, but we reigned in our beasts enough to stop the outright fight here on a human street. I'd beat his ass back at headquarters, if he wanted, but it'd have to wait until after I slaughtered that piece of shit ma—

Suddenly, a scent swirled in the air above my head.

I sniffed, breathing in deep, practically tasting the pungent flavor of stale closet. The mothballer was nearby. *Yes.*

I regathered my focus and turned away from Easton. I followed the trail for a couple blocks before it banked a hard right and slithered down an alleyway.

"You smell that?" Easton asked as he came up beside me.

I glared at him as he took stock of our surroundings. "No, I just wandered back here to admire the trash. Of course I smell that."

"Not the mothball smell, you arrogant dick. The sugary smell. It smells like... magic."

The word had no more than left his lips when a dark cloud of magic surrounded us. It swarmed like millions of tiny insects, scraping and burning our skin like coarse sandpaper.

"Fucking pixie magic!" I shouted at Easton.

I couldn't see more than bits and pieces of him through the vortex of black.

"You think?" he cried sarcastically. "Whatever gave you that impression?"

I snarled. "Keep it up, Goldilocks, and I'll leave your dumb ass bleeding in this alley after I wring that pixie's neck."

He fucking chuckled. Who chuckles while they're getting slowly skinned by pixie magic? Crazy bastard.

"Looks like you're making a lot of progress with the

pixie situation," he goaded me as I swatted senselessly at the undulating blackness around me. "Maybe Larry'll be able to use what's left of our bones in one of his potions."

"Seriously, man? What the fuck is wrong with you?" I'd always considered Easton the most level-headed of the three of us, the peacemaker. But clearly, he was off his rocker. Going after my mate. Making cynical jokes. He wasn't himself.

All at once the magic stopped, the black smoke cleared, and I could see a tiny pixie fluttering in the air in front of us. Her hair was neon pink and she had both fists held firmly on her hips. "Do you two ever shut the fuck up?"

I glanced over at Easton whose skin was pink and bleeding in places from the countless abrasions. Pieces of his shirt now had holes. Looking down, I realized I hadn't fared much better. The pain... it was there. But my shifter side would heal it pretty damn fast, so I wasn't worried.

But what the hell was a pixie doing in this alley? Especially one wearing a uniform that marked her as Mage Police.

"We didn't do anything," Easton immediately led with a line that ended up making most shifters get fucking arrested.

The pixie snorted. "First you were fist fighting on the street, two seconds from shifting and going wild animal on each other. Then you argued like gorillas in this alley. For fuck's sake, you were even bickering while I blasted you with magic! What the hell is your deal? Lover's tiff? One of you forget to put the toilet seat down?"

I glared down at my feet, making the little pixie think I was ashamed of my actions. Then faster than light, I lashed out and grabbed her. Her body was in my right hand, her head in my left, as I prepared to snap her neck like a twig. Like twisting the lid off a soda bottle.

"Wait!" she screeched. "You're the ones who took Aubry, right?"

I locked gazes with Easton, whose eyes had suddenly lit up at the sound of her name. That mother fucker. It took everything in me to keep from headbutting his dumb ass since both my hands were currently occupied.

"Aubry was last seen with a giant red head male shifter at a bar. A couple patrons said he smelled like a bear shifter." The pixie eyed Easton. "Hair dye is easy enough to come by. I should know. Bear shifters... tend to like to live farther north."

God fucking damn it. Rage shot through me like a bullet. I shouldn't have asked Easton to help. Where the hell was my head? The fucker was conspicuous on a good day.

Fine. This bitch knew who we were. Not for long. But I'd pump her for information first. "How do you know Aubry, you flying rat?" I growled at her. "You have three seconds."

"She's my friend!" the pixie shrieked. "You can't kill me until I kick your asses and bust her out of your evil lair."

I cocked my head and squinted down at her. "Are you fucking kidding me? What kind of a half-assed incentive is that to keep me from murdering you?"

"Uh... shit." She hesitated. "How about—I'm Aubry's second in command. Don't kill me when you can use me for ransom too!"

I scoffed and rolled my eyes. "If the princess wasn't worth shit to the mages, what do you think that makes you?" I reached my second hand up to cover her head. I could snap her neck—make it fast.

"Don't," Easton whispered, putting his hand out to stop me from going over the edge. "She's a friend of Aubry's."

"I don't give a fuck if she's a friend of Satan—and with magic like that, it sure as hell wouldn't surprise me." My wounds had started to ache as my shifter metabolism healed them.

Easton bit his lip and turned away, staring off down the alley, which was empty except for us and one very normal, non shifter rat. "Fine. Then kill her. But I don't think Aubry will ever forgive you for it."

God fucking damn it, Goldilocks!

My grip on the pixie tightened for just a moment before loosening slightly.

I took a deep breath, fighting like hell against the grating of my nerves. It felt like nails on a chalkboard, scraping the underside of my skin. "Call Larry."

Easton immediately pulled out his phone and dialed the mage's number.

I couldn't believe what I was about to do. It went against over a decade of self-preservation tactics. But I had to try something. Aubry was my mate whether she liked it or not, and if I wanted to strengthen our bond, and somehow make it about more than just mind-blowing sex, then I needed to do something for her. Something I'd never done before.

I didn't leave survivors. Ever. That's why, though Drake was The Shadow, I didn't even have a name. I didn't exist to the mages. Because I took out anyone who knew about me.

Except for today.

I was gonna show Aubry that *I loved her* by letting her friend live.

AUBRY

"WELL, DON'T YOU LOOK WORSE THAN A SHRIVELED cock!" Tee exclaimed the moment she saw me, her bright pink hair the boldest thing in the forest.

My jaw dropped to see the six-inch-tall pixie in Easton's huge hand. I was relieved, shocked, mortified —I didn't know what I was. It was like a toddler was fingerpainting my feelings, blurring all the colors together into a muddy mess. I rushed toward the front door of the cabin, which Drake had left open. I figured he'd done it to mock me with the taste of freedom while he went and drank his instant coffee on the cabin's porch steps.

I could only get as far as the open front door before my chain ran out. My eyes traveled up to Easton and Bodie who stood side by side. Behind them was a beat up car that I hadn't even heard drive up; I'd been too busy cursing Drake under my breath and watching the one and only children's movie in the place for the eightieth time.

Last time I'd seen Easton, he'd looked wrecked. Even now, his eyes were shuttered, like he was trying hard to keep whatever was going on inside of him locked up tight.

Bodie, though, he looked at me with fire in his eyes, and I couldn't tell if it was fueled by desire or hate. Not until he said, "According to the flying rat, the two of you are friends. So I didn't kill her for you."

My hands flew to cover my mouth, shock and disgust my first reaction. Unlike the finger paintings from a moment ago, *these* emotions were very distinct. Then came anger. I launched myself at Bodie, but the chain around my ankle halted me so abruptly that I smashed face-first into the floor.

Fuck me.

No, fuck them*!*

I glared out at Bodie and Easton. "You can't go kidnapping the people in my life."

"You'd rather I kill them?" Bodie asked, pulling out a giant hunting knife from his jacket and turning toward Tee. The knife glinted in the early morning sunlight as he stepped closer.

"Jesus-fucking-Christ! No! That's not what I said!" I held up my hands and clambered ungracefully to my feet.

Easton stepped away from Bodie and his giant Bowie knife, lifting his elbow to shelter Tee by blocking the wolf shifter. For once, Tee seemed to have no words.

"Well, those were the options." Bodie smoothly slid the knife back into his jacket as if he was discussing financial statements or some shit. "She saw me, so it was either kill or kidnap."

He had no emotion in his tone whatsoever. His light green eyes stayed calmly focused on me. *Psychopath.* And to think I'd been starting to wonder if we were truly mates.

No. No way. I refused to believe it.

I turned away from the rabid dog shifter and held my hands out to Easton. I spoke through my teeth. I couldn't even look at Bodie again just then or I was going to try to shoot fire from my hands and melt his fucking face off. "Can I please have Tee?"

He shuffled forward along the gravel drive, still avoiding eye contact with me.

Drake stood from his perch on the stairs, allowing Easton passage, before walking off in the direction of the piece of shit car the other two had rode in on.

He doesn't care that his wolf pup almost killed my friend?

Of course he didn't. Drake only cared about himself. That ass.

Easton thrust Tee toward me and I gently scooped her up, brushing his hand softly in thanks. I had no doubt it was Easton, not Bodie, who'd spared Tee. He pulled back like my touch had stung him and then shuffled over to Bodie's side. I glanced between them.

Bros before hoes, huh? Fine.

They were three of a kind. Three peas in a fucked up pod. Three strikes and I'm out. The rock, paper, scissors of my tumultuous existence. A match made in hell.

I had Tee. I didn't need another friend... or 'good captor' or whatever the hell they were.

My sarcast-o-meter was apparently broken, but that didn't matter. Tee was safe, and she was here— that's all I cared about. I hugged her tight against my chest as another thought came to me. If she was here, there was no way Aaron wasn't searching for us already.

If Bodie could feel me leave, surely Aaron could feel Tee. Or was he used to her leaving? Would he assume nothing was wrong if their mate bond stretched because it often did in the MP line of work?

I shuttered my face so the guys wouldn't know that seeing Tee had given me hope for another rescue attempt. A better one. The fact that Trite had only brought one Portal Potion had been rubbing me wrong for days. I mean, if he'd been planning on rescuing me, then why the hell hadn't he brought *two*?

I walked Tee into the living room and curled up on the broken couch with my back toward the buttlicking shifters.

I stared down at her, noticing she had small iron cuffs around her wrists. *Of course.* "Tee, are you okay?"

She glared up at me. "No, I'm not okay! Those floppy-eared fucks stemmed my magic! I can't fly, can't hurt anyone. I'm like a fucking infant that has to be carried around." She flopped down on a couch pillow, stirring up a cloud of dust. After coughing for a moment, she lowered her voice and leaned in close to me. "And why the fuck haven't you broken out of here yet?"

Her dark brown eyes gleamed, full to the brim with conspiracy theories.

"*What?*" I leaned back as if she'd slapped me in the face.

"You know the council expects you to break out and bring these fuckers in, right?" Tee raised a brow, like *I* was the one acting crazy, not her.

"Excuse me!" I intended to whisper, but it came out as more of a shout.

I glanced over my shoulder. Bodie stood in the doorway, watching us as he leaned against the doorframe, as casual as could be. I left the couch and stormed over to him.

"We're having a private conversation! Get the fuck out!"

"Not before I get my *thank you* kiss," he murmured, his green eyes dropping to my lips.

"Thank you? You think I want to fucking thank you for stealing my friend away from her life?" I marched right up to him, rage billowing around me as I leaned in close. "You want me to thank you for hunting down my best friend with the intent to kill him? No. You are dead to me, mutt."

Bodie's eyes lost their calm and something fierce lit up beneath them. They turned that mixed shade of gold and green again as he grabbed my upper arms roughly and pulled me against his chest. He snarled and fur started to erupt from his arms and down the sides of his neck.

I narrowed my eyes and glared up at him. "Get away from me, filthy shifter."

With a howl, Bodie's head shifted and he shoved me to the ground. I fell hard on the chain as he ran out the front door and into the dawn in werewolf form.

I sat there, staring after him, my heart dragging through the brush along the ground, tripping over stones, getting caught on sticks, brutalized... but still chasing after him.

I had to swallow down the urge to call out his name. Fuck emotions. I could live without a heart.

I turned away from Drake and Easton, who stood in the kitchen holding grocery bags of food as they watched me. I was starving, but suddenly, eating sounded like the worst thing in the world. Or maybe the best. I wasn't sure. My body was going haywire. I felt like I'd fallen into a hole like Alice and I had emerged somewhere unidentifiable. Somewhere insane. Nothing in my life made sense anymore.

I stumbled back to Tee and tried to hold back the tears of confusion and frustration.

She shook her head and stared up at me, thoughtfully blinking a couple times. Then she leaned forward and whispered. "Honey, are they drugging you? Like with human stuff?"

I pressed my lips together and shook my head. "I wish."

Tee's eyes popped and she glanced over my shoulder at the kitchen, where Drake and Easton were shuffling around and putting away boxes and shelving fresh vegetables. Shit that smelled like real *food*, not just the canned gruel Drake and I had choked down every night for dinner because neither of us could fucking cook worth a shit. Not even rice. How could we fuck up rice?

"What's going on, then?" Tee wrapped her hand around my little finger.

I squeezed my eyes shut. I was nervous to say it. No, not nervous. Humiliated. No, furious at the fucking stars for aligning like this.

"That taint curd who shifted and ran off... he thinks we have a mate bond." I peeked out at Tee, whose jaw had dropped and left her mouth gaping.

"No! A mate bond with a shifter? Who not only gives off total serial killer vibes but is one of your kidnappers?" Tee climbed up my arm and sat on my shoulder to give a full body hug to my cheek. "I wish I had a growth potion right now, so I could get larger and squeeze you. You poor thing! No wonder you haven't gotten away."

Her sympathy broke my shell of anger that covered the sadness hiding deep inside. A single tear escaped. But I quickly wiped it away when footsteps headed our direction. I pulled Tee down onto my lap and cradled her, determined to take the brunt of whatever anger Drake was about to throw my way.

That asshole was always angry. The only time I ever saw him smile was when he'd walk outside at night and shift to expel the tiniest bit of fire. He'd stand there and stare at the flames, entranced. But I was pretty sure I was about to get reamed for telling Bodie to eat shit. I straightened my back and tensed, ready to give back as good as I got.

But it wasn't Drake who walked up. Easton stood off to the side of the couch, holding out a bowl of Pho. My eyes widened and my stomach turned traitor. It grumbled, begging him for the food.

"I got your favorite." His words came out in almost a whisper, like it was hard for him to be near me.

Tee climbed up and peered around me to see the steaming bowl of soup with all the fixings.

"Damn. Well, if that's how you treat prisoners, I'm gonna like it here," Tee sat back in my lap and kicked up her feet, playing cool. "I personally am a pizza girl. Got any of that?"

"Not today," Easton said. "I could grab some tomorrow—"

"I'll take some Pizzeria Mozza pizza, the lemon one with capers. Tell them light on the fried parsley though," Tee spit out her order like Easton was a waiter and not the slightly-less-evil warlord who had barely spared her life.

Easton pressed his lips together, but Drake yelled from across the room. "You just be glad you're breathing right now, and leave it at that."

Tee glared and Easton set the takeout on the table before turning and actually looking at me. His eyes swam with hurt as he asked, "Can I talk to you for a second?"

Shit. I didn't want to talk, but I found myself gently scooting Tee off me and standing. My heart fluttered nervously as Easton moved out to the porch. I followed him until my chain held tight, just outside the door.

"Look," Easton ran a hand through his blond hair and sighed. "You need to understand something. Bodie... he doesn't like witnesses."

Just the mention of Bodie's name had me looking toward the woods, searching for that stupid wolf. My heart sent out a signal, like radar, and a tiny ping came back. Bodie was far away, probably running, probably still in his wolf form. But didn't he deserve it? I mean, what the fuck?

"You mean I should feel grateful that he managed to curb his killer impulses?"

"Yes, that's exactly what I mean," Easton replied.

"You can't be serious."

Easton shook his head. "Bodie's not like other guys. He's got a huge pack to defend. He became alpha at fourteen. He's had ruthlessness pounded into him. If he wasn't vicious, his pack would suffer."

I shook my head. "Maybe if he wasn't vicious, the whole magical community wouldn't suffer," I retorted with sass.

"That's not how this fucking works and you know it!" Easton growled, his bear rising to the surface and changing his eyes gold. "Why the fuck don't you say the same thing about the Mage Council, huh? Larry told me about the bones from murdered people they use for their strongest spells. I saw a fucking mage let his friend die so he could use the dude's bones. They're fucking sick. Why aren't you down on them?"

My stomach dropped out. Trite never talked about what the council did. No one ever talked about mage spells or how they were performed. That shit was classified. Even when we'd gone to college together, certain buildings had been for mages only. No one else had been allowed inside. I knew my parents were terrified of stepping out of line. I'd always thought that was because they were social climbers, sycophantic assholes. And maybe they still were… but… murder bones?

"That's *one* asshole," I said, holding my head high despite how lost and confused I felt. "You can't tell me it's all of them."

I turned my eyes from Easton and stared out at the trees, trying to process his words.

Why would mages have *kill* orders instead of *arrest*

orders? Why would we send the bodies off to the Mage Council afterward? Bile crept up into my throat.

No. That couldn't be right.

"Larry's wrong," I decided with a nod as I turned back to Easton. "He's not a very skilled mage. He had to come out here while Drake was babysitting me, just to fix my spell. Maybe *he* has to use bones for spells but that doesn't mean—"

"Deny all you want. I can see by your eyes you believe it." Easton cut me off. He tugged down his shirt and pointed at his neck. "When I was younger, I didn't see the war as necessary either. That was before Iris."

Immediately, that name set off a spike of irrational jealousy in my chest. I swallowed hard and leaned toward him. "Who is that?"

"The siren who helped push me to this," Easton took a step closer and I could see an old scar on his neck. It looked like rope burn.

Horror flashed through me and I reached for his hand.

No. He couldn't be saying what I thought…

Easton didn't let me touch him. He shook his head and stepped back, biting his lip as he stared off the side of the porch into the mix of deciduous and pine trees.

"We were secretly together when I was seventeen," he admitted quietly. "I already had a hard enough time at home with my parents and she said she had it the same. But she was lying. One night she tried to lure me out so that the mage she was *actually* dating could off me."

Easton laughed, but the sound was cold and dead, without a trace of humor in it.

"I only just realized *now*, that the asshole probably wanted my bones. I killed him. And when Iris came at me…" He stopped talking as tears gathered in his eyes. "When she was *gone*… I tried to end it. Drake found me. Stopped me. Saved me."

"Easton," I reached for him again, aching to touch him, my heart split open by his story.

The silence stretched out between us like a lonely desert road.

He stomped down the porch, away from me, but turned back after he was halfway to the treeline. "We live in a shitty reality. Shifters especially. Bodie's had to deal with more than you could ever imagine and has become harder than you could ever imagine. That pixie in there? Leaving her alive leaves him fucking vulnerable. Which leaves his pack vulnerable. And you just spit in his face."

It felt like I'd been slapped. My cheeks stung. My neck heated. And worst of all, my heart felt like it had been shoved into a meat grinder.

"Don't be just like everyone else, Aubry. Don't just stay on the other side of things because you were born there. Open your eyes. The two sides to every story? You can see them, if you just fucking bother to look."

Easton turned and I watched him walk away from

me, into the forest. Part of me wanted to call him back. But no words came. I just stared as he disappeared into the brush, my entire body aching under the weight of his absence.

It was nearly an hour before I went back inside. By then, my soup was cold, ruined. I curled up on the couch and stared at one of the iron curtain covered windows.

Tee walked over to me, stumbling a little on the lumpy cushions. "Ok, spill all the tea," she commanded.

"You didn't hear?" I asked with an eye roll, knowing full well that she had.

"I wanna hear your version."

My head sank into my hands. But a second later I sat up and twisted around. Where was Drake? Why wasn't the asshole silently gloating in some corner, smoke rings rising from his lips?

"Where'd he go?" I asked Tee.

"The sour-faced one? Upstairs," Tee answered.

I listened for the tell-tale sounds of Drake punching stuff but it was silent.

"He took a bowl of that Vietnamese stuff with him," Tee added. "Now, come on… tell me, are you really mates with that shifter?"

I sighed. "I dunno, Tee. There's some sort of a connection, yeah. But .."

"But you like the other one, don't you?" Tee shook her head, her pink hair flopping back and forth.

I gave a hopeless shrug. "I like them both, I guess,

299

which doesn't make sense. I'm so screwed up. I should hate them, shouldn't I, Tee?"

Tee smacked a hand to her forehead. "Oh, girl. This whole thing is all sorts of fucked up."

A mocking grin invaded my lips. "And the award for shittiest parents ever, who've totally messed up their daughter's sense of relationships and romance so she equates it with all kinds of drama, goes to—"

Tee interrupted me with a laugh as loud as a bull-horn. "You can blame a lotta things on your shit parents, Princess, but not this. A mate bond is a different thing altogether. It's inherent magic. It doesn't discriminate."

"What the hell does it really feel like, Tee? How do I know? And if it is real, what the fuck am I supposed to do about it?" I ground out in a furious whisper. "He's a criminal."

My voice broke. Bodie was the opposite of everything I'd ever pictured for my life. The opposite of everything I'd wanted, aspired to be... but there he was. And I was drawn to him like a fucking sailor to the sea, a faerie to a flower. There was this pull between us, like gravity, and as much as I swore I hated him... part of me didn't. Deep down I didn't hate him at all, even though I should have.

Tee climbed up the back of the couch and straddled it, her police uniform a black stain that didn't really look out of place on the beat up old material. "Those are some tough questions. And I've got answers. But I don't know if you're ready to hear them. I think you need to calm down first. So… instead, I'm gonna tell you something else."

"Good news, I hope?" I asked.

"Well, I get to say 'I told you so' but other than that, no. Not good news."

I groaned. "You are not trying to deflect and tell me about scented gunpowder or something are you?"

"That wouldn't just be *good* news, it'd be *great* news. No. Not that. Triton, whom I've always said is a creep, is under investigation by the Mage Council. When your boys caught me, I was tailing him."

She was right. Her news completely sideswiped me, like a mud slide during a car chase. My mind was the car, completely uncontrollable and about to break through the guardrail and tumble down the cliff.

"This information is supposed to help me *calm down*? What the *hell*?" I leaned forward on pins and needles. "The council has clearly gone mad."

Tee gave me a regretful look. "I don't know if they've gone mad as much as *he* has, hon. Trite's the one who's been running around starting fires."

I shoved back, scooting away from her. "No way."

Tee just stared at me with her large eyes, blinking sadly.

Trite's face rushed into my mind. The last time I'd seen him… he'd smelled like smoke.

"But that was *after* the fire," I muttered to myself. "We all smelled like smoke."

"What?" Tee leaned over. "You talking about the Tuesday fire? That's what the news is calling it. That was definitely a mage fire, hon."

I shook my head. "I know, but it couldn't have been him."

But then a memory popped into my mind. Of the night Trite and I had gone out, the night the fucking Mage Council had demoted me, the night I met Easton… Triton had smelled like smoke then, too. I'd thought he'd taken up a stress-induced habit. But maybe I was wrong.

"I've been shadowing him for the past five days," Tee said softly. "It was him."

"Why? Why the hell would Triton do that—"

"He's looking for me." A deep voice interrupted us.

I spun on the couch and turned to find Drake. He stood in the middle of the room, tray in his hands, half-forgotten. My own hands started to shake. The world was completely falling apart.

"Is *nobody* who I think they are?" I bit out in irritation. "What the hell did you do?"

There was a long beat of silence. And at first, I thought Drake was gonna pull his standard asshole move and just walk away from me. But he didn't. He actually looked down at the ground. Almost like he was ashamed. Which couldn't be right. Alpha a-hole never admitted he was wrong. Even when he tried to serve us a can of expired beans the other night and I refused to eat them. He hadn't admitted he was wrong even when

I heard his stomach grumbling later in protest. He'd just disappeared.

Probably into a bathroom for three hours thanks to food poisoning.

"When I was younger, I didn't have as much control," Drake began.

I instantly froze, not wanting to interrupt him. He'd never made small talk before. Ever. Let alone important talks about his past.

He didn't look at either of us as he continued. "I used to have a problem controlling my fire. Well, not controlling it. I didn't want to control it. It was too beautiful. I love how fire just does whatever the hell it wants and says 'fuck you, outta my way or I'll destroy you.'"

Drake abruptly stopped talking. He turned and marched toward the kitchen, setting his tray down on the counter and leaning over it.

I glanced over at Tee with wide eyes.

"Is he the unhinged one?" she whispered.

"He's *The Shadow*," I replied softly.

Her eyes widened. "No!"

I nodded then glanced back over at Drake. "Your story didn't really fill in any of the gaps there, Horntail."

Tee gave me a high-five. "Nice HP reference."

"Thanks."

Drake shook his head and started up the stairs. I turned and glared at his back over the rear couch cushion. "You're just gonna leave it like that? Why the hell is Trite after you?"

Drake stopped on the steps, back still to us. When he spoke, he almost sounded sad. "Because I killed his parents."

What! It felt like Drake had punched me in the mouth. Then it felt like Triton had too. He'd always told me the fire that killed his family before we met was a random accident. Was I fucking Alice? Had I gone through the looking glass?

The dragon shifter stomped the rest of the way up the stairs and disappeared.

I flopped around in my seat for a bit expelling my pent up anxiety and shock. Then I dragged my fingers through my hair, raking it back. "Trite." I felt pity, anger, and disbelief all braided together.

Tee shook her head. "What the council knows and what they tell everyone... I wonder if he found out the truth when he got a minor seat on the council last year?"

I pressed my lips together. "He didn't even tell *me*."

"Might not have been allowed to. They told me I couldn't even tell Aaron about this investigation assignment on penalty of treason," Tee said.

My eyes widened. "Then why the hell are you telling me?"

"I'm a prisoner. In a near-death situation. *Duh.* What better time than now to break all the rules?"

"They're not gonna kill you, Tee."

She gave me a skeptical look. "Mark my words, that scaly one's gonna try."

I glanced back at the stairwell, even though I knew Drake wasn't there. Would he try? I couldn't be certain. The past few days, I'd loosened up around the asshole. He was still one of the most intolerable people on the planet. But evil?

Ugh. I was letting my stupid mate bond with the others interfere. It made me forget how many fucking "jobs" this asshole had pulled off. How many people on my force had been taken out on his orders? Jake, Kimberlee, Mason. My jaw clenched. Maybe Drake *was* that bad. I mean, he'd killed Trite's parents. He seemed so remorseful, I assumed it'd been an accident, but dead was dead. It didn't matter if the end result was the same, did it? My jaw clenched.

Tee studied my eyes. "And you're back in business. Aubry the Asshole has officially returned."

"Excuse me?"

"That's what we call you at work behind your back."

"You don't defend me?"

"Oh, sure, yeah. I'm gonna go defend the boss to my co-workers. Great way to build morale. Come on. Hating the boss is a universal bonding mechanism."

I shook a finger at her. "When we get back to the office—"

She raised a brow. "You don't really delude yourself into thinking you're getting out of here, do you?"

"*What?*" It was like she'd punched the air out of my lungs. "Why would you say that?"

"You are mates with a criminal. One who's so fucking good he's invisible. And you're hot-to-trot for his best friend too."

"But that's all just insanity, right? Like, it's not real." I didn't address the fact that I didn't deny her accusation. "Prisoners hallucinate and shit. Get attached to their captors."

"You feel it when he leaves the room, right?" Tee asked.

My heart and face fell at once. "Yeah."

Tee shook her head, her smile sympathetic in a way that made me realize the worst. *It was true.* Whether I wanted it or not, Bodie and I had a mate bond.

Tee tried to soften the blow of that gut wrenching realization a bit by grabbing my hand and saying, "When I met Aaron, he was dating my cousin. But the pull we felt was intense. And I kissed him—against my better judgement—and everything in our lives just... flipped. Do you know how that made me feel? I was the *bad guy*, Aubs. *Me.* I was the asshole who broke a happy couple apart."

She sighed and rubbed a nervous hand across the back of her neck.

"It took years to reconcile myself to that," she continued. "But circumstances change. Time changes things. People change. Who's the good guy and who's the bad guy, who's the boss and who's the bitch—that

306

can all flip on a dime. Days are good, bad, ugly, beautiful, brutal, and everything in between. But mate bonds..."

She shook her head, and I felt a weight sink down to the pit of my stomach, pulling me under the waves of my own misery.

"Mate bonds are *forever*."

AUBRY

O<small>UTSIDE, GRAVEL CRUNCHED, AND AN ENGINE</small>
sputtered as *yet another* vehicle pulled into the drive.
What the fuck was this, a pump and dump? Were we
selling gas, soda, and snacks now? I mean, Jesus…

The car door shut, and footsteps sounded across the
pebbles. Slow and shuffling. Not anyone who was in a
hurry, so not likely a bad guy—or a good guy,
depending which side of the war you were on. The
floorboards creaked as the newcomer strode across the
porch and turned the doorknob.

"Sorry, I'm late," a familiar voice said just before
entering the cabin. "I needed to restock my supplies.
The fire from the other night really depleted my stash,
and after spelling the pixie…"

I rolled my eyes. *Larry*. Of course. *The Wizard of
Waverly Place* was back for another episode.

"No worries, Lar," Easton said from out in the kitchen. The bear shifter had returned from his little jaunt in the woods and was now stirring something in a pot that smelled mouth-wateringly delicious. The scents of tomato and red pepper wafted into the living room, along with the rich smell of cheese and bread. Italian food, if I had to guess, not Vietnamese, but I no longer gave any fucks. I was just starved for something that wasn't cold or scraped from a can.

Easton hadn't spoken a single word to me since he got back, and while I hated it, I hadn't allowed myself to speak to him, either. If this was some sort of cold, silent war we had going on, then damn it, I was going to win. It didn't matter how much I may have... *liked* him. My pride was the only thing I had left, and I was determined to hold on to it.

Bodie hadn't come back yet. I ignored the unsettled feeling that bubbled in my stomach at that thought— probably just a shitty consequence of Drake's horrid cooking. I grinned at my own pun.

And Drake was still upstairs, probably beating the hell out of a punching bag with my face taped to it. I still couldn't believe he'd admitted to killing Trite's parents. Talk about a small, fucked up world I lived in. The supernatural community was a fucking B-list soap opera.

My captor-slash-mate's alpha killed my best friend's parents, and my bestie wants revenge so now my mate and the other shifter I have a crush on are hunting down my friends. What a shit storyline. How the hell could this end in any way but tragedy? Soap operas pulled it off with random surprise babies that made everybody go goo-goo.

Somehow, I didn't think a surprise pregnancy would end the Drake-Trite feud.

I glanced over at Tee, who'd curled up at the far end of the sofa and fallen asleep. Her words about mates floated around in my head, like decaying leaves drifting to the ground. If Aaron was on his way to rescue her right now, would I be able to leave with them? Or was I stuck here? Not just physically, but spiritually and emotionally stuck?

"Whatcha cooking?" Larry asked Easton, taking a deep breath as he moseyed closer to the stove.

"Parmesan chicken penne with fire-roasted tomato," Easton replied with a grin. "I had to have something other than chips and ninety-nine cent burgers. That shit was getting old."

"Well, it smells delicious," Larry told him before he wandered into the living room.

"You staying for dinner, then?" Easton called out over his shoulder. Of course, he had an easy grin for the mage. Not for me though. Grumpy bear.

The mage's typically dull eyes lit up as he sat down across from me. "Yes, please, that'd be wonderful." Then he brought his attention back to me. "Evening, Miss Summerset. It's that time again."

I rolled my eyes. "Isn't it always?"

He tipped his head in Tee's direction. "Is your friend doing okay?"

I nodded. "Yeah, I think she's just tired. It's been a long…"

What? *Day*? Few weeks? I didn't even know.

"It's been a long *life*," Larry supplied wearily with a sad half smile. "I'm just going to get this over with so that we can eat in peace, okay?"

"Sounds good," I muttered.

With a sigh, I glanced back over at Easton. His upper body flexed as he sprinkled something into the pot, muscles rippling beneath the soft beige shirt which he'd rolled up to his elbows. His blond hair was combed to the front with a breezy wave at the top, making him look as sexy and cool as a SoCal surfer. And his light blue jeans hugged his ass and thighs in all the right places before draping down over a pair of tan work boots.

He squatted down to check on the loaf of bread in the oven, and I bit my lip as I imagined him mostly naked, wearing only a tiny white apron. In my vision, he stood up and turned around, grinning at me before gesturing to the kitchen table.

"Climb up here, baby, and spread those legs. I'm ready to devour you."

Pain flared in my chest and I blinked, crashing back to reality as Larry's magic coursed through my system. His eyes were shut, and he was muttering intently, a bunch of pig Latin mumbo jumbo that reminded me of ancient priests and demon slayers.

How the fuck had this become my life? Living in the woods, lusting over Goldilocks, falling for the big bad wolf, being held by a dragon... I was living a fairy tale gone wrong.

The front door rattled again, and suddenly Bodie strode into the room, glistening with sweat, his shirt plastered to his torso. My eyes locked onto him and wouldn't leave.

"Have a good run?" Easton asked him without glancing over.

Larry opened a single eyelid to assess the state of the room, then immediately shut it, never missing a beat of his incantation. I grit my teeth as the pain intensified, grateful that we were almost finished with this shit.

Bodie grabbed a bottle of water from the fridge and chugged the entire thing, while rivulets of sweat and condensation slipped down his neck and soaked into his shirt. When he was finished, he chucked the bottle in the trash and nodded. "Yeah, the run was good. Can I talk to you for a minute?"

I hoped he'd turned and started talking to me, but he was still focused on Easton.

The burly bear shifter took a moment to turn off the stove and pull the bread from the oven—damn, the scent was mouthwatering. Then he turned and followed Bodie toward the door.

My traitor eyes trailed over both of them. Bodie's running shorts left little to the imagination. But even Easton's jeans couldn't hide his package.

This one's dick was too big. And this one's dick was even bigger. But they both felt just *right.*

The image of me moaning, hands chained above my head and getting double teamed by the two of them, filled my mind and sent a wave of heat crashing through my core and settling low between my legs.

Fuck, that would hurt so good.

Even the captive fantasy aroused me in all the right ways.

Dino dildo, where are you? My lady bits cried mournfully.

There's a dragon *dildo upstairs*, my mind bit back.

I shook my head to try and clear the image of Drake that'd been burned into my pupils the other night. Dripping wet and shirtless, a splash of water slithering down his demon trail to hell.

Nope, no way was I going to pound-town with a dragon… or a dragon dildo. I tried to scrub my brain clean of that thought. But I didn't have enough mental bleach to do the job.

Bodie and Easton came back inside a few minutes later, just as Larry finished up his spell. What the fuck had they been talking about? I let suspicion take over and shoved horniness aside.

"I'm gonna grab a quick shower," Bodie announced. "You guys go ahead and start eating without me."

I turned on the couch and nudged Tee but she barely even stirred.

"Tee," I whispered, not wanting to startle her. Last time I'd done that, I'd ended up with abrasions on my freaking eyeballs. I didn't really wanna go through that again. "*Tee.*"

She groaned and snuggled into a tighter little ball.

I sighed. "Tallulah, it's time to eat."

"Go away," she mumbled with a furrowed brow. "There aren't enough rakes for all the unicorns."

I raised a brow. What the ever-loving fuck was she dreaming about?

"Come on, Tee," I tried once more, gently prodding her shoulder.

"Get a bucket," she muttered, rolling onto her other side and falling fast asleep again.

I grinned and shook my head. *Whatever.* I'd save her a plate.

Easton, Larry, and I ate in silence at the small, janky dining table next to the couch until Bodie and Drake came downstairs. They murmured between themselves, but I didn't even care; my mouth was too busy orgasming over every delicious flavor that touched my tongue.

Easton was a fucking god of cooking, and we were nothing more than mortals scattered amongst the silverware in his kitchen. Damn it. His amazing skills made the war-of-silence we had going even harder to focus on. I wanted to compliment him. But I didn't.

Drake took his plate and jogged back upstairs without even a thank you. The self-isolating dick. But Bodie stayed. When he sat, he shared a knowing look with Easton who immediately wiped his mouth and stood.

"Mind if I borrow your car for a couple hours, Lar?"

"Sure," the old mage replied, taking the hint and standing, too. "Let me just grab my airpods."

I gripped the edge of the table tightly and broke the silent feud. "Why do you need Larry's car? You have one." A sinking pit grew in my stomach. The guys did have a car. But I knew them by now. Drake's paranoia had rubbed off a bit on all of them. Easton would want a new car if he was going somewhere they'd gone before. Like wherever they'd picked up Tee. "Where are you going?"

Easton swallowed hard and tried not to look at me, but his baby blue eyes drifted over anyway. "Unfinished business."

My mouth went dry. He was referring to Triton, he had to be. "Please don't kill him," I begged softly.

Easton's throat bobbed once more. "I won't. But I can't guarantee that no one else will." With that, he strode through the doorway leaving Larry to trail clumsily behind him.

Fuck. I lost my appetite and shoved my plate away. *He promised he wouldn't kill Trite,* I told myself.

The engine turned over in the background, gurgling

to life like a smoker choking. Gears grinded and brakes squeaked. The sounds grew fainter and fainter, and before I knew it, Bodie and I were alone at the table.

He finished and turned towards me. "You wanna take a walk?"

I crossed my arms. "Can't. Chained to a couch, remember?"

Bodie rolled his yellow-green eyes as a grin tugged at his lips. "It's almost like I have a key to those chains, isn't it?"

That made me laugh out loud. "Oh, so you want to take me for a walk? Like I'm some fucking German Shepherd on a leash?"

"No," he replied without missing a beat. "If anything, you'd be a poodle, or maybe a spaniel. Something uptight and prissy."

I scoffed, immediately drawn in by his insult. "I am *not* uptight."

"Yeah, you are." He scooted back from the table and crossed his ankle over his knee. His fingers threaded behind his head and he smirked. "You probably don't even want to walk in the woods. I'll bet you're scared of spiders, of mud... and the big bad wolf."

Oh my cross-dressing Jesus, this man. If my eyes rolled any harder, they'd be knocking down bowling pins. "I am definitely not afraid of any wolves. Especially ones who think they're big and bad, and really, they're just all talk."

Bodie was *not* all talk, but I couldn't keep from poking the beast with a stick anyway. It gave me a sick sense of satisfaction to irritate him. Kinda like playing Russian roulette, it was thrilling in a death-defying sort of way. It brought out his wolf a little, which was kind of like a dom. And that made me hot as fuck.

He stood and took a couple long strides into the living room, unlocking my chain from the couch. Then he wrapped it around his hand a few times and slowly stepped toward me like he was reeling himself in.

"You and I," he said darkly, making my pussy swoon, "have shit we need to discuss."

I swallowed hard and gasped for air. Had someone turned off the fucking oxygen in the room? Jacked up the heat? Slipped me some fucking crack in my noodles?

My heart hammered as my body practically screamed for him. I wanted another taste of those delicious fingers, that supple tongue, and his rock-hard cock.

Bodie stopped a few feet from me and closed his eyes, inhaling deeply before biting his bottom lip. "I can smell your arousal from over here, little Butterfly. Come and take a walk with me. We can talk... and then I can rail you until you're screaming my name at the moon."

I took a deep, shuddering breath and clenched my trembling fingers into a fist. He didn't need to see how powerfully he affected me—he could already *smell* it.

There was no sense in denying what he'd said, but I could at least do my best to ignore it.

"We *do* need to talk," I agreed. "I have some shit I need to get off my chest."

"Like your bra?" he teased as he tugged on my chain, leading me out the door and into the night.

I waited until Larry passed us, earbuds in already, fuzzy head bobbing side to side to his music. When the mage had entered the cabin and shut the door, I turned back to my wolf.

"No, you leg-humping bulldog!" I hissed in reply to his question. "Like how sorry I am."

Bodie paused, the grin on his face momentarily slipping when he looked back at me. "Sorry?"

I caught up to him and he fell into step beside me, my chain rattling softly in his grasp.

"I owe you an apology, Bodie." God, this was painful for my ego. My tongue tried to twist, and my lips twitched to purse, but I fought the urge to clam up. "I've been fighting this mate bond thing tooth and nail, and I've been pushing you away at every turn. I honestly didn't believe it was real at first, and then, once I did, I just wanted to pretend it was still fake. It was... easier that way."

He nodded, staring straight ahead as we slipped between the trees. Tiny twigs snapped beneath our feet, muffled slightly by the soft moss and dewy leaves covering the forest floor like a living carpet. He wasn't looking at me. I couldn't read his expression so I wasn't sure how he was taking all of this. Nerves crept over me.

"And I..." my voice broke, and for a moment, I didn't think I had the courage to say what needed to be said.

Come on, Aubry. Time to face the facts. Being a badass isn't only about battening down and buckling up. It's also about being vulnerable and taking risks. Telling the truth when it's easier to lie. Admitting your feelings when it's easier to light them on fire and watch them burn...

I swallowed hard and tried again. "I never meant to hurt you. When I left with Trite... it wasn't because I wanted to leave YOU and US behind. It wasn't because I cared about him in any way other than friendship. I just... I can't be your prisoner forever. How are we supposed to feel something real in a completely fucked up situation? How am I supposed to fall for you with my hands bound in iron and my true self stemmed with mage magic?"

Bodie sighed and stopped walking. "Did you ever ride a wolf?"

I blinked, completely blindsided by his abrupt subject change. "First of all, fucker, I was in the middle of pouring my heart out to you. And second, I feel like this is some perverted innuendo-slash-pickup-line that is going to fall *so* flat and backfire *so* hard."

He chuckled, running a hand through his feathery brown locks. "It's really not. I meant that in the most literal way possible. I want us to continue talking, but there is someplace I wanted to take you to talk. So I want to shift, and have you ride me, so we get there faster."

"Oh." I didn't really know what else to say. "No, I've never ridden a wolf."

His grin was a mile freaking wide. "Alright, so after I shift, just straddle my back like you'd do a bicycle."

"And hold your ears like handlebars?" I crossed my arms and smirked.

"You pull my ears, I'mma fuck you up."

He was teasing—I thought. But if he wasn't... My pussy clenched tight, imagining all the glorious ways Bodie might manhandle me while he 'fucked me up.' Would he spank me? Deny me orgasms? Getting in an actual fight with him would also be epic. I imagined us sparring on the mats, panting and sweating. One wrong move and a fist to the face could be replaced with *lips* to the face. And then before I knew it, I'd be getting pounded in the most delicious way possible.

"Not the ears," he continued sternly. "You grab a big fistful of fur and hold on tight, okay? Think you can manage?"

I glared at him, pursing my lips and drawing his heated gaze. "I can handle it."

"Good."

He shifted quickly, and his beast roared into place as his skin stretched and his bones snapped and popped. Jet black fur erupted along every inch of his body as his clothes disappeared and he dropped onto all fours. His wolf was huge, way bigger than I imagined, as big as a horse.

He stared at me intently, intimidating the hell out of me, as he bent down and took my chain in his powerful jowls. Then he lowered onto his belly and waited for me to clamber up.

I hesitated for a moment, gently raking my fingers through his ebony coat before squeezing tight and hopping on when he knelt. "So help me god, if you drop me, we are *not* continuing this conversation."

His wolf let out a low growl, which somehow emboldened me.

"And if you whack me on a branch or some shit, you can totally forget all the words I've said so far. Got it?"

He shook his fur like I was some big, wet storm cloud raining on his parade.

I was about to reply to his cocky, non-verbal comment, when he lurched into a run. *Shit!* I tightened my grip on his fur and fought the urge to squeeze my eyes shut. I wanted to see the whole world as it blurred past. Wind rushed at my face and pulled tears from my eyes. The sounds of crickets and cicadas blended with the images of glowing fireflies and the silhouettes of scurrying forest animals. My breath synced with Bodie's as our bodies aligned rhythmically on our race through the forest.

Before I knew it, we broke from the trees, leaving

the spongy dirt behind and climbing out onto a large boulder. Bodie dipped his head and I slid off right at the edge of the giant rock, staring down about twenty feet or so into a tiny pool. A waterfall cascaded on our left and all around the pool a ring of boulders separated it from the forest. The moon's reflection wavered in the water. It was beautiful.

Bodie shifted back into human form as I sat there dangling my legs over the edge.

"You almost dropped me off a cliff," I scolded, as he sat down next to me. I wasn't quite ready to admit how much I liked that he'd picked out a romantic spot for us. I wondered if he'd seen it earlier, when I'd hurt him. That thought made my heart clench a little. That he could be mad at me and see a place like this and still want to share it with me.

Bodie chuckled as he pulled his sneakers and socks off and set them aside. "Yeah, but I didn't drop you. So all your words still count, and we get to continue our conversation."

I grinned and stared up at the stars. It was so different from the smoggy city lights. Peaceful and pure. Real.

"I don't know..." I teased.

He scooted closer to me until our thighs brushed. "I believe you were saying, 'I'm falling for you so hard, Bodie, and I'm sorry for leaving with that dickbag mage who smells like an old lady's underwear drawer.'"

I laughed out loud. "Why the hell do you know what that smells like?"

"Unlucky guess."

"Doubtful. Admit it. You have a granny fetish."

He laughed and grabbed my hand. "Caught me."

We sat together for a second in comfortable companionship. Then I nudged him with my shoulder as I kicked my feet, looking down at the rippling water below. "I really am sorry for hurting you when I left with Trite." I glanced at him, but the smile was once more missing from his handsome face. "I'd thank you for not killing him, but I have a feeling that's exactly what Easton is trying to do right now—on *your* orders."

His eyes narrowed slightly and his lips puckered just a touch, but it was enough for me to notice he was irritated. So, I was probably right.

I sighed and pushed myself to keep talking. We could stop and argue about Triton now, but I'd rather get all the shit off my chest first. Pile it all on the ground between us like a bag of dirty laundry, then sort through the mess after.

"And I'm sorry about Easton."

"What about him?" he asked. He never glanced my way, but I could tell he was listening intently, waiting with bated breath.

I swallowed hard, studying the dark water rather than his face, trying to buy some time while I thought up a response that made sense. What about Easton? What drew me to him? What broke my heart when I saw him hurting? We hadn't connected on some undeniable spiritual level like Bodie and I had, but on an emotional level? I related to the bear shifter. I felt for him and cared about him. He'd made me see things differently.

"I'm sorry for... making you jealous of your pack mate."

He smirked, leaning back on his palms as he gazed into woods beyond the pool. "Look, I... I know Easton saw you first. And I know I kinda just rode in balls-blazing, helicoptering our mate bond around like an unsolicited dick pic. I was so ready to sweep you off your feet, I hadn't even bothered to consider if you two had caught feelings. I know now. Goldilocks has it bad for you. And... I know you have some sort of a crush on him in return, so..." He bit his lip and shook his head. "So, I'm sorry, too."

My brows furrowed as I turned to look at him. What was he apologizing for? For nature doing its thing? I knew he couldn't control the mate bond any more than I could.

He turned toward me, and our eyes locked as if our souls had reached out to one another through our pupils. "I'm sorry because... no matter how much you *like* him, I can guarantee you that I *love* you even more. And no matter how much you *want* him, I will never fucking let you go."

He leaned closer and took my face in his warm

palm, caressing my skin more delicately than I thought he knew how.

"You're *mine*, Butterfly."

His possessiveness sent a shiver through me that made my heart kneel and my nipples pebble.

Bodie's smile was full of warmth and promise. "I will spend the rest of my life making sure you're the happiest woman in the world, but I will not share *my mate*."

God, he'd gone straight for the jugular. Breaking my heart just as fast as he'd wooed it. I loved the way his words made me feel—warm and fuzzy, hot and ready. But I hated the thought of hurting Easton. Or more precisely, the thought of not *having* Easton. This wouldn't just hurt him, it would hurt *me* too.

"Easton…" Bodie continued, gliding his thumb across my bottom lip, "he's like a brother to me. I'd give my life for that man. Take a bullet for him. Give up a kidney for him. Even share my gummy bears with him, the damned bottomless pit."

I giggled, accidentally leaning my cheek into Bodie's hand as my eyes started to water.

He continued, "Wolves are born into packs. We're used to sharing. I have eight damn brothers and sisters for god's sake. I couldn't even get a glass of milk to myself growing up. There's only one thing in life that wolves don't have to fucking share. Our mates. I won't share *you*."

I nodded, pulling my face away to stare down at the

rock beneath me. Damn it. Why did I feel elated and distraught? As much as Tee might have said I couldn't blame my parents, there was something fucking wrong with me if I couldn't just be happy with my mate's possessive declaration. It was twisted and unhealthy that a little piece of me ached at how Bodie cut Easton out of the equation.

"You admitted our bond was real," he said softly. "Are you willing to give it a real chance?"

I glanced up at him, my eyes searching for... something. Anything I could cling to to keep from going under in the sea of my fucked up emotions. I took a deep breath, and calmness slowly leaked into me as I gazed into his green-gold stare.

I am not defined by my goddamned parents. Their dysfunctional relationship does not have any effect on me. I will not fuck up my one true chance at happiness because of them—the assholes who clearly never gave a shit about me, anyway. Whatever I was feeling for Easton, it came from their shitty self-sabotaging ways. I needed to bury those feelings and weep at their grave site, then walk away without looking back.

Finally, I nodded in response to Bodie's question.

His eyes twinkled in the moonlight, lighting up with a happiness that his stoic features couldn't entirely contain.

"Are you willing to take a leap of faith?" he asked, standing and offering me his broad hand.

His palm was warm and soft and his fingers zapped

energy into my skin like lightning, heating my blood until I wanted to slide more of my flesh across his.

I stood and glanced down at the small pool of water below us. My lips tugged at the corners. "You're not talking about a literal leap of faith are you?"

He grinned and pulled off his shirt. Holy mother of sweet baby unicorns, I would never get tired of that view. His skin was a dark tan, but the moon illuminated the rise and fall of his muscles with delicious contrast. My fingers ached to rove up and down his chest and abs, but I held myself back, waiting to see what he would say.

He unbuttoned his jeans and dragged them down his legs before tossing them onto the pile with his shirt. "What do you think?"

I bit my lip and squeezed the hem of my tank top. An adrenaline rush and a challenge? Hell yes. If this crazy wolf wanted me to jump twenty feet into a tiny-ass pool, then damn it, I would. I'd fucking go first.

I slid my shirt up over my head, putting my heavy breasts and hardened nipples on full display. "That's right, asshole. No bra. Wonder who made damn sure that didn't happen?"

He grinned devilishly, clearly pleased with himself and his moronic wet dreams.

I slid my pants and undies off, but it left that insidious iron chain directly touching my ankle. Hissing, I did my best to grit my teeth and bare it. I wasn't a fucking pussy. I could handle a little burn if it meant getting my rocks off.

But to my surprise, Bodie bent down and unlocked the cuff around my ankle, adding the chain to my pile of clothes. "Don't make me regret this, Buttercup. Remember, if you run, I will catch you. And I love the chase."

I grinned while he distractedly admired my body with his heated gaze.

Now or never.

I launched into a short sprint and leapt from the edge.

Wind tangled through my long silver hair as the sensation of weightlessness hit me. My pulse quickened. I tucked my wings so I'd fall fast and straight. The pool rose up to meet me and I'd barely taken a deep breath before I crashed through its inky black surface. My body went into instant shock. What the hell? Was this pond fed directly from the Arctic?

As my brain drifted out of shock and back into reality, I realized I needed to swim. Kicking my feet, and pulling with my arms, I broke through the surface just as Bodie crashed through it a few feet away.

Gasping, I smoothed my hair back and rubbed the water out of my eyes as he resurfaced with a wild and sexy grin on his face. God, he was entrancing when he smiled. I couldn't look away. All I could do was tread water and stare as he glided closer to me.

"You're not running," he said, surprise crossing his face for just a moment. "You took the leap."

I rolled my eyes, my chin bobbing beneath the water for a moment before rising back up. "Nice assessment, Captain Obvious. I can see why you're the best of the best. You literally asked me to jump."

He bit his lip and his eyes darkened at my taunt. I tried to glide away backwards, but his hands gripped my hips and held me firmly.

"If we're gonna do this," he said, staring down at my lips as his hands squeezed my ass, pulling me right up against him until my legs wrapped around his waist, "then we're going to set some ground rules."

Mmm. Rules. That made me so fucking excited, when a normal girl might've been freaking out.

"First of all, let's address this sassy mouth of yours." Bodie leaned in and bit my bottom lip, tugging on it with his teeth before sucking and stroking it with his tongue. "I like your fiery attitude, it makes for some intense foreplay. But I don't ever want to hear you putting me down or questioning my skills in front of anyone else. Understand? Teasing me is one thing, insulting is another—one I won't tolerate."

I couldn't help myself, I slipped into submissive mode and lowered my gaze as I nodded. I wasn't ashamed or anything, though, just extremely turned on. Which he probably knew, considering my nipples were pressed into his chest like marbles.

"If you want something acceptable to do with that

sassy mouth," he continued with a grin, "I have a cock with your name—and your name *only*—on it."

I glanced up, briefly meeting his hooded gaze before looking back down at where our skin pressed firmly together. A big part of me wanted to drop to my knees and suck him off like he'd just suggested, but I'd probably freaking drown, so that was a no-go for now. The other part of me wanted to roll my hips until he was positioned just right, then allow him to make good on his 'screaming at the moon' promise from earlier.

"Second of all," he said, and I realized he was slowly walking us toward the smooth boulders along the shore. "No more cozying up to Easton. I know he's attractive—we all are."

Conceited much? I fought hard not to smirk and roll my eyes.

"I know he's cuddly," Bodie continued, sinking his fingers into my hips, "he's like one of those giant, over-sized teddy bears, for fuck's sake. But I can't be worried about my mate cheating on me with my brother. Because that's basically what he and Drake are to me, *brothers*."

I nodded once more, but that didn't seem to be good enough this time. Bodie took my chin and lifted my face, staring deep into my eyes. Could he see the sadness there? The trepidation at having to give Easton up? The fear that I might not truly be able to commit because of how fucked in the head and heart I was?

"I want to hear you say it, Butterfly," he murmured,

reaching down to roll one of my nipples between his thumb and forefinger. "Tell me I can trust you. Tell me you'll be loyal to me and only me. Tell me Easton isn't an issue."

Pleasure rocketed through me at his touch, sending an explosion of heat straight to my core. My lips parted and my eyes fluttered shut as his clever fingers short-circuited my brain. His hand drifted lower, skimming my stomach before gliding past my pelvic bone and dipping into my heat.

"You want me to keep going?" he asked seductively as he stroked me.

Fuck yes, I did.

He seemed to hear my non-response loud and clear. "Then tell me what I want to hear."

He lifted me up sat me down on a boulder behind me, leaving my exposed sex just inches from his face. Heat rushed everywhere, lighting my entire body up with need and anticipation.

"I..." I could barely fucking think straight as his fingers delved even deeper inside of me. "I can't help what I feel, but—" He suddenly stopped moving, watching me with a dark glower that told me I needed to finish that sentence *very* carefully. "But, I can at least promise to put some distance between us. I won't actively seek him out. If he's the only one in the room, I'll leave. I won't let us be alone together."

Bodie glared at me for a moment longer as he considered my words. Then slowly, his fingers began to move, stroking until he found my g-spot, making me moan. I took that as a yes, that I'd told him what he wanted to hear. Thank fuck. I could hardly wait for him to take me.

He strode closer, water raining down his pecs as he nestled between my thighs. "This pussy, is mine now." He bent down and gave it a long hot lick from bottom to top, pausing briefly to flick my clit before continuing.

"Any man who's been here before me is officially gone. I'm going to eat you so good it erases any signs of them ever being down here, any memory of them ever touching you."

He licked me again, his tongue slipping between my folds and dragging so maddeningly slowly up to my clit that I thought I might burst.

"There will never be another man but me down here ever again," he said. I wasn't sure if it was a threat or a promise, but I could feel the heat in his words. "And if, for some godforsaken reason there ever is, they'll be officially gone, too. Because I'll fucking kill them. Understand?"

Goddamn it, why were homicidal maniacs so fucking hot? I shouldn't be turned on at the prospect of him murdering someone over me, and yet...

Yep. I really am fucked in the head. There's no denying it at this point. Doms had threatened me during scenes before, with dark, delicious things. And at the time, those had made me hot. But knowing Bodie actually meant it, knowing he would take someone out… that was beyond hot. It made me molten.

Bodie suddenly bit my inner thigh, making me yelp. "I said, do you understand?"

Mmm. More delicious desire coursed through me as his dominant side took over. "Yes, sir."

His lips twitched slightly as he looked up at me. "I know you're a sub. But mate bonds are different. They're deeper than sex games. I don't mind playing that way sometimes, but when you're coming hard with my fingers, head, or cock between your legs, I want you to scream my name. None of this *sir* shit. Got it?"

I nodded. "Yes." I had to swallow the 'sir' down. But even doing that felt good. Because I was submitting to what he wanted, whether he knew it or not. That thought brought on a grin. And I slipped just the tiniest bit into sub space.

His lips spread into a satisfied smile. "That's good, little Butterfly. Now let's see how my name sounds when I make you come."

He lurched forward, digging into me like a starved man eating his first ever dessert.

This is the real *reason they call it 'eating out,'* I thought with an uncontrollable moan. Bodie seriously looked like he was trying to devour me, his mouth swallowing up my clit and lighting my girly bits on fucking fire.

"Pull my hair," he said, briefly coming up for air. "Put my face exactly where you want it, baby."

I wasn't used to being in control, but since it was technically a command, I did as he asked, positioning him just right to set off a soul-shattering orgasm. Honestly, it was more like a possession and exorcism in one. My body wasn't my own as it bucked and throbbed under his hot tongue. His lips sucked and his thumbs stroked my thighs and my eyes rolled back. My hands acted of their own accord as they shoved his face harder into me. My voice sounded like some kind of demonic succubus as my head tipped back and I shouted his name at the sky.

God, Bodie was right. He'd completely wiped any of my previous oral orgasms straight from memory. Not a single one of them had been more than a ripple compared to this wave of ecstasy.

As I came back down from my high, Bodie smirked. "Yeah, I like the sound of my name like that. I think I might have to hear it again with my cock buried deep inside of you."

He lifted himself out of the water and onto the boulder beside me, water rushing down his hardened body in greedy streams that vied to touch every inch of him.

"But first," Bodie said, stroking his cock slowly, "I want you on your knees."

I immediately pushed off my ass and onto my knees as ordered.

His cock jumped as I complied. He could say what-ever he wanted about mate bonds being deeper, but he totally had a dom streak in him, whether he knew it or not. And, as a sub, I enjoyed pleasing him. So this was a win-win, really.

I made a show of licking my lips, wetting them as seductively as I could before taking the head of his dick in my mouth. The wolf was huge. Relaxing my jaw, I opened wider, drawing him in deeper until I damn near started to gag.

"Fuck, yes," he groaned as I bobbed my head up and down his shaft, the earthy, rosemary-laden taste of his precum driving me forward with lust.

I was just finding a rhythm he seemed to like, when he grabbed my face and pulled away from my lips.

"Bend over."

Biting my lip, I quickly did as he said, moving around on the uneven surface of the rock until I found a comfortable position. I was so ready for him it was almost painful. Even though he'd already given me one orgasm, my body was greedy for another.

But instead of thrusting into me, Bodie paused to stroke my wings, driving me wild. My eyes had just drifted closed when his hand came down hard on my ass. The sting jerked me back into the present moment and caused even more desire to flood my aching cunt. Then he stroked my wings once more, lulling me into a false sense of pleasure before bringing the pain again.

If my ass was as red as it was hot, then I'd bet there was a ruby red hand print burning there. You could probably pull a fingerprint off of it. I shuddered as those thoughts mixed with the sting of my flesh and the pleasure of his fingers once more gliding up and down my wing. This was the blissful fucking torture I loved and missed so much. This was the punishment my body needed in order to fully let go.

"Are you sure you're not a dom?" I whispered. But it wasn't loud enough for him to hear. Or, if he did hear, he didn't respond.

Bodie positioned himself at my entrance. I felt the hot tip of his dick slide over my lips once, eliciting a full body shiver right before he rammed in hard, jabbing his dick all the way to my cervix. The painful punishment stole my breath. I fucking needed more of it.

But instead, he pulled almost completely out and stroked my wing again, bringing me right to the brink of an orgasm before slamming into me once more.

"You're wet as fuck, Butterfly," he taunted me. "You're quivering all over." He squeezed my stinging ass cheek with one hand while stroking my wing with the other. "If you want to come, I wanna hear you say you're my mate again."

He thrust into me, rubbing my wing between his thumb and forefinger, beautifully mixing the pleasure with the pain. Fuck, I wasn't going to have time to say anything. I was going to come in seconds.

As if he instinctively knew that, he pulled out, leaving me high and dry, a little frustrated, and a lot turned on.

"Fuck me, Bodie," I whimpered, willing him to push back inside and drag me over the edge.

His hand came down hard on my ass. "You were about to come without saying it."

I moaned as more heat pooled between my legs. "Please, Bodie," I gasped, swimming in a haze of lust. "Please fuck me. You're my mate. My only mate."

With a growl, he quickly flipped me over until I was gazing up at his dark silhouette in front of a big, full moon. "Say my name."

"Bodie," I whispered.

He thrust into me and kept pumping this time. "Say it again."

"Bodie."

He rocked into me harder and faster until I could barely breathe, until I was so close to coming my head started to spin.

"Say it louder."

"Bodie... " I moaned with a bit more force. It was a warning of sorts, letting him know how close I was to coming undone.

"Louder, baby."

"Bodie!" I cried, cresting that delicious peak and tumbling down the other side hard. "Oh, fuck, yes! Bodie, yes!"

Again, I writhed and twisted as if he were wringing the very soul from my body with his cock. My back arched and I came up off the rock, clawing at the hard stone beneath my fingers. Bodie reached down and wrapped a muscular arm around my waist, holding my hips flush against his own as he pushed deeper and deeper inside of me. Sweat glistened on his intense face, his eyes glowing a brighter and brighter gold as his pleasure built and built.

He suddenly stood, wrapping both arms around my waist and lifting us up. The breath flew out of me and my legs wrapped tighter around his waist so that I wouldn't fall. Bodie chuckled. One hand curled around my ass, holding me up and digging into my crack, while the other hand reached up and rubbed that erogenous spot on my wing.

"Come for me one more time, baby. I'm almost there."

He didn't have to tell me twice. I clenched all around him as another orgasm wrecked me, tearing me apart before gloriously piecing me back together. His eyes flashed gold and suddenly he pumped fast, slamming me up and down on him where he stood. Then he was growling—roaring—his pleasure echoing off the silent tree trunks before being muffled by the cascading falls.

Fuck. *Yes.* I knew his eyes would glow when he came.

When we were finally finished, panting as we held each other tight, I couldn't help but stare into the eyes of... *my mate.* A man I was falling in love with. *My captor.*

I glanced up at the top of the waterfall where we'd stripped and discarded my chains.

As good as this was, as perfect as it felt, would I still stick around if those chains weren't going back on?

If I had my freedom and my freewill, would I choose Bodie and the shifters, or would I run away and never look back?

DRAKE

MY BEST FRIENDS WERE TOO FUCKING DISTRACTED TO listen to reason, which meant, if we were gonna defeat the mages, I was gonna have to do it alone. And I needed to do it fast. I had a council member hunting me down. With the amount of power and resources behind him, I was sure it was only a matter of time before he found me. My clock was ticking. I needed to make the most of whatever time I had left. I needed to get a mage jewel. *Now.*

I opened the upstairs bedroom window of the cabin and climbed out onto the ledge. The old wood creaked under my weight. I leaned out as far as I could before I shifted, trying to avoid punching any holes through the walls. Then I flapped my wings and took off into the night sky, leaving Bodie, Larry, and the pixie behind.

And Aubry.

The snooty little princess had my guys wrapped up

in knots. The only good thing I could say about the situation was that it appeared she hadn't done it on purpose; so she hadn't quite fallen to *mage* levels of evil yet. That was her one redeeming quality.

That, and her ability to pull off a lie. That first time she'd bluffed about being able to cook, I'd actually believed her. A small grin broke out across my face as I remembered her salty attitude after I'd complimented her *burning* skills instead of her *cooking* skills.

She always bit the corner of her lip when she got annoyed. It made me want to grab her, pull that bit of lip free, and tell her that I had something else she could do with that smart mouth.

Fuck me. Having her around twenty-four-seven was clearly distracting *me* too. The three of us had always taken our pleasure elsewhere, and left it there. None of us had ever brought a girl back to the crew before. Just went to show that having a woman in the mix messed up our dynamic. I couldn't even be all that pissed at the guys when half the time seeing Aubry in those chains made me so hard I had to go punch things for hours just to get my blood away from my dick and into other places.

Focus, you stupid reptile, I cursed myself.

I caught an air current as I made my way back toward the light blotted streets in the distance. Los Angeles gleamed in the darkness, as if it were a mage jewel itself.

I swallowed hard, realizing what I'd have to do—go

for one of the mage jewels at a council member's house. According to Larry, they each had one. Most of the mages lived in different parts of the world. With their fucking Portal Potions they could just teleport to wherever they needed to be in moments.

Only two members lived in Los Angeles.

The first option was Triton Vale, who was fucking hunting me. I'd bet my left nut his place was jerry rigged full of magical traps.

The second option was Aubry's parents. From what I'd heard, they were too busy scrambling around trying to find Aubry—the only people on the Mage Council actually concerned with finding her—and setting up her cousin as Chief Enforcer in the interim.

With all the distraction surrounding them, they would be the easier targets. And because of my research on Aubry's background, I knew exactly where they lived and what spells they used to guard their home, making it even easier.

I headed west toward L.A., but landed before I got into the city. Too many lights. Instead, I shifted to human and pulled out my phone. I called an Uber. Then I called Larry. If I made it out of there, I was gonna need to meet up with him. If I didn't... *someone* needed to know where I'd gone, so the guys would at least be able to learn the truth.

"Don't you think you should tell the others?" Larry asked.

"Nope." I responded bluntly. "People will need them."

I hung up the phone before he could say anything else or I could change my mind. I chucked it out the window of the Uber, smashing it hard against the pavement below.

My driver's eyebrows went up in the rearview mirror, but my death-glare silenced him.

Or so I thought.

He asked, "Um, man. How you gonna tip me?"

For the first time in days, I laughed. *Of course*, that's what he cared about. I took a twenty from my wallet and handed it up to him.

He gave me a head nod. "Thanks."

I turned, looking back out the window without responding. I needed to visualize the layout of the mansion. I hadn't looked over Aubry's file in weeks, not since the negotiation had gone south. But I remembered her parents having a first floor bedroom. If I could get past the mage spells to get in there... I'd be in business.

The mage jewel we'd stolen from that shipment belonged to a mage who'd been moving across the globe for this very reason. Mage jewels were typically well protected by their keepers; the council had the most powerful jewels and keepers around. Their mastery of magic would ensure their mage jewels were harder to touch than a dragon's dick.

The joke that my father used to make had flown

into my head out of nowhere, but I blinked, refocusing on the traffic blurring by outside the car window, and shoved it away just as quickly. It was a distraction. Just like any thought of the guys or Aubry. This job was going to be difficult. Probably the hardest I'd ever attempted.

I'd be lucky to get past the Confusion Spell that I was pretty sure surrounded the stone. That kind of spell was intended to make you forget what you were doing, who you were, and where you ought to be. It made people into sitting ducks. The Summersets could wake up in the morning and find me sitting on their marble floors, drooling on myself.

Damn it, Drake. Get a grip. I wasn't typically this full of imagination. Possibilities. Negative outcomes. *Where the fuck is this coming from?*

A little voice in the back of my head told me it was because of Aubry.

That infuriating little fae. Somehow, she's made me soft. Somehow, she's made me worry about getting fucking hurt. But why? *Stupid.* This was stupid. I wasn't like the other two. I wasn't fooled by her looks. Those would fade. I wasn't hamstrung by her. Not a fucking chance.

Her furious face popped into my mind—that sexy, deadly glare she'd given me the moment she'd realized I was working out and she couldn't. *No! Erase. Erase.*

I scrubbed a hand down my face and took a couple deep breaths, trying to center myself again. My leg bounced against the shitty fabric of the backseat, creating a small plume of dust.

Doubt could sabotage me before I even got started on the mission. Instead, I started thinking about goals and the steps I'd need to take in order to reach them. First step, getting into the area by pretending to be a tourist.

"Where's Hugh Hefner's house?" I asked the Uber driver, trying to sound casual. Pretty sure I just ended up sounding like an irritable dick. "You know, the one that sold after he passed?"

That got the driver's lips moving; it *always* got the locals talking. Whether they liked him or not, the humans always had an opinion on the Playboy mogul. The driver rattled on, which gave me time to nod as if I gave a shit, but also time to think of my next few steps. As soon as we drove by the mansion that used to be the Playboy Palace, I tapped on the window. "You can let me out here."

The driver stopped mid-sentence and pulled over on the side of the road. I climbed out and pretended to care about the fancy gates and the big house beyond, until he drove off. Then I hurried down the street, past a tour guide who was using a bullhorn to spread gossip and a paparazzi with a camera waiting for someone to leave their house.

The Summerset's place was just around the next corner and two houses in. It was a big, three story white mansion. I knew the fae had a ton of money.

Their glamour let the sneaky shits just walk into any bank and pretend to be anyone. The unethical ones cleaned out human and shifter accounts on the regular. I wasn't sure if Aubry's parents were the ethical or unethical type, nor did I particularly give a shit. They were hateful assholes, either way. Especially for what they did to their own daughter, refusing to negotiate at all—even if word on the street was they *were* supposedly looking for her now.

I stepped behind an old cypress tree and studied the house.

Fae only had elemental magic, so I wasn't too worried about the kind of magic they might use directly against me if I actually encountered them. Particularly summer fae, since I'd be fighting fire with fire. The spells around the stone were going to be harder.

I lingered by the cypress and let out a low growl. Immediately, I heard footfalls pad toward me and barks sound. They had dogs. Okay. I could deal with that. My eyes scanned the fence surrounding their property and the overhang on the pitched roof. I counted at least three cameras.

I pulled out another burner phone and dialed. A shifter buddy of Easton's answered. I gave him the address and said only one other thing. "Cut all the electronics."

"Gimme half an hour," he replied.

I paced for that half an hour, walking to the far end

of the block and tossing the burner phone into some rich asshole's yard before I walked back. I checked my watch every thirty seconds, growling whenever the damn dogs got too close.

Eventually, it was time. The sky was finally dark enough and the streets were clear of tourists when the lights on the Summerset house winked out.

I shifted into dragon form.

It only took two seconds for the dogs to run away whimpering with their tails tucked between their legs. I huffed out a laugh in my dragon form, which resulted in a puff of smoke. I cracked my neck, and swung my wings in a circle, giving myself one last deep breath before I squatted down and then launched into the air.

Fae were tricksters. That was one stereotype about their race that ran true no matter who the fae was. Their downfall was thinking they were more clever than I was. Dragons were sharp-witted too, and as a bonus, we knew all about treasure.

If I were an arrogant ass fae who loved to revel in his own cleverness, and I had a glowing jewel to hide… I knew exactly where I'd keep it.

I glided up and over an air current, and then dived. Not for the house—for the pool. The giant, kidney shaped body of water was beautiful in the moonlight. The underwater lights that would normally illuminate the space like some magazine-worthy oasis were all out. Except for *one*, glimmering under the water at the deep end.

Bingo.

I dove down, tucking my wings to streamline my descent and hopefully avoid any unnecessary splashing. I'd smash the pool wall, grab the jewel, and be back in the sky before the Summersets could even make it outside.

I broke through the surface of the water and seconds later I was in front of the glowing light. The yellow beam was misshapen because the jewel behind the cover wasn't a perfect circle. It was chipped. My claws smashed the cement wall once, twice, a third time. But the cement didn't crumble.

The water currents swirled around me as I stared at the jewel, which was just out of reach.

Of course, the fucking mages had probably reinforced the wall somehow. Damn it! My plan to smash and grab wouldn't work. I might have to melt the thing out. But to do that, I'd need another breath. I shoved off the bottom of the pool and swam toward the surface.

But I just swam and swam and swam.

What the everloving fuck?

I tried not to let myself panic. I tried to think through what might be happening. The water was endless… just like those pouches Larry made for us. *Aw shit!* I was stuck inside a goddamned Expansion Spell.

Where the fuck does all this extra water come from though? Are they pulling it from the entire damn ocean? I wondered as I stroked my arms through the water, not feeling any closer to the surface than I had just a minute ago.

I stopped swimming. I had to think.

This was why we hadn't gone after any of the damn council members' jewels. This *right here*. My breath was slowly giving out, and I didn't want to have a damn fae leer at and lord over my fucking corpse when it washed up.

Think!

Expansion pouches only had one opening. You could only get items in and out of one hole. Even if you cut a slit in the pouch, nothing would spill out.

This pool, then, only had one exit. And even though I'd entered from the surface, those water currents had swirled as soon as I'd touched the far wall. *Fuck.* I wouldn't put it past a damned fae to somehow magically spin that expansion spell around and mix shit up to ensure the opening no longer faced the direction I expected. Fuck them and their cleverness.

Goddamn it!

I turned around and swam toward the fucking pool floor, feeling like an idiot.

My lungs squeezed harder and harder, begging for a breath, as black flecks started to swim before my eyes. I could almost hear Easton's eulogy, because Bodie would never give one. "Drake was my friend. And he was a good guy. Until he decided to be an idiot and sneak off by himself."

The throbbing in my temples from the water pressure... the heaviness of my wings under the water... I started to become conscious of every tiny bit of it. I was almost out of time.

The last few bubbles escaped my mouth as I neared the mage jewel. *Almost to the bottom,* I told myself. But even my internal voice sounded weak, labored. I swam, but my strokes weren't strong enough. I could feel my mouth start to open. My lungs were about to fill up with water and drown me.

Right here. In some dickheaded fae's pool. And I won't even get to tell the guys I'm sorry.

I won't even get to tell Aubry how endlessly annoying she is.

Because my body was going to betray me.

I tried to shift back to human, to see if I could buy myself another second, another swimming stroke. But I couldn't. I was too weak to shift. The magic didn't even start.

One more stroke, I told myself weakly. *One more before you open your mouth.*

I forced myself to push through the water one last time despite the burn in my chest, despite the desperate need for oxygen in my body. My clawed hand reached out to brush against the bottom of the pool.

I at least had to know if I was right.

But my claws scraped against nothing. Only air.

Air!

Hope and adrenaline filled me, giving me just a tiny

bit more energy. I gave three more weak strokes before I burst through the illusory bottom of the pool, dropping through thin air a few feet before my dragon hit onto the hard concrete below.

I was in some kind of underground room. A set of stairs went up at the far end. It wasn't too different from the place we kept Aubry. My mind appreciated the irony even as my lungs rasped and took in deep, gulping breaths of pure, sweet oxygen.

Holy fuck.

My heart started whipping me as hard as I'd ever whipped any sub during a sex session. *Asshole, asshole, idiot!* I could hear it shouting with every beat. My entire black scaled body lurched as my heart lashed out and my lungs struggled to suck in enough air.

That's why it took me a second to hear the fae descend the stairs.

I spun around, but I was too late. Fire engulfed my body and my face. As a dragon, the fire didn't bother me. The fact that the fire stole my precious oxygen *did*. At least I'd gotten enough to regain my senses. Enough that my mind was functioning again.

So when I dove back into the water, it wasn't to escape. It was because I'd just realized how a fucking fire fae would retrieve a mage jewel.

I floated in front of the plastic light cover and opened my mouth. Fire spewed from my glands and turned the water into a steaming, hissing, boiling mess. Slowly, the plastic contorted under the heat, bubbling until I could reach a claw underneath it and rip the fucking thing off.

Tossing the cover aside, I reached into the little mage-made grotto. I grabbed the jewel and held it close, tucking it into my claws. Then I used my wings and legs to propel myself back to the bottom of the pool, and I burst through the surface.

This time, there were no flames in the underground room to greet me. There was no one around. The fae must have realized that the fire wouldn't affect me. He must have run back upstairs.

I had to hurry. With their portal potions, the Mage Council could travel anywhere in moments. They could disappear in a puff of colored smoke and reappear on the other side of the world. I had no doubt that King Summerset had run off to call them.

I ran up the stairs and found myself crammed in the pool house—the pool itself a glittering, innocuous-looking mirrored surface once more. There was no sign that it had just tried to swallow me up.

I shoved through the doorway of the poolhouse, still dripping wet, and taking down chunks of the wall on either side because of my size. I shook out my wings, trying to rid them of water and debris as quickly as I could so that I could fly out of there. The droplets and splinters scattered like rain. I was about to jump and put on a burst of speed, when a white sleep grenade hit my stomach and exploded.

Everything seemed to slow down when it detonated, as if my mind was working so fast that the world was in slow motion. I watched in horror as a cloud of white dust billowed up around me.

Fuck.

If I inhaled, I'd be knocked out for hours.

I'd *never* wake up.

The council would make sure of it.

With only half a second to spare, I plunged back down into the water to avoid the white powder. I made sure to stay far from the mage jewel's cage. The water currents didn't seem to spin. The spell didn't seem to activate again, perhaps it only went off if someone touched the jewel's hidden location. When my clawed foot hit the bottom of the pool, it was actually the bottom of the pool.

I waited a moment and held my breath as the sleep dust cleared. Then I shot back out of the water into the night sky, sending a stream of fire from my mouth. I didn't pick a direction for my flame, I just turned my head from side to side and sprayed. I kept the heat low, hoping the smoke would make the fae cough and give up his location.

I assumed it was Aubry's father attacking me, but it could have been some security guard. They had enough fucking money. Or even one of the council members showing up. I'd certainly wasted enough time.

My ears twitched as I heard the tell-tale cough. *There.* To my right, standing between me and the house. I swiveled my head in that direction and let out a billowing puff of smoke without flame.

I heard the coughing intensify as he started to fly after me, but I didn't care. I flapped my wings as hard as I could, straightening my tail for maximum velocity, and I shot up into the sky.

But pain ripped through my tail only seconds later, making the appendage curl in agony. I lost my aerodynamic shape and tumbled back down, smacking against the roof tiles until I fell to the ground. If it weren't for the scales that protected me like armor, I'd have been dead. As it was, I saw double. My head pounded. My tail throbbed. Sanity and humanity left me, and the frenzied fury of an animal in fear of death stole over me.

I *roared*.

Someone had fucking *shot* me.

I whirled around, stomping through perfectly manicured lawns, shoving aside planters and firepits until I came face to face with an older male fae, who hovered in midair and held a gun. His wings had the same pink dots along the tips as Aubry's, but I didn't register that fact in the moment. I could hardly see anything beyond the scarlet rage tinting my vision.

My fire couldn't end him nor could his hurt me. I'd have to defeat him some other way.

I blew smoke again and dove sideways as the gun went off once more. I tucked and rolled through a set of bushes, hitting the house so hard it vibrated.

355

The second bullet missed me. So did a third as I crept around on the ground, continually blowing black smoke rings so that the fucking fae couldn't see a thing.

Prey! my beast mind screamed.

I heard a whoosh behind me, which meant that someone else had just arrived—probably via Portal Potion.

I'd be surrounded soon.

I blew more smoke and finally heard a cough. I lunged forward, fangs latching onto the fae's shoulder just as more footsteps sprinted around the corner. I used the claw that wasn't clutching the mage stone to wrench away his gun and heard a horrid pop in his shoulder.

The beast in me didn't give a fuck when he screamed. The man in me didn't give a fuck. My enemy was disarmed.

I launched into the sky with my treasure and my prey, determined to take both far away from the dangers here so I could better enjoy them.

I had to focus intently in order to force my injured tail to stay straight. My muscles ached, even as they started to heal and knit together. My wings flapped vigorously.

I was getting away. I was doing it. I knew I was succeeding based on the furious yells coming from the tiny people dotting the lawn below.

But my prey didn't hold still. He struggled, still

fought, even as my free claw accidentally shredded one of his wings as I tried to get a better hold on him.

The fae's hands shot useless fire at me. It did little more than momentarily obscure my vision. But when he started kicking and swinging his legs in my hold, he fucked up all my aerodynamics, and that made me furious.

My rage grew as hot as my fire and I just... let go.

I dropped him.

But he kicked one last time as he fell from my grasp, his foot wrenching the mage jewel out of my claw before he tumbled through the air, one wing flapping uselessly, the other—the one I'd shredded—dancing like streamers in the wind.

The glowing yellow jewel plummeted down after him.

NO!

Before I could tuck my wings and dive after it, before I could react *at all*, both of them smashed into the concrete pool surround, pulverized. I hovered for a second, in some suspended state of disbelief.

Did all of that actually fucking happen?

Shots whizzed through the air at me, confirming that it had.

I ignored the bullets, wondering if I could plunge down there and fly off with a tiny chip, if a piece of the jewel would do any good, make any of this worth it. But the fragments of the mage jewel had lost their glow, returning to tiny, ordinary crystals dotted with blood.

It was a few seconds before I could pump my wings and soar off into the sky, away from the mages who had started to appear out of thin air.

Fuck. Fuck. Fuck.

The angry beast within me subsided, and my horrified human side took its place, as the reality of what had just happened sank in.

All my hopes for shifter kind were shattered along with that stone.

And a piece of my heart splintered too as I realized... I'd just killed Aubry's father.

22

AUBRY

WHEN DRAKE SWOOPED OUT OF THE SKY IN DRAGON form, my heart clenched tight with worry.

Bodie and I had just emerged from the woods, returning from our "walk," when Drake landed in the gravel drive. He quickly shifted to human, stumbling slightly as if he were drunk or hurt, and said only one thing, "Time to run."

My chest grew heavy and my hands started to tingle. Drake was in trouble. Probably with the fucking mages, if his eagerness to flee was anything to go on. Did I want him to get away? Did I want them to succeed?

I looked over at Bodie. I couldn't answer that question because my pussy still ached from his cock. My heart still ached from the words and emotions we'd shared.

"What the fuck happened?" Bodie asked, grabbing

my hand and the chain he'd reattached to my ankle, pulling me from the trail over to the porch. It seemed like these shifters couldn't go two seconds without some kind of drama popping up.

The fact that Drake had left without telling us riled me up in a way I didn't expect. It made my heart beat frantically, almost like I was fucking panicked. Probably just because I'd gotten so used to his annoying presence over the last several days stuck in the damned cabin together, but still.

"Where the hell were you?" I demanded as if he owed me an explanation. As if he'd give me one.

Drake didn't. He just walked into the cabin, with Bodie and I on his heels.

I spotted Larry, who was passed out on the couch, EarPods still in his ears. Tee was snuggled up near his elbow, muttering again about unicorns and hoes. I couldn't tell if she was having gardening dreams or dirty ones.

Drake lifted a phone to his ear and I could hear Easton's curt, "Yes?" on the other end of the line.

"Come back now," Drake ordered. "We have to disappear."

Drake hung up and dug another phone out of his pocket. Before he dialed, he turned and looked at Bodie. "Anything you need, grab it. Weapons too. We need to clear out of town. Code Black."

I saw Bodie's shoulders stiffen at that code. I had no fucking clue what it meant, only that it was bad.

Drake made a call on the second phone, but that didn't give me any more damn information than the first call. He just ran a hand through his jet-black hair and said, "Code Black," again. What the fuck was happening?

Did Trite find him?

That thought froze my heart. Shit. I hoped they didn't find Triton. But I also hoped Trite didn't find them. I didn't want anyone to find the other. I didn't want these separate worlds to meet. *Ever.* I had a feeling it would be like stars colliding.

Bodie dropped my hand and sprinted up the stairs without explanation, leaving me in the middle of the cabin's living room with a twenty-foot chain coiled at my feet like a pet snake.

I just stared at Drake with a question on my face. He grimaced, and I thought I saw a spot of blood on his lips, but he turned away quickly and shook Larry awake.

"Huh? Huh? What?" Larry mumbled. When he opened his eyes and realized the dragon shifter loomed over him, he shoved himself as far back into the couch cushions as he could. "Damn, Drake, you scared me!" the old man shouted.

"We have to leave," Drake said softly.

"What? Oh, hold on a second." Larry dug his EarPods out of his ears and grabbed the charger from his pocket to replace them. "What was that now?"

"We have to leave. I need you to…" Drake glanced at

Tee then over at me. Then he gave a loud, long-suffering sigh. "I need you to spell the pixie so she doesn't remember anything."

My heart jumped into my throat. Did asshat just do what I thought he did? Was he actually taking my feelings into account? Holy shit! Was the world ending?

Drake didn't look at me again, which only confirmed my conclusion. And it made me scared—more scared than when he'd first landed and freaked us out. Drake didn't do nice. He was acting out of character.

Shit.

He was worried.

Larry scrubbed a hand over his face and gave a yawn. He shook his head, trying to wake up. "You know that Memory Wiping Potions aren't really my specialty. And they're typically only for use on humans."

"You want me to kill her?" Drake's fury heated the room.

"Nope. Nope. Just gimme a minute." Larry scrambled to his feet and went over to the kitchen. I turned to watch the mage, because the alternative was staring at Drake's furious eyes as they flickered between gold and blue.

Larry puttered around in there, opening the cabinets that Easton had recently filled with food. He pulled out some nuts and an avocado. "Is there a mortar and pestle?" he asked.

Bodie came back downstairs with a sawed off shotgun strapped to his chest, pistols at his hips, and two cases in his hands full of what I assumed were more weapons. "Yup. We keep a mortar and pestle right next to our magic cauldron," he quipped. "What the hell are you doing?"

Larry shrugged. "Drake wants a memory wipe for the pixie."

Bodie sighed. "You got time for that?"

"I wasn't given a timeline—"

"Never mind. Where's Drake?"

I turned, realizing the dragon shifter was back outside. Two flaming hunks of plastic lay on the ground near him—the cell phones. Fire danced above a disgusting mess of plastic and black smoke billowed into the night. The stench wafted in and made me cover my nose.

Bodie stopped next to me. "Wait here while I go check on him."

"What?" My jaw dropped. After everything we'd just done and confessed, my mate wasn't going to trust me? What the ever loving fuck? Anger rose and smacked my cheeks, turning them red. "You just want to—"

Bodie shook his head. "Drake looks like he might flame out. I don't want you getting hurt, Butterfly."

His stupid nickname softened my rage. Or maybe it was all the orgasms he'd just given me. I decided to blame those instead. Bodie leaned down and kissed my forehead. "I'll be right back," he said.

I huffed but turned to watch Larry instead of going out onto the porch and eavesdropping. Their stupid shifter ears would have heard me and my chain coming from a mile away, making it impossible anyway.

Larry used a meat mallet to smash up some walnuts. Then he put them in a bowl and cut open some avocado and dumped it in. He reached into his pocket and pulled out some white dust. He sprinkled that onto his mixture and grabbed a spoon.

"What was that?" I asked him.

"You don't wanna know," he responded, using a spoon to mash the whole thing together. "Unfortunately, I'm gonna have to ask you to be quiet because I don't want to mess this up."

Larry started to chant as he finished the mixture, the words sounded like gibberish to me. From what Trite had told me over the years, mage magic used some long-forgotten language out of Mesopotamia. It made it harder for people to learn and impossible for non-mages to just steal spells or potions and replicate them.

He began waving his arms in wide gestures as he chanted. He even did a strange little shuffle-step.

I looked out the front window when Larry started to do some squats and his pants slipped a little. I didn't want to break his concentration, but I also felt awkward as a plumber's crack issue started to develop.

Outside, I saw Drake was now as armed as Bodie. Both of them stood sentinel, staring down the road, waiting for Easton. My heart pinged around in my chest like an old-school screensaver. I knew traffic was bad in Los Angeles. But waiting on Easton made me nervous that something had happened to him. It made me want to chew my nails.

Instead, I dropped and did push ups. If I was gonna have anxiety, I'd rather burn it up than let it burn me up.

No worrying for you, I told myself as I extended my arms and lifted my chest from the ground. *You're the mother fucking Chuck Norris of the fae. When you do a pushup, you push the earth down. When fear knocks at your door,* it *runs away screaming.*

I didn't know how much time passed. Half an hour? An hour?

I'd moved from push ups to sit ups to lunges by the time Larry finally made his way over to the couch and spread the paste he'd created on Tee's forehead. Instead of being brown or green, like I expected, it was a soft lavender. Larry kept chanting, and I watched as the lavender paste soaked into Tee's skin and disappeared.

I swallowed hard. I was used to magic, but Larry was the only mage who'd ever performed spells in front of me before—I didn't count whoever my parents had hired to spell me upon birth and make me reversibly infertile. Part of me was fascinated. And the other part of me couldn't help but wonder why the hell mages ran the world when their magic was slower than a snail riding a turtle.

Those thoughts didn't have time to expand into metaphors that *didn't* suck, because Easton pulled up just then, his headlights cutting across my vision.

I ran out onto the porch. I couldn't stop myself.

My heart thumped wildly until I saw him climb out of the driver's seat unhurt. Until I realized that his back seat and passenger seat were both empty. He hadn't been harmed and he hadn't found Trite. Good. The knot in my chest eased.

"Go time," Bodie was at my side in seconds, grabbing my chain and escorting me down the steps. He opened the back door of the car for me and I climbed into the seat.

"Nope. Scoot over, Buttercup," he said, shoving his ass in next and coiling my chain at his feet. "Hurry, Larry!" I heard Drake call out. Then the dragon shifter slid into the driver's seat.

Larry came scurrying down the steps moments later, lugging a cat carrier that came from... where?

Drake just jerked his head at the car and the mage got in. He took the front seat next to Drake. "I can't just leave her behind, not knowing if someone would take care of her. I brought Tallulah. No arguments," Larry stated, with a sense of authority I'd never seen from him before.

It made me smile. But that smile was wiped right off my face when I realized that the only open seat left was next to me. I gulped as Easton slid into the back seat on my other side.

I was caught between the wolf and the bear, each of them cozying up against my legs just as they had my heart. The irony was not lost on me. In fact, the irony felt like a shaft of iron had just been shoved up my ass for a nice little 'fuck you.'

Neither man looked at me. Both checked their weapons and kept their eyes out the window. I took a deep breath and tried to keep my adrenaline from fueling my desire. If I had known any sports stats, I would have started reciting them.

"Where are we headed?" Bodie asked.

"Away." Drake's monotone response was all we got for the next half hour.

We left the forest and wove through Pasadena and Glendale before coming to a stop outside of Union Station. The old Spanish mission style building had a modern clock tower with Roman numerals on the exterior. The time read 12:50 a.m.

Drake jerked the car toward the sidewalk, cutting someone off, and ramping Larry's ride up the curb for a second before parallel parking in a spot that was just long enough that Larry's bumper didn't touch the car in front of it.

"Out," Drake ordered.

The street was empty at this time of night, but I could hear people inside the station. The depot served trains *and* buses, and typically hummed with life no matter the hour.

Before we climbed out, Bodie bent and unlocked

the chain around my ankle. But then he kept a tight grip on my hand and slid out of the car with me next to him.

How the fuck are these shifters going to walk inside with all their guns? I wondered.

But then Drake opened the trunk and grabbed some coats. The long rain coats were out of place given the weather, but better than nothing. Bodie tossed a coat on me to cover my wings since I couldn't use glamour.

Larry carried Tee's cat carrier and also grabbed a duffel out of the trunk before he gave Drake a nod. What the hell that meant, I wasn't sure. But the four assholes tramped toward Union Station like they owned the place. Despite my anxiety, I couldn't help but revel a tiny bit in how hot their badassery was. Like the Boondock Saints of L.A., they were totally movie-worthy.

I hurried to catch up to Bodie. "Where are we going?"

He shrugged.

"You're okay with just leaving everyone and every-thing behind?" I asked incredulously.

My mind flashed to all the little shifter kids that Bodie and Easton watched. The guys could just walk away from all of them? What about all the shifters they supposedly helped?

"We *have* to go," Drake replied darkly as he shoved open the door and held it for us.

"But why?" I asked as I passed him and entered the

station. The glass ceiling overhead, the intricate, shining tiles below, and the giant mural in front of us barely got half a glance from any of us.

Drake didn't answer me, he never fucking answered me, just strode toward the ticket counter. "What bus leaves here next?" he asked an elderly gentleman perched behind the glass.

"We have a Greyhound to Palm Springs leaving at 1:20," the man replied.

"Good. Four tickets." Drake pulled out cash.

So we were leaving, and it didn't matter *where* we went, only that we left quickly. I pressed my lips together. Easton hadn't found Trite. But had Trite found Drake? Is that what this was about?

"Four tickets," Easton said, interrupting my thoughts. "We need five."

Drake shook his head. "I'm not going with you." He wouldn't look at us, but I saw his jaw tick.

Shit. The worry that had been stewing in my stomach started to boil.

"*What?*" Bodie stepped away from me and moved closer to Drake. "The fuck you aren't." He turned to the ticket man. "*Five* tickets." Bodie slapped additional cash on the counter as Drake walked off.

The old dude raised his bushy eyebrows and added an extra ticket.

My eyes drifted toward the front door. Was Trite out there right now? Or was it someone else? Who was coming for Drake? Why?

My feet shuffled after Bodie and Easton, who crowded Drake where he stood in a corner, glancing out the windows every few seconds, trying to keep it together. But I knew, somehow I knew, that he was fighting for every bit of fake calm he could muster.

"What the fuck is going on?" Bodie got in Drake's face.

Drake's eyes flickered to me, then back to Bodie. Then he turned and walked off without a word.

Bodie was on his heels in an instant. "Don't you walk away."

"I'm going to the bathroom," Drake replied tersely.

"Nope. Not buying it," Bodie stayed on his ass.

Larry, Easton, and I exchanged long looks.

Easton shook his head. "He's pulling the fucking martyr card."

He started after the other two shifters. He was probably going to try and break the inevitable fight up before it could begin.

I glanced at Larry, who looked over at me with a sad smile. "Please don't run. This night has already been draining enough."

Run? Then it hit me. *Why the fuck was I* not *already running?*

My eyes drifted back to the three shifters, and then out the giant arched windows of the train station. I saw a man materialize on the street, wisps of colored Portal Potion smoke rolling off his suit and dissolving into the night air.

"Bodie!" I yelled, running toward him. "Mage Council!" I pointed toward the window, where another mage appeared near the first. Then a third. And a fourth.

"Fuck!" he shouted.

Bodie thrust the hilt of a knife into my open palm.

He stared deep into my wide-open eyes, his own irises glowing gold. "Use this, Aubry. I don't care who you have to cut down, you just keep yourself alive. Understand?"

My head nodded, but I barely registered the movement.

The battle for Los Angeles had officially begun, and I was now officially free... but which side would I choose: the mages or the shifters?

23

AUBRY

WHO'S THE GOOD GUY AND WHO'S THE BAD GUY... THAT CAN *all flip on a dime.*

Tee's words echoed in my mind as I watched the battle unfold.

The metaphorical dime had been tossed; it flipped over and over in midair, and I held my breath, unsure what side the coin would land on. Because it wasn't mages versus shifters anymore—black and white—at least not for me; shit had gotten mixed together until my life was *Fifty Shades of Grey*, all hot sex and hard decisions.

Fuck me.

The doors to the depot smashed open, along with several of the huge, three-story tall arched windows. Glass shards scattered across the marble floor like stars, gleaming in the cheap artificial light of the circular chandeliers above us.

Two mages in suits walked in through the empty doors.

My throat dried out and I swallowed hard, wondering what the hell I was going to do, and why the future always had to get pinned down in life-or-death moments like this.

Why can't life altering decisions be slow and well thought out?

Wind blasted my cheek from the window and I turned. A fall fae named Mollie appeared in the window frame, shooting jets of air at us so fast and low that we were literally swept off our feet and tossed on our asses.

That put a stop to my philosophical ramblings real quick.

Instead of choosing a side, why don't you just try and come out of tonight alive? my inner snark scolded me.

I lifted my knife, but Mollie was Mage Police. Could I really attack her if it came down to it? Did I *want* to?

Martyr complex isn't really my style. But...

I whirled behind Drake, who'd partially shifted so that he had huge black wings. I needed more time to think.

Shit, if it was only mages from the council... it would be different. Those assholes had treated me like shit. But Mollie? Others who'd been under my command?

Maybe I could just run for it?

But then Bodie would chase me. That would leave

him exposed. And they wouldn't hesitate to eliminate him.

I closed my eyes and rubbed at them, the stress making me dig in hard.

I heard shuffling sounds and opened my eyes to see Easton and Bodie also ducking for cover behind Drake's huge ass wings. They were seriously big enough to be a small circus tent.

As I watched the guys checking their guns, I felt the loss of my utility belt and my powers fiercely. Fucking Larry. I was gonna have to stick out this fight as if I were human. While I liked fighting, I liked having the upper hand even more, so this was just great. Damn it.

I ruled out attacking Mollie, whose wind power made it impossible to get close to her anyway. Plus, I'd met her husband and kids at a company picnic. I just... couldn't.

I peered around Drake's wing as another mage popped into existence over by the ticket counter. Was there anyone out there I hated enough to fight? Or was I gonna sit here behind Drake like a pansy-ass preschooler until the sun rose?

I squinted through the shadows. There were now three mages and Mollie here in the station with us. I didn't recognize the mages, so that left them open as potential adversaries. But I *did* recognize the formation. They were setting up a perimeter. We'd soon be surrounded.

"Well fuck me in the ass with a donkey cock," I grumbled.

"I like how you think, babe, but now's not the time," Bodie quipped, racking a sawed off shotgun before he whirled out from behind Drake's wings and fired off a shot that hit its mark. A mage's head burst apart like a watermelon, the potion in his hands falling to his feet and exploding, fire dancing out of the broken glass and licking up the dead man's legs as his headless body toppled forward.

The few humans left in the vicinity screamed as they ran. Nothing like a flaming, headless body to cause panic and mayhem. A winged fae? Unexplainable wind? Dragon wings? *Nah*, the humans probably just thought they'd stumbled onto a badass movie production and had somehow gotten lucky enough to be an extra. But when bodies started dropping, humans peaced the fuck out.

I didn't have time to feel anything, much less horror, because the new mage by the ticket counter pulled out a white Sleep Grenade and lobbed it at us.

Hell fucking no!

I dove forward, landing right on top of the potion as it broke. My abdomen blocked the dust from billowing up and knocking us all on our asses, useless and snoring for hours. Drake reached an arm down and helped me up, retracting his wings, which arched over his head like huge shadows. Something about him resembled Goliath, from that kid's cartoon, *Gargoyles*.

I was momentarily distracted by that image, when the impossible happened—Drake complimented me.

"Quick thinking," he said.

"We train for it at PD," I responded. Part of me hoped for a head nod or a tiny smile. But those two words were a bigger compliment than I'd ever seen Drake give anyone, even the guys.

Another mage lobbed a glowing potion at us, catching my attention a moment too late. This time, the glass globe held a mix of orange and blue smoke.

"Damage Potion incoming!" I shouted.

Drake scooped me into his arms and tossed me high into the air before flapping his wings to fly out of the way. He caught me just as I started to fall, and then hovered in midair right next to one of the hanging circular chandeliers.

"Oof!" Drake's chest smashed into me as he spat fire down on the mage who'd thrown the Damage Potion. The man used a Portal Potion to disappear just before the flames reached him.

A shot rang out and Drake dodged the whizzing bullet. Barely.

"Burn their pockets," I told him in a rush, "it's where they keep their potions."

The tip slipped off my tongue before I even realized what I was saying. Was I actually helping the criminals? What the fuck? I hadn't decided that. I hadn't decided anything, other than trying to stay the fuck *alive*.

Drake propped me on the chandelier before swooping down and doing as I'd suggested.

My eyes scanned over the faces of the furious mages below. They surrounded the depot almost completely. There had to have been at least ten of them who'd portaled there now. That meant they'd all been sent by the council or were members themselves. Only council members were given unlimited Portal Potions, because the damn things were so difficult and time consuming to make. Two years, from what I'd heard.

I watched a mage fall as Easton slashed through him, huge black claws protruding from his human hands like a goddamned X-man. Was this battle seriously going down like some kid's Saturday morning cartoon? Goliath and now Wolverine? What was fucking next? Balto versus Mickey the Magician?

My sarcasm felt like the only weapon I had; the knife Bodie had given me was too insignificant. I needed a sword or a gun. I wanted my goddamned fire magic back.

Below me, a mage started to wave his arms in a big arc and chant. "Fuck! Compulsion Spell!" I cried.

Drake flew up and grabbed me, tossing me down toward Bodie before swooping at the mage with fire spewing from his mouth.

Bodie caught me and quickly set me down, not pausing to cradle me for even a moment. "Be careful, Aubry," my mate scolded.

Aubry... when was the last fucking time Bodie had

called me *that*? He was too in love with his annoying-as-shit little nicknames. Was he pissed at me for some reason?

I stared at my mate as he lifted his gun... and pointed it at my heart.

My heartbeat tripled. *No.*

"Bodie?" I whispered in shock and confusion.

His eyes narrowed and his head thrashed, his teeth scraping over his bottom lip in an incredibly strange gesture. It was almost like he had an itch he wasn't allowed to scratch.

Oh shit. I grabbed for my knife, but with his gun already aimed at my chest, I was too late.

A shot rang out.

Bodie crumpled in front of me, blood dripping from a ten-ring hole in his forehead.

I felt dazed as I stared at Bodie's body on the ground. My vision flickered. No, his *body* flickered. Bodie's face disappeared, and a fae I'd never seen before lay on the ground, dead.

Fuck me. No. Fuck him. Fuck that fly and his goddamn glamour.

I wanted to kick him, but that kind of shit was only good in video games or the movies I created in my head—where my hair looked fucking epic, and a sunbeam always shone from behind, making my ass look fantastic as I jumped up and roundhoused a motherfucker. In real life, badassery came from paying goddamned attention. Maintaining control of the situation.

And I hadn't been.

I was never this off during a fight. Normally, I loved the adrenaline rush, lived for it. Anxiously anticipated it while my beat cops did stake outs and found my targets. But I was used to springing traps on others. I wasn't used to being on the surprise end of an attack. I wasn't used to being unclear about what side of the fucking fight I was on, either.

Everything about tonight was different.

But at this point, the asshole fae had proven they didn't give a shit about my hostage status. One had literally just attacked me—not just the guys near me, not just with wind or Sleep Grenades that knocked out everyone. Some asshole had just tried to *shoot* me.

"Fucking fae glamour," my mate's voice said from behind me.

I swung around to see the real Bodie, looking fierce as fuck, his face streaked with gunpowder and blood. He lowered his handgun and slung an arm over my shoulder, pulling me in tight.

My mate bond freaking sang.

I pulled the knife Bodie had given me out of my waistband and moved so we were back to back. If nothing else, I knew my mate would protect me. And I'd do the same. But did that make me a criminal? Was I one of the bad guys now?

Fucking hell! Stop thinking and just smack some fucking skulls together, my adrenaline shouted.

A mage approached from my left. His pockets were burnt to a crisp. It looked like Drake had succeeded in following my suggestion. I grinned. That meant he had no potions—no Sleep Grenades, no Mage Fire, no Damage Potions, or Portal Potions. Fucker had hand to hand combat left, and that was it.

Or so I thought.

That was before Big Nose pulled out a gun. "Life tip: if you don't wanna die, don't bring a knife to a gun fight." Schnoz laughed as he lifted his weapon at me.

I kicked out hard and fast, so that his gun-arm swung wide, then lunged forward and stabbed him right in the gut.

"Great tip. Gonna file it under 'fuck you,'" I sneered.

A car engine roared outside along with the screech of tires. A moment later, four wolf shifters burst into the station, fangs gleaming. Echoing howls bounced around the room as the wolves joined the fight.

Fuck! Would those assholes attack me too, just because I was fae?

One of them lunged right at me, answering my dumbass question in a hurry.

Easton appeared out of nowhere. The massive man, who was still in human form except for his claws, ran in front of me and blocked the new wolf. Raising an arm and shaking his head, he pointed across the room at three new mages who'd just portaled in with a *pop*.

One of those mages was Triton.

Fuck!

My heart clenched when I saw him immediately go after Drake. The dragon spewed flames at him, but my best friend dodged and tossed out a portal potion. He disappeared. Seconds later, he reappeared behind Drake and started a spell.

Bodie, now a pure black wolf amongst his gray and white packmates, leapt through the air and latched onto Trite's arm.

"No!" I started to run forward, but I slipped and fell across the blood striped marble. I twisted as I fell so that I could land on my ass rather than my knees... And that's when I saw Mollie, slowly lifting a gun to the back of Easton's head.

He couldn't see it, and the other two weren't there to help. There was only me.

Fuck.

The thought of Easton getting hurt threw shadows across my chest. Those shadows felt like voids in the sky, where planets used to spin, and the potential for life used to exist, only to be wiped out entirely. If he died, the shadows would take over. The void would ensure there was nothing left to explore. Nothing left to reach for. No possibilities. No hope. Only blackness. Soul-crushing blackness.

I glanced left, watching in slow-motion terror as Drake and Triton each fought to gain the upperhand.

I glanced right, fear and dread curling in my gut as

Mollie clicked off the gun's safety, preparing to end Easton's life.

Half a breath.

That was all the time I had to make a decision.

Easton or Trite.

I shoved myself onto my feet and yanked out my knife. I wrenched my arm back and focused on my target. Just like throwing a dart. The blade left my fingers, twirling soundlessly through the air, as it rushed toward Mollie's neck.

I didn't wait to see if my aim was true, because she'd already pulled the trigger. I heard the crack of her shot reverberate through the air around me, as I raced her bullet, desperately sprinting to get to that big, giant, overstuffed teddy first.

I smashed into his shoulder, trying to push him out of the way.

But it was like tackling a mountain. I hadn't moved him far enough. Not nearly far enough...

The slug tore right through Easton's back and out his chest, splattering me with his blood.

EASTON

I turned to look at Aubry in shock and in wonder... She'd just saved my life.

Even as pain tore through every fiber of my being, even as her scream echoed on repeat in the back of my mind... She'd still saved me. If she hadn't pushed me, that bullet might've gone straight through my heart.

A potion flew through the air above me, smashing somewhere in the distance and making someone scream.

I grimaced and glared over my shoulder at the bitch who'd shot me. She lay motionless on the ground, the gun a few feet from her right hand, a blade lodged deep in her throat. Bodie's blade—the one he'd given Aubry at the beginning of this shit show.

Scratch that earlier thought. If she hadn't knifed that chick *then* pushed me, I might've taken a fucking bullet to the *head*.

As it stood, a bullet to the chest was not much better. Agony sizzled through me as my entire body seized and blood gushed through the wound to the erratic beat of my heart. I stumbled and crashed to the ground. The pain caused my eyes to see double.

This wasn't normal. Not that I'd ever been shot before, but seriously. Something was very, very wrong. Usually, if a shifter suffered a terrible injury or wound, all we had to do was *shift*—into one form or the other, it didn't really matter, and inevitably our bodies would begin the healing process. But I couldn't shift, and there was damn well no healing going on.

Aubry dropped to her knees on the ground beside me, her fingers shaking as they hovered over my bloody white t-shirt. Her lips moved as if she were screaming at me, but I couldn't hear the sound or comprehend what she was saying. A marching band was playing in my head, symbols crashing together over and over, pain a humming vibration that undulated through my bones. I was in a daze... and the only thing I could sense for sure was blood-curdling *anguish*.

The wooden waiting bench in front of us wasn't much of a barrier. Wood sprayed through the air and Aubry ducked down beneath the bench's back and covered her head, a bullet just missing her.

No! Shit! Not her.

I wanted to do something. To get up and protect

her. To beat the fuck out of whatever dumbass mage had turned his back on her. But I couldn't even move.

Aubry's head popped back up when the coast was clear, and before I even realized what was happening, she was behind me, dragging me farther back between two rows of pew-like bench seats. My eyes squeezed shut against the urge to vomit and when I opened them again, the world was spinning. Smoke curled from my chest, tainting the air with the scent of burning meat.

Oh fuck. The bullet that hit me must've been silver. That would explain my inability to shift, and also the reason why my body was fucking barbequing itself alive right now. I needed to get it out, and fast.

I flopped a heavy hand onto my chest and fumbled with numb fingers, trying to find the source of all my pain. My hand slid through the mess of hot, sticky blood, but it all felt the same to me—excruciating.

"Silver!" I tried to shout, but I had no idea if my lips even moved.

Aubry's brown eyes drifted down to my chest before she grabbed the material of my shirt and ripped it apart. Under different circumstances, I might've gotten hard at a move that sexy, but at the moment, it was all I could do just to stay conscious.

Her eyes fluttered shut and she bit her bottom lip before plunging her fingers deep into my flesh. My chest spasmed and it felt like my entire rib cage had caught fire. My muscles tensed like I was screaming, squeezing hard until I cramped up everywhere, my

387

mouth frozen in a grimace, my eyes squeezed tightly shut.

Then suddenly, the sizzling sensation was gone. My eyes flashed and a roar ripped up my throat as my bear finally took over my body. Cells and tissues mended back together as my body stretched and realigned. Bones broke and extended. My skin sprouted golden fur and my nails elongated into claws.

I'd taken on full-bear form for less than a second, when my body shifted back, putting me through yet another invigorating round of rapid healing. By the time I was human once more, the wound in my chest had stopped hemorrhaging. All that was left was a sore, meaty hole and a soaking shirt-full of old blood.

"Easton!" Aubry cried as she leaned down and latched onto me.

Finally I could hear the beautiful sound of her voice. Before I could think better of it, my fingers raked through her silvery hair, and I held her tight. I wanted so badly to take her face in my palms and kiss her for all that she'd done. Saving my life over and over again. Making me feel alive in a way I never had before. She was like the first day of spring, like emerging from the darkness of a cave and the cold of winter and being hit with the scent of life and warmth.

She leaned back and as I gazed up into her precious face, she slowly shook her head.

"I'm so sorry, Easton. I..." Tears fell from her eyes and streamed down her cheeks, creating clean rivers in the wake of all the dust and soot and blood spatter on her face. "I'm so fucking glad you're okay. I wouldn't have been able to live with myself if you'd…"

Again, she trailed off. She swiped a hand across her cheeks, smearing the dirt and debris like mud.

A window shattered and magical wind blew shards through the room. Only our bench saved us as the glimmering slivers pierced the wood like a thousand tiny daggers.

My chest clenched once more, but not from my wound—from my fucking heart. She was about to break me all over again, I just knew it.

More tears left her eyes and her chin quivered as a sob escaped her throat. "I care about you, and that's why this hurts so fucking much. But I made a promise to Bodie. A promise to give us a real shot. And I can't do that if my heart is still half attached to you."

My breathing grew shallow. It was like I wasn't getting enough oxygen. She cared about me? Her heart had felt attached to mine? It wasn't all some sick, one-sided infatuation on my part?

Not that it mattered, now that she had just cut me loose…

I licked my cracked lips, trying to process all she'd said and all she'd meant beneath the surface of her words.

"Aubry," I croaked as I struggled to find something to say, anything that might make her change her mind. "Please, don't—"

"I'm sorry," she said, quickly cutting me off. "I'm *so* sorry. But I have to go. I'll send Bodie over to get you when the fighting's over. Just… stay safe, Easton."

She bent down and, ever so slightly, brushed her lips across my forehead.

I took a deep breath, committing her smell to memory. Like an orange orchard. I memorized the feel of her delicate skin on mine, warm and silken like honey. The way she said my name, it rose like a bubble inside my chest, but instead of being filled with air, the bubble held all the unspoken words, the emotions that spun through the air when we saw each other.

And suddenly, my eyes flashed once more. I didn't shift. Not physically. But something inside of me definitely changed.

It was like my soul had just exploded into a million metallic pieces, all of the shards drawn like a magnet toward the fae in front of me. Pure, unadulterated love coursed through my veins like molten lava. My heart filled with it, overflowed with it, drowned in it.

The kiss she'd placed atop my head had inadvertently awoken nature's most primal bond…

I gazed up into Aubry's wide, chocolate brown eyes and I knew she was feeling exactly the same things I was. Shock. Wonder. Fear. Excitement. *Gravity*.

She had suddenly become… *my everything*—dark, winged, fierce, and beautiful. She had the power to wreck me like an apocalypse, or save me like a miracle; to reject me and punch a hole through my chest, or accept me and offer me every tomorrow with her at my side.

She may have been Bodie's mate, but she was also mine.

My mate.

I was usually the peacemaker, the compromiser, the self-sacrificing dude-bro willing to take one for the team.

But not with this.

If one of us was going to walk away from the best thing that ever happened to us, then I knew who I was betting on.

Because it damn well wouldn't be me.

THE END

CONTINUE THE HOT AND SEXY ADVENTURE WITH AUBRY and her mates in *FAE UNCHAINED*!

ACKNOWLEDGMENTS

Special thanks to all of the people who helped us get these books together. A huge thanks to our husbands who not only watch our crazy kids but also help support us and turn our dreams into reality.

A huge round of applause goes to our beta readers for their feedback to make these books better than before. We're listing them in alphabetical order so we can't be accused of playing favorites. Allison, Brittany, Ivy, Jessica, Jessica, Lysanne, Raven, Thais.

Thanks to Sue for being our British phrasing consultant.

And thank you Lori Grundy for the beautiful covers.

ABOUT THE AUTHORS

Ann and Elle are both cool and amazing people. If you've read their books before, you'll know that one of them is sweet and the other is a demon with a human mask.

In their free time, they like to... wait, what free time? Both women are mothers. Elle has three wonderful children. Ann has two. Add husbands on top of that and you might as well nickname each of them Miss Hannigan (aka the witch that ran the out of control orphanage in the musical *Annie*). Oops. Ann's theater nerd popped out. It does that sometimes.

Unlike Ann, Elle is totally cool. One of her favorite things to do is play video games. Which is totally fun. But if you add wine or brownie batter, it's even better.

Both of them hope you enjoyed this book. Or at least don't want to use it to start a forest fire. Because forest fires are bad. So says Smokey the Bear. And Easton... also a bear.

And with that ramble, we'll let you peruse a few of our other books.

Taken by Storm (Storms of Blackwood Book 1)

A Crown of Blood and Ashes (Enchanted Royals Book 1)

Magical Academy for Delinquents (Pinnacle Book 1)

Knightfall (Tangled Crowns Book 1)

Made in the USA
Monee, IL
15 February 2021

59626366R00236